THE WRONG DIMENSION

Paul A. Coscia

DEDICATION

To Linda, for your love and support.

To my sister Denise, for always believing in me.

To my good friend Rich, for your encouragement.

To Kathy, for your thoughtful beta reading and feedback.

To Jen, whose middle name found a place within these pages along with Spotford.

And to my editor, Rose Winters, for your guidance and skill in shaping this book.

***

CHAPTER 1

Down on one knee, hiding behind the lifeguard stand, PC watched the soldiers coming toward him. He counted three soldiers bearing down on him. Being that the weather was cooperating with no wind, this would be easy pickings.

The soldiers picked up their pace as they spotted PC. Quickly, he lay down in the sand and crawled underneath the lifeguard stand. He put himself in position with his M82, scoping the first soldier, who went down on one knee to take aim at PC. Before the soldier could pull the trigger, PC took him down. The second soldier slowed down to see what happened to his comrade and was taken down quickly. The third soldier kept charging and was also shot dead in no time.

PC looked up from his scope to view the casualties. He crawled from underneath the lifeguard stand, stood up, and wiped the sand off himself.

"Nice shooting."

He spun around toward the voice, raising his rifle in the air and pointing it at the lifeguard in the stand, who didn't even flinch as he sat with his arms spread out across the back of the stand. He was perfectly tanned, with straight brown hair and dark sunglasses. He looked out to the ocean as the waves crashed onto the shore.

PC slowly lowered his M82 noticing the lifeguard was no threat to him.

"Who are you, and..." he moved his head back and forth looking around the beach in bewilderment. "...where the hell am I?"

"Do you remember where you were last?" the lifeguard said, still looking straight out to the ocean.

"Remember?" PC started moving around the lifeguard stand with his head still moving from left to right. "Remember?"

He stopped in front of the lifeguard stand, also looking out at the ocean, trying to get his bearings down to remember where he was before he'd appeared on the beach. "It was just about to start raining. I was driving my car."

He continued to stare out to the ocean as he recounted, "Somebody cut in front of me; I saw a white flash." He looked up at the lifeguard. "And here I am. How did I get here? Who the hell are you?"

The lifeguard laughed. "My name is Lambert; I'm here to guide you home out of this dimension."

"Dimension?" PC lowered his weapon. "Just what dimension am I in?"

"Well, you're in your own dimension." PC looked at Lambert in a confused, inquisitive way. "There are three dimensions that your world knows about, defined to you as length, width, and depth of all objects. Time is considered an additional fourth dimension but is an abstract measurement."

PC shook his head in confusion. "Not a dimension."

"But there are seven other dimensions the world does not know about. Scientists still haven't figured them out," he said with amusement in his voice.

"So, where am I? What dimension?"

"Like I said, you are still in your dimension, the fourth dimension. But here lies the issue. The fifth and sixth dimensions have collided with the fourth, creating as people would say, a FUBAR."

"FUBAR," PC said. Fucked up beyond all recognition." He leaned his rifle on the lifeguard stand and looked around the beach.

"I know this place, this beach. I grew up here." He spun back around and looked at Lambert. "Hey, this is Jones Beach, on Long Island."

"Field Four to be exact," Lambert said.

"Yes! I know this well. I spent my youth here."

"And this is the way home."

"What do you mean?" PC looked up at Lambert.

"We need you to get you back to your dimension."

"Well, wait a minute, you told me I am in my dimension."

"Yes, you are. But, since the fifth and sixth dimensions have collided, they've created FUBAR in your dimension. Because you were thrown out, you, and one other, are the only ones effected. You are the only ones who can straighten this out."

"Wait, wait, wait." PC held his hands up in the air at Lambert. "You mean there is someone else?"

"I'm afraid so." Lambert sighed. "Both of you must trek to the lighthouse together to get things back to normal."

"Lighthouse; what lighthouse are you talking about?"

"The Montauk Lighthouse."

"That's ninety miles away. A hell of a walk."

"Yes indeed," Lambert said.

"And this person?"

Lambert nodded his head quickly, "Oh, this person will be along soon. You will be supplied with what you need to make this trek at a hideaway that you will locate."

"And how is that going to work?"

"Did you ever hear of Miriam's well?"

PC looked at Lambert. "Something biblical."

Lambert pointed his finger at PC. "Correct. Miriam was the sister of Moses. She was named after a spring that would appear and follow the Israelites as they traveled for forty years through the desert."

"So, this hideaway will follow us as we travel the beach?"

"Correct." Lambert continued. "You will come across things that you may not understand. Contrasting times that happened some time ago will be mixed into this dimension. You may see people or things you know or knew from the present or past. I will help you in every way to get where you want to go. Forces will try to fight you and stop you from getting back to your destination. That's why I'm here." He smiled through his pearly white teeth.

"You said I will be supplied with what I, or we, need; what are we talking about here? Food, water," he looked down at his M82 and pointed, "Ammo? And how did I end up with this M82? I used it in the military but haven't picked one up in years."

"You did pretty good when you landed here."

"Yeah, I took those guys out rather good. Like riding a bicycle," he said as he scratched the back of his head. PC looked over to where the soldiers lay, and noticed they were gone. "Hey! What happen to their bodies?"

Lambert smiled again with his pearly white teeth. "Remember what I told you, you may come across things you may not understand. Those soldiers went back to where they came from. They were most likely killed in battle somewhere in Earth's history."

PC scratched his head again. "I didn't get a good look at their uniform, but it was definitely familiar."

"Don't be surprised if you come across them again. One other thing I must tell you; do your best to make it to the lighthouse before the cold weather begins. Ninety days of good weather is what you have."

"And what happens if I don't make it in ninety days?"

Lambert looked up into the sky, took a deep breath as he exhaled, and brought his head back down. "We don't know. Just do your best to stay alive."

"Well, that's nice to know." PC turned around to look at the ocean again.

"One more thing; notice you have a ring on your finger."

PC looked down. He hadn't even noticed he'd had one on. He wasn't much into wearing rings. He looked at it oddly. A gold ring with a yellow stone. "What's this for? I don't wear rings."

"This one you will. It's kind of a beacon. It will always tell you when trouble is ahead or when you come up to locations where you can rest and refresh your supplies. So, keep it on if you want to stay alive."

PC looked to Lambert and said, "I'll remember that."

"Go." Lambert said, "Begin your trek east." He pointed his finger with his arm stretched out. "Be well."

PC looked toward the direction Lambert was pointing in, turned around, and said, "But what about this—hey, where'd he go?"

PC looked at the empty lifeguard stand, looking around him. Nothing but sand surrounded him.

He looked up into the sky since he did not have a watch on, to see if he could figure out the time of day. The sun had just come up from the east, so he figured it was early morning. He picked up his rifle still leaning on the lifeguard stand, looked around some more, and was on his way east, wondering when he was going to meet up with this other person. He was still confused about what was happening to him, hoping the person he was to meet could help clarify things. Or maybe be just as confused as he was.

CHAPTER 2

The weather seemed nice as PC walked. Light breeze with some clouds in the sky. He figured the temperature was somewhere in the seventies. The air was refreshing. He noticed beachgoers were starting to enter the beach. PC was getting nervous walking around with this sniper rifle in tow, that people might get alarmed by him. But they didn't seem to notice he had a weapon of war with him. One lady passed him by and said, "Top of the morning to you," and smiled at PC as she passed by. PC remembered that Lambert said there would be different encounters.

"This must be one of them," he said out loud to himself.

Still, he wondered what else would be coming after him, and when. He kept alert, not knowing what to expect. What concerned him now was that if shooting were to start, there might be civilian casualties with people on the beach, and the thought made him feel cold.

PC was feeling kind of hungry and thirsty, too. He wondered out loud to himself, "How long would I have to walk till I find one of the safe havens Lambert was talking about?"

He kept close to the shore since it was easier to walk on wet sand than dry. More bathers walked by him, a young couple, and they didn't even notice his sniper rifle.

"Gorgeous day," the young lady said.

PC smiled nervously, holding the gun low. "It certainly is." He continued his walk. A flash of light made him flinch, and he noticed his ring was blinking. "Must be getting close to something," he said to himself. He continued to walk as he looked at his ring. Abruptly, it stopped flashing. He halted again.

"Damn," he said. PC walked backward in his tracks, still looking at the ring. It started flashing again. He looked up and said, "Well, it's not forward." He looked to his right at the ocean, "and it's not that way, either." He looked to his left and saw a boardwalk.

"Hmm." He walked through the dry sand, trekking his way to the boardwalk.

Still staring at the ring, he walked up the step onto the boardwalk. The ring stopped flashing. He stopped again.

Now what? He walked back down the stairs and looked around. He went left of the steps, but the ring stayed silent. He stopped after a few feet, turned around and went the other way, past the steps.

The ring flashed again. "Now were getting someplace," he said. He continued walking along the bottom of the boardwalk and the ring stopped flashing.

"Shit," he said under his breath. He walked backward and the ring went off. He stopped walking and pointed the ring at the boardwalk. PC started feeling around the boards. He fingered the wood and found some loose boards.

Okay, he said to himself. He found four loose boards and leaned his gun on the wall of the boardwalk. He looked around to see if anyone was watching him. He pulled all four boards down and entered underneath the boardwalk.

Click.

PC knew that sound. It was the coil of a rifle.

"Don't even breath."

CHAPTER 3

Frozen on all fours, PC didn't twitch. At the corner of his eye, he could see a rifle about three inches from his face. He could just see enough of the rifle to know what type of weapon was being pointed at his head.

"Looks like you have a Winchester rifle there, maybe 1892? I'm guessing you have a large loop."

"How do you know that?" the female voice asked.

"Well, I'm bit of a gun guru. Spent some time in the military, learned a lot about guns."

"What's your name?"

"PC."

"PC? What kind of name is that? Does that stand for something?"

"Almost anything," he cocked his head with a little smile. "Do you have a name?"

She remained silent.

"Come on now, if we're going to get along here, and be friends, be nice to know your name."

"Who says were going to be friends?" She pressed the Winchester against the side of his head.

PC looked down and noticed she wore a ring similar to his. "Well for one thing, we have something in common."

"And what's that?"

"Check my left ring finger."

She glanced down and back up quickly. She slowly looked down again at her own left ring finger. They both were the same, both blinking yellow stones. She lowered her rifle, backed off a few feet, and sat in the sand, rifle pointing up. "My name is Ren."

PC relaxed and sat in the sand also. "Glad to meet you, Ren." He noticed Ren looking around in confusion, shoving her long black hair behind her ears, her slender body sitting in the sand. "Confused?"

"Confused isn't the word," Ren said.

"Yeah, join the club. What do you remember last before you showed up on the beach?"

She looked at PC as she thought. "I was at work sitting at my desk. There was a thunderstorm moving in. I got up to look out the window at the oncoming storm, saw a flash of lighting. And here I am."

She looked at the rifle. "This looks like my grandfather's Winchester rifle." She looked toward the butt end and ran her fingers across it. "This *is* his rifle. I remember the markings on the end, like someone was making notches for everyone they killed."

As she examined the rifle, PC, with his legs crossed, looked around and noticed the supplies Lambert was talking about. He saw several plastic containers.

He got up, walked over to the containers, and opened them. Food, water, camping supplies, sleeping bags, flashlights, but he wasn't noticing any ammo. *How are we supposed to walk ninety miles and face whatever might be coming after us with just one clip of ammo where I've already used three shots?*

He walked to the entrance of the hideaway, took out his clip, and noticed it was full. *How could it be full,* he wondered as he stared at the magazine. *I fired three shots.*

"Hey, Ren, have you fired your rifle since you got here?" Ren looked up.

"What? Me? No, I haven't fired a shot since I got here." She looked left and right. "What the hell is going on here?"

"Have you talked to anyone since you got here?" PC asked.

"No, just you. What about you, have you? How did you get here?"

"Well, kind of like you, but I was driving into a thunderstorm when someone cut me off. I saw a flash, and..." he smiled at Ren, "here I am. I did talk to someone when I got here."

"Tell me everything that has happened to you since you landed here."

"I talked to this guy Lambert. He was sitting in the lifeguard stand about a mile or two from here. He told me I was going to meet someone," he gestured with his head, "Which is you. And we need to walk ninety miles east to the Montauk Lighthouse at the end of Long Island. There we can get back to where we belong."

"Long Island, as in Long Island, New York?"

PC nodded his head. "Yep, that's the one."

She looked into the hideaway, which was big enough to crawl through. She looked at the sand, then at the ocean, listening to the waves crashing on the beach.

"Wow," she said, "I've never been here before. Been landlocked all my life."

"Where are you from?"

Ren gazed at the surf. "Indiana. Long way from home." Her voice trailed off. She turned her head to PC. "How the hell are we going to get back where we belong by going to... what did you say... the Montauk Lighthouse?"

"Well, from what Lambert told me, we're in a different dimension. To get back where we belong, we must get to the Lighthouse."

"And what do we do when we get there?"

PC shrugged his shoulders. "I don't' know, he hasn't told me that part yet. He says he will guide us through this."

"And you believe him," she said sarcastically.

PC threw his hands up in the air. "I don't know what to believe, but I'm not going to stand around here. He said we have ninety days to get to where we need to be, or we may be stuck here the rest of our lives."

"How so?"

"I've already been shot at by three soldiers."

"Shot at! Holy shit. Who were they?"

PC shook his head. "I don't know, I couldn't make out the uniform markings, but they looked familiar. We may run into them again. In fact, Lambert said we may run into a lot of crazy situations."

Ren swatted the sand with her hand. "Terrific."

"Let's start gathering things for what we need and be on our way," PC hoisted his gun over his shoulder.

"Are you going to lug around that cannon for ninety miles?" She pointed to PC's M82. "There are some lighter rifles behind you."

PC turned his head to look at the other armament behind the rifles. He saw a pair of binoculars with the rifles and grabbed it quickly knowing they would need it. "No, I'll stick with what I have. Let's collect what we need and get going."

She laughed to herself and said under her breath, "Your funeral."

CHAPTER 4

Ren popped out from underneath the boardwalk with a backpack in tow, her Winchester hanging from a leather rifle holder slung over her shoulder. PC then stepped out with his backpack and M82 in hand.

Both searched the beach to get some bearings. PC finally got to see Ren in full view instead of in the semi-dark underneath a boardwalk. Ren stood about five-foot-five, long black hair and blue eyes. A slender girl he thought, and incredibly attractive. PC himself stood at six-foot, with brown curly hair that he kept short because he hated curly hair, he was in athletic shape and wore a goatee, which he also kept short.

"Which way are we headed?" Ren asked.

"This way." PC pointed east. "Oh, and here," he pulled two pairs of dark rim sunglasses out of his backpack. "We're going to need this. No shade where we will be going."

Ren put the glasses on and looked at PC.

PC smiled. "You can pass for Trinity on the Matrix."

She stared at PC with a straight face, not finding it amusing.

This is going to be a fun trip, he thought.

Both put their backpacks over their shoulders onto their backs. "Okay, let's go," PC said quickly, as the two of them set out.

PC and Ren were quiet for the first few miles, both wondering how they got here and if this Lambert person was on the up and up. PC had been in worse situations, but this one was quite different. He kept wondering if the government was up to something and screwing around with his head. He'd been to the VA hospital to get his annual and was wondering if something had been in the flu shot the doctor had given him. He dismissed that quickly and didn't want to be like his buddy in the Army who thought the government was poisoning the water when they were in Iraq. His friend ended up losing it and PC didn't want to be like him. Besides, Ren was with him, and she certainly seemed real to him. *Maybe I've been watching too much of The Matrix,* he thought.

Ren was quiet on the trek, staring at the ocean; it relaxed her, and wanted to keep her wits together. She didn't realize how soothing it was. But she kept thinking, *what the hell am I doing here all this way from home?*

"So, you're from Indiana."

Ren looked at PC quickly. "What? Oh, yes, Indiana."

"Hear it's a nice state."

"Yeah, it is. Want to get out of there, though."

"How come?" PC looked at her with curiosity.

"It's cold, windy and cloudy, like seven to eight months out of the year. Must be like that here on Long Island."

PC nodded his head lightly. "Yeah, but not seven to eight months out of the year. Winter gets kind of gray, but, when spring rolls around, things get pleasant weather-wise."

"Do you still live on Long Island?" Ren lifted her sunglasses and flashed her blue eyes.

"No, live in Florida now. Have been for quite some time."

"How come you left?"

PC looked up to the sky.

"Oh, the cold, the wind, the cloudy days."

PC looked back down from the sky and looked at Ren with a smile. Ren smiled back at him, breaking the ice between them.

Suddenly, their rings began to flash. An explosion in front of them knocked them both off their feet. PC sat up from the sand as Ren pulled herself up.

"Okay?" PC said.

"Okay," Ren replied. "What the hell was that?"

PC pulled his backpack off, ripped open the top, and pulled out his binoculars. "I've got a feeling...." he scanned around to see what was in front of them. The beachgoers had disappeared. "Where did they go?"

"Hey, the beachgoers are gone," Ren frowned.

PC stopped scanning as he spotted what he was looking for. "I thought so." He put the binoculars down. "Those soldiers I told you about are back again."

"What did they drop on us?"

"Mortar, and we better get moving cause they're reloading and have us in their sites."

As PC and Ren stood up, the soldiers launched another mortar.

"Shit let's go!" PC pulled Ren up and they ran toward the boardwalk. They got about one hundred feet away when the mortar exploded behind them.

"Quick, get near the lifeguard stand."

"They're going to pick us off if we stay near the stand," Ren said. "Shouldn't we keep moving?"

"There's a method to my madness!"

Another explosion hit behind them. They kept moving, finally making it to the lifeguard stand. PC got underneath and quickly pulled his backpack off. He pulled out two pair of noise cancelling headphones and put one on.

"Here." He threw a pair at Ren. "Put these on. This cannon I have can be loud. Stay low behind me."

Ren quickly put the headphones on and ducked low behind PC as he lay underneath the lifeguard stand in a sniper position. Ren pulled out her Winchester aimed her rifle at the enemy, on high alert.

PC focused in on the soldiers with his site. *Two of them,* he thought to himself. There didn't seem much of a wind. He made the necessary calculations. The one soldier was just about to put the mortar in when PC exhaled and softly pulled the trigger. The large noise startled Ren at first, never having experienced such a powerful gun. A second shot was made.

Ren saw the second soldier go down. She pulled the binoculars out of PC's open bag and lay on PC's back, looking at the now dead soldiers.

PC tried to look up at Ren but was forced down by her weight. PC exhaled. "Comfortable?" he said.

"Wow!" she said. "Checking out your handiwork."

"Did I get them?" he said somewhat sarcastically.

"Oh yes. You really fucktarded them."

"Thank you. I'll take that as a compliment. Now if you would kindly get off me, I would like to check out these soldiers and see what Army they are with. They're not US soldiers; I know that."

Ren stayed frozen on top of PC.

"Well," he said, "are you going to unsaddle yourself from me?"

"Uh oh," Ren said, still looking in the binoculars.

"What—more trouble coming?" He looked in his scope and scanned the area.

"No, that's not it," she said. "Those soldiers you took down are gone – they disappeared!"

"What! Again? Get—get off me already."

Ren rolled off PC and he stood up. "Come on, grab your stuff." He headed toward the spot where the soldiers had been. Ren grabbed her backpack and followed PC.

When they got there, nothing. No empty shells, no blood, no sign that anyone has been there. Clean.

"What the frig?" PC said.

Ren finally caught up with him. She looked carefully around. "You said this is the second time this has happened?"

PC looked around somewhat bewildered, then turned to Ren. "Yeah, second time this has happened. Happened to me when I first appeared here." PC exhaled and scratched his head.

"Hey," Ren said. Who's that guy on the lifeguard stand?"

PC looked back toward where they'd just been. There he was, sitting in the Lifeguard stand, laid back with his arms spread out across the back of the stand with his mirrored sunglasses.

"Come on," he said to Ren. "I'll introduce you to Lambert."

CHAPTER 5

"So, the adventure has begun," Lambert said as PC and Ren approached the lifeguard stand. "Well, hello young lady. Sorry we didn't get to meet earlier so I could introduce you to myself and explain why you are here."

"Yeah, well, I've already explained that to her," PC said with a smirk. He turned to Ren. "Ren, meet Lambert, Lambert meet Ren. But you already know who she is."

"Quite true!" Lambert said with a smile.

"How did I end up here?" Ren asked, looking up at Lambert.

"It's hard to explain. To make it simple, you were at the right place at the right time." He swiped his dark hair from his face and raised his sunglasses.

"You mean the wrong place," PC said under his breath.

Ren held back a chuckle as she glanced at him, then back at Lambert. "How long are we going to be here for?" she asked.

"Well, that depends," said Lambert.

"On what?"

Lambert shot a look under his sunglasses at PC, till PC could feel the heat of his eyes. "Thought you got her up to speed."

PC was agitated now. "Well, why don't you enlighten the lady? She's been dragged out of her life and has ended up on a beach, in the middle of, well, Long Island, and she wants some answers. More clarity than what I have told her. I'm just as confused as to why I'm here, too. So, spell it out so we can understand what we're doing here."

Lambert's smile disappeared and his head looked down at his lap. He sighed and looked back up. "Right now, I can't give you that information. All I can tell you for now is to follow the path I have explained to you. When I can give you more information, I promise you I will. But for now, just keep going. Young lady, I'm sorry you're being dragged into this, but yes you were in the wrong place at the wrong time—that much I'll tell you. Stay close to PC, and work together. I'm sure you're a strong woman and you can handle yourself since I see you toting that rifle."

He stopped and looked out to the ocean. "I must be going now, I'm being summoned."

"Who's summoning you?" PC asked.

"There are others working behind the scenes to repair the damage. It is not an easy task, and we're not sure if we can, considering the amount of damage that has been done. We may be able to repair some of it, but not all." He looked at the two of them. "That's where you come in."

PC put his arm out toward Lambert. "Yeah, but…"

…and just like that, Lambert disappeared. PC put his arm down, staring at the empty lifeguard stand.

"Well," Ren said, "that was an interesting conversation."

PC glanced at the sand, then at the ocean.

"So, what do we do now?"

PC put his backpack on and looked at Ren. "We keep moving." He nodded to the lifeguard stand. "Like the man said."

Ren put her Winchester rifle back in its holder and walked with PC. "How long do you think it will take us?"

PC was silent for a moment. "Hard to tell. Not sure what we're going to run into and how much we're going to be slowed down by weather, soldiers, and whatever else we might come up against. He told me we had ninety days to get to our destination. It shouldn't take us ninety days to walk ninety miles. So, I'm guessing we're going to run into a few things on our trek." He studied Ren's face. "Is this coming any clearer to you?"

She laughed. "Fuck no. The only thing that's clear is that I'm not in Indiana anymore, which is kind of a good thing. Well, in a way."

He raised a brow. "How so?"

"How so? It's kind of a good thing not to be in Indiana. Well, even though this is quite strange, I've always been an adventurous person. I like to see and do different things and go to various places. I've seen the wild horses on the Carolina Islands recently. I was in Mexico a couple of years ago to see the Aztec ruins. I did some hiking in caves that went back deep into the mountains."

PC nodded his head quietly. "You want to see the world. That's good."

"What about you, don't you want to see the world?"

PC sighed. "I have, but the ugly part of it." He stared out in the distance.

"I'm guessing you were a soldier in the military since you seem to know how to handle the bazooka you carry."

PC nodded his head. "You are correct. I was a sniper. Spent a lot of time in Iraq and Afghanistan."

"Oh," Ren said sadly.

"I'm lucky," PC said.

"Lucky? How so?"

"A lot of the guys, and girls too, came out of the war with issues."

"PTSD?"

"Yep. Some even killed themselves. They just couldn't handle it after they left the military. Some others learned to deal with PTSD. War was too much for them. Some are even living in the streets."

"And you?"

PC shook his head. It didn't bother me for some reason. I left, went back to a normal life, and I was fine. Not sure why. Doctors can't even figure it out. They think it might affect me later in life, but it's been ten years, and life has been normal."

"And this bothers you," Ren said.

"It does."

"Why so?"

"Because I came out normal and they didn't. What did I do so right that they didn't do? We worked together, lived together, trained together, drank, laughed, and cried together. Yet, I came out normal, and they didn't. I don't get it."

Ren looked down and said softly, "Difficult. I wish I had an answer for you."

"I'm not sure there is an answer." PC noticed more people lying on the beach now. He pointed.

"Looks like the beachgoers are back."

He looked over by the boardwalk. "Let's go over there by the boardwalk, in the corner where the stairs are. Let's eat something, I'm starving."

"Okay," Ren said, and they deviated from their path and headed for the boardwalk.

CHAPTER 6

A s they sat in the corner of the boardwalk in the shaded sand, PC noticed something odd. "Hey, does anything look peculiar to you?"

Ren bit into her sandwich and looked around as she chewed. "Well, more people on the beach," she said with a mouth full of food.

PC pulled out a water bottle from his backpack, twisted open the top, took a quick sip, and looked around them, behind him. "Yeah, yeah, there are more people here, but that's not it. Look at where we are near the boardwalk."

She looked at the boardwalk. "Looks like the rest of the boardwalk."

"You're getting close," PC said.

"What are you getting at?"

This is the same spot you and I met. I mean, we had to have walked at least five miles from the spot we started, and…" PC grabbed his binoculars, stood up, walked a few feet out, and looked to his west.

"There," he pointed. "Look there."

Ren stood up and walked toward him. "What are you pointing at?" She took another bite of her sandwich.

"See the tower? That's the Jones Beach Tower. We started right around that point. We've walked at least a few miles away from that, yet we seem to be at our same starting point."

Ren swallowed her mouthful of sandwich. "That's impossible, how can we be at the same starting point but have walked five miles toward the east?"

PC's eyes widened. "Lambert told me about Miriam's Well."

Ren stared, incredulously. "Miriam's Well?"

"Yes, it's biblical. When Moses traveled to the desert for forty years, this spring followed them wherever they went in the desert. So, they always had water. Lambert told me our hideaway would follow us on our trip."

"So, where we go, it follows us?"

"Exactly," PC said.

Ren looked around. "This is getting more fascinating by the minute."

PC looked at the wall along the boardwalk and scratched his head. Then he noticed something. "Come here," he said to Ren. He walked up to the wall in the sand and kicked it. Four cut boards about four by four feet fell in. Ren stood with her mouth open and sandwich in hand. He walked toward the entrance, got down on his hands and knees, and crawled in. Ren was close behind him.

"Oh, my God," Ren said.

Both looked around and noticed the same surroundings. The food, the weapons, sleeping bags. All that they would need on this trip.

"Look over there," she said, That's my red bandana. I thought I lost it when we were walking. I usually hang it out of my back pocket. Could this be the same place?"

"There's one way to find out. Leave your bandana here. Let's see what happens down the road if we come across this again and if the bandana is here." PC looked around. "Put it on top of the sleeping bag and we'll see if it's here when, or if, we come across it again."

Ren put the bandana on top of the sleeping bag. "I'll grab some more bottles of water for us."

"Yes, a few more bottles of water won't hurt." They tossed the bottles of water in their backpacks. "Okay, let's get trucking."

Both crawled out of the boardwalk and put the boards back up securely so no one else could get in. They stood up, put on their backpacks, and walked toward the shore.

Ren scanned the beach, and a thought popped into her head. "Um, is New York an open-carry state?"

"No," PC said.

"Then why are people not looking at us cross-eyed for carrying weapons?"

"I don't know," PC said. "They seem oblivious that we have weapons."

"Everybody keeps smiling at us as we walk by. I know I wouldn't be smiling if I saw someone carrying a cannon on the beach like you are. What the hell is that, anyway? Looks like it can do a lot of damage."

"Oh yes, it can."

"Then why do you carry it?"

"Well, it wasn't exactly my choice when I was dropped here. I did use such a weapon when I was in the military."

"What kind of gun is that?"

"It's an M82 sniper rifle. The rifle was made to destroy equipment at long distances.

"What kind of equipment?"

"Usually, parked aircraft, radar units, light-armored vehicles, trucks, fuel silos."

"But why use it to kill people? You can probably blow a hole in someone with that cannon."

"Well, it's a good long-range sniper rifle. It can neutralize enemy snipers at standoff range. It's also good if someone is behind a wall. Will take them right out."

What's the range?"

"Anywhere from nine hundred to a thousand meters. Couple of snipers during the Iraq and Afghanistan made a record of over two thousand meters. Those guys were good."

"Wow, guess that outdoes my pea shooter."

PC laughed. "I presume you know how to use that."

Ren smiled back at PC. "Oh yes, this was my grandfather's rifle. He loved those old westerns with the cowboys and their Winchester rifles. He used to go hunting with this." She pulled out the Winchester. "He used to take me hunting with him and taught me how to use it. Used to take me target practicing in his backyard. I became rather good with it. When he died, he made sure that I got the gun. He knew it would be in a safe place with me. Not sure how it made its way here, but glad I have it."

"Original Winchester?" PC said.

"Oh yes. Not sure where my grandfather got it. I had it checked, and it is authentic. 1892."

PC nodded his head. "Impressive."

"Ren? Ren!" came a voice from behind. Both PC and Ren stopped to see who was calling her.

"Oh no," Ren said. "No, no, this can't be."

PC looked at the man coming toward them. "Who is that? Do you know him?"

"Unfortunately," she sighed.

"Who is he?" PC looked at him hesitantly.

"I work with him." She sighed again. "His name is Kevin. What the hell is he doing here?" she said, annoyed.

"Hey Ren," Kevin said with a big smile.

"Hey Kevin." She tried her best to put a smile on her face.

Kevin was six-foot-two and overweight, with short brown hair and a little moustache. PC wondered if he dyed his hair. *Seems he should have more gray hair for a man his age. He doesn't look like a spring chicken. Quite goofy,* he thought.

"What are you doing here on the beach?" Kevin pointed to PC. "Is this your boyfriend?"

Ren darted Kevin a look. "No", she said sternly. She composed herself. "This is my friend PC. We're just out for a walk and chatting."

"PC? What does that stand for?"

"Almost anything," PC said with a smile."

"What are you doing on the beach, Kevin?" Ren asked.

"Oh, I'm here with my wife and son Kevren, you know, soaking up the rays."

PC looked him up and down again. Kevin was wearing a pair of Army fatigue shorts with sneakers with a T-shirt that read: 'Make America Great Again.'

Ren gave Kevin another stern look. "You told me you hated the beach."

"Kevren?" PC said. "Not Kevin?" Kevin nodded his head up and down like a puppy dog.

"Yes, Kevren." Suddenly, his son came walking up dressed up like he was a construction worker, looking like a younger version of his father, except with long blond hair and a beard. He walked and looked just as goofy as his father.

As he walked up next to his father, Kevin smiled and put his arm around his son, who had a matching smile.

"Do you hate your father for giving you that name?"

Kevren smiled and said, "Every day."

PC was rather enjoying the show when Ren grabbed his arm and said, "We must go. Meeting some people up the beach. Good to see you, Kevin," as she whisked PC away.

"Good to meet you Kevin, Kevren," PC said, as Ren yanked harder on his arm. PC laughed as she led him away. "Where did you find him?" he continued laughing.

"Shut up." She pushed him along, and PC wiped the smile off his face. "God. I just want to know what the hell he is doing here."

"Well, Lambert said we would see some strange things." PC looked back at Kevin. "I think that qualifies. What is it you do for a living?"

"I work for a construction company as the Accounts Payable Manager."

PC pointed his thumb over his shoulder. "And him?"

"He does the purchasing for the company. He's a good person, but can be quite annoying. Bad bedside manner if you get my drift."

"How so?"

"He likes to talk, and he doesn't know when to stop. He tries to be helpful but gets in the way most of the time. Gets involved in things he shouldn't. He once gave a vendor names and numbers to two of our managers, who, by the way, hate him to begin with. The vendor started calling the two and Human Resources had to step in. He's not well liked, but I'll never understand why they got rid of the person who was working with him instead when the company was sold. He's the one who trained Kevin and was the most respected in the company. Corporate bullshit, I guess."

PC smiled. "Well, I've never had to deal with corporate bullshit, but being in the military can be pretty damn close."

Suddenly, PC stopped. Ren stopped with him. "What's wrong?" she asked.

"Look around." Ren scanned the area.

"Where did everybody go?" PC was frozen in place. He lifted his sunglasses up over his head and turned a complete three-sixty. They both looked down at their flashing rings.

"We must find some cover. I have a bad feeling."

"We're out in the open, where the hell are we going to go?"

"Quick," PC said, "head for the boardwalk." PC started running with Ren right behind him.

Suddenly, twelve soldiers appeared about fifty yards in away from them. They were all armed. They yelled "Halt!" and began firing at PC and Ren.

"Come on!" PC shouted at Ren. "We can take some cover behind the ramp; it's our best bet."

PC heard what sounded like rapid shots going off. He stopped to see that Ren was not behind him. He spun to face the soldiers with his M82 pointed at them, but noticed all the soldiers were shot down. He looked at Ren, who was about twenty feet behind him. The butt of her rifle was up against her rib cage. She spun the rifle as the large loop snapped back, and then back into place when the rifle came full about.

PC stood amazed as Ren walked toward him. "Wow. I didn't realize you were Annie Oakley in disguise."

Ren stopped beside PC and looked at her rifle. "You know, I took twelve of them down. And this rifle only carries ten shots. This rifle seems to be endless when shooting."

"Probably why we haven't seen any ammo in our safe spot."

"That's strange," Ren said. "How can a rifle reload itself? Doesn't make any sense."

Ren put the rifle back in the holder behind her back, looked at PC, and said, "None of this does."

PC sighed. "I know. And the only person we can trust to guide us back to our real world is Lambert. He did say we would see strange things and people we may know."

PC and Ren noticed movement. The beachgoers had reappeared. PC looked quickly behind him. "Damn it! The soldiers are gone."

Ren looked over to where the soldiers had been.

"Is that a terrible thing?"

"I wanted to look at them to see where they came from. Damn it!" He sighed again as he put his hands on his hips. "Okay, okay. Let's start moving again.

"Well, at least we know when the beachgoers disappear, trouble is ahead," Ren said.

"Yeah, yeah, that, or our rings flash at us," PC said. "Seems like Lambert lives at the lifeguard stands. Hopefully we'll be coming up on another one soon." He smiled at Ren. "Onward, McDuff." She smiled and both started walking.

CHAPTER 7

Ren looked down. "Hey," she said, "My ring is flashing."

PC looked at his ring. "Yeah, so is mine." He looked to see where the sun was to gauge the time. "Getting late," he said. "We've been walking for a while."

"Ten miles at least."

"Yes, I'm thinking ten miles also. The rings going off must mean we're near a place where it will be safe for us." He looked around the beach. "Most of the people have gone home." He looked toward the boardwalk. "God damn."

"What?" Ren glanced at him.

"We've moved, and the scenery has changed, except the boardwalk remains the same." He scratched his head.

"You think that's the same spot where we met?"

PC continued scratching his head. "Certainly, seems to be. We're moving, but the background remains the same."

Ren looked at the boardwalk. "So, fucking odd."

PC looked at Ren with a cocked eyebrow. "Come," he said, "Let's head up to the boardwalk. I've got a feeling it's the same spot and we'll be safe there for the night. I was hoping we'd find Lambert again, but we'll try to locate him in the morning."

They treaded through the soft sand, both tired from the day's walking.

When they approached the boardwalk wall, PC pulled out the four-by-four-foot sections. He set them down in the sand and went ahead to look inside. He pulled his head out and looked at Ren. "Yep, this is the place. Your bandana is still here."

She looked inside. "Well, I'll be damned," she said. Both went inside and put their backpacks down.

"I don't think we'll need our rings to find our hideaway since it is always close by."

PC looked around to see what they had. He grabbed the two sleeping bags. "Here." He reached and gave one to Ren. "Something to sleep in."

Ren took the sleeping bag. "Thank God. Would have hated to rough it in the sand."

"I've done worse," PC said under his breath.

He spotted some camping lanterns. It was not a traditional lantern, but LED. He flicked one on.

"Oh," said Ren. "Pretty bright."

"Eh, it works," PC said.

"PC, what are we doing for..." she looked around, "you know, bathing."

"Well, I guess the ocean is our bathtub." He continued going through the supplies. "Here are a couple of bars of soap, towels, and..." he spun around to look at Ren, "some shampoo for the hair." He smiled.

Ren sat there with her arms folded, giving PC the look of death. "Bathing in salt water?"

"Well, it's either that or we both stink and offend each other."

She unfolded her arms and crawled toward PC before letting out a sigh. "What else do you have there?"

"A small camping grill, and all sorts of camping food, a pot to cook in, couple of plates, water, toothbrush, toothpaste, couple of brushes, razors, shaving cream."

Ren grabbed one of the brushes. "A must—right there." She put it in her back pocket.

"Got some pasta in a bag here, freeze-dried, that we can cook." PC looked at the package. "Lots of veggies."

"That will work," she said. "Let's get cooking; I'm starving."

They cooked their meal in the bottled water that was there, knowing they couldn't use the salty ocean water. Both downed their meals. The sun started setting and Ren got herself in the sleeping bag and passed out.

PC looked outside to see if any more soldiers were around. Still some people walking along the shore. A good sign no soldiers were around. "Wait a minute..." he saw a lifeguard stand. *Wasn't there before,* he thought to himself. And on top sat a person. PC came crawling out from underneath the boardwalk and walked toward the stand. "So here you are."

Lambert looked down at PC with a smile. Still with arms spread out on the stand and his mirrored sunglasses on. "Ah, so there you are, my friend. I see you found your hideaway. Good, good."

"Are we going to be safe here during the night, Lambert?"

"Yes, you will be."

"Will I be able to sleep at night without keeping one eye open?"

Lambert laughed. "They will not come near you when you are here at night. We created this haven for you for that purpose, to be safe."

PC walked around the lifeguard stand with his head down and his hands on his hips.

"Things will get worse before they get better," Lambert said. "Always stay close to the boardwalk. There will be times you don't see the boardwalk, but it will appear when you walk toward it."

PC spun around and looked at Lambert. "And that's another thing. What about this boardwalk? It doesn't seem to change. It stays the same. It moves with us even though we are moving. And now you are telling me there will times we don't see it, but it will always be there?"

Lambert moved forward and looked down at PC. "That will be the only constant you will see. Behind the boardwalk is your world. It moves with you. Once you carry out your trek, things will go back to normal. The boardwalk is a reminder of your dimension that is waiting for you. The boardwalk keeps you safe."

"A lifeline?" PC asked.

Lambert leaned back in the stand. "A reminder you don't belong in this world."

"That's for sure."

Lambert looked to the horizon as the red sun faded over the ocean.

"Time for me to leave. I will see you soon. Remember what I have told you."

Suddenly, PC stood alone. Lambert and the lifeguard stand were gone. PC looked around, astonished. "Well, what the fuck." He walked back underneath the boardwalk.

It was almost dark out now. PC flipped one of the lanterns on. Ren was sound asleep. PC thought he should be too, considering the long trip they would be taking. But he wanted to see what other supplies were there.

Ren was right, he thought. Carrying around the M82 for ninety miles might become a burden.

Let's see what other weapons are available, he said to himself.

PC felt a side arm would be good. He found a Taurus G2C stainless twelve-round semi-auto 9mm handgun. "Perfect," he said. He found a second one. Looked at Ren, said "Yeah, I'm sure she can handle this," and he located two shoulder holsters. He found a watch and put it on. A plastic band, but it would work.

At least I can keep track of time.

Next, he spotted what he was looking for. "Oh yeah, this is what I want."

He sat in the sand and looked at it. An AAI LSAT Light Machine Gun with a scope.

"Twelve and half inch barrel, excellent. Lighter to carry. Now we're getting somewhere."

He looked further back with the lantern in hand, crawling on all fours, and spotted a MG CS/LM1 machine gun.

"Wow!" he said. "This can take out some people."

He pulled the machine gun up front and positioned it near the opening off to the side so he could pull it in front of him, just in case. Lambert said they would be safe here. PC wanted to have some insurance just in case things changed.

PC sat by the entrance. He wanted to watch things on the beach for a while. He wasn't sure he felt safe. It was a whirlwind day, he thought, but was feeling too tired to collect his thoughts. PC finally faded into sleep.

CHAPTER 8

"Wake up, wake up!" Ren shook PC. "Come on, wake up!"

PC was slumped asleep along the entrance to the boardwalk. "What, what?" He opened his eyes. "What's that rumbling noise?"

"That's why I'm waking your ass up. Look outside."

PC looked outside, trying to focus. His eyes went wide. "Holy shit."

"What is it?" Ren asked.

"What the fuck." He looked at Ren. "It's a half-track." He pulled his binoculars from his backpack, put them to his eyes, and focused in. He was looking for markings.

He put his binoculars down, looked at Ren, put them back up, then, back down.

"What?" Ren asked. "What are you seeing?"

"It's a World War II half-track. The markings on it are German."

"German?" Ren asked, shocked.

PC but the binoculars back up. "There's about a dozen soldiers behind it." He focused in on the soldiers. "And they're SS soldiers. What the fuck?" He dropped the binoculars from his face.

"SS? They were a brutal bunch back in the day." Ren picked up the binoculars to look for herself.

"Yeah, they were, and looks like they will be again."

"They're turning toward us," Ren said. "What do we do? I thought we were safe here."

"At this moment, we're not." PC grabbed the LM1 machine gun and aimed it outside the entrance. "Have you ever fired one of these?"

Ren looked at him incredulously. "No."

"Good, you're hired. I'm going to run out on the beach. I'll act as bait and make them turn the half-track to its side. Once it's turned, take them down.

She grabbed PC by the shirt sleeve. "Are you shittin' me?"

"You can do it," PC said. "You took out those other soldiers."

"Yea, but with a little old western rifle."

"I have faith in you. Just don't shoot me."

She said gruffly, "Just don't get in the way."

PC smiled again and ran out onto the beach.

"Holy shit, what did I get myself into," Ren said to herself. She watched PC as he ran out and turned left. The half-track turned and exposed the soldiers behind the beastly vehicle. Ren put her hand on the trigger, took aim, and let loose on the soldiers. One by one they went down until no one was standing. She looked up and smiled to herself. "Piece of cake."

The smile ran away from her face as she saw the half-track turn toward her.

"Oh, shit," she said.

Boom!

She saw an explosion and the right track came forward off the vehicle as it rolled to a stop. Three soldiers came out. Ren took aim again and took the three soldiers down.

She looked up. Nothing was moving outside. She grabbed her Winchester and came out. She looked around and saw PC coming toward her.

"Oh," she said with relief, "thank God you're okay."

PC stood there with a deadpan look on his face. "For someone who never shot a piece of armor like that, you did pretty good."

"Well," she looked around quickly, "It was the thrill, really."

"The thrill of killing twelve men?"

"Oh, no," Ren said. "The thrill of just shooting a gun like that. It was a thrill for me. I like thrills. I'm always searching for a good thrill. Besides, it's kill or be killed, right?"

PC still sat there, his expression unchanged. "Right."

"I think she did rather well," came a voice from outside.

PC turned around and there, in the lifeguard stand, sat Lambert.

"Well, I'm glad you think so," PC said with a bit of sarcasm in his voice.

"Hey," Ren said. "Look, everything is gone. Soldiers, half-track, gone."

"They have gone back to where they belong," said Lambert.

"And when do we go back where we belong?" PC asked angrily as he walked toward Lambert.

Ren grabbed his arm. "Stop. Yelling at him will not get us anywhere."

"You should listen to the young lady, PC. I know you both don't want to be here; we're doing the best we can to get you out of here. Right now, the only way is for you to continue your walk until you get to your destination."

"And what is our destination—a lighthouse?" PC yelled back at Lambert. "What the hell are we supposed to do when we get there?"

Lambert sighed and looked at both of them. "Just go to the Montauk Lighthouse, where you need to go. When you get there, I will tell you what to do."

"Why can't you tell us now?" Ren asked.

"We're still getting things in order so this will work. For the most part, it will work once we iron out a few details. I have no reason to lead you astray. Please, just trust me."

PC looked at Lambert, then at Ren.

"We have to trust him," Ren said. "What else are we going to do?"

PC nodded to Lambert. "Alright McDuff, we will follow you."

Lambert smiled. "The day is young. You must get to it."

And just like that, Lambert was gone.

PC just looked at the empty Lifeguard stand as he shook his head. "Let's get ourselves together and move on." PC headed toward the boardwalk.

"What about a shower?"

PC stopped in his tracks. "A shower? No showers here. Remember, the ocean is our bathtub." She looked toward the ocean with disgust. She looked back at PC. "Besides," he said, "it's broad daylight now and everyone is going to see you buck naked in the ocean. Unless that is a thrill for you." He winked at Ren and walked under the boardwalk.

She sighed, looked down with her hands on her hip and kicked the sand. "Shit," she said under her breath.

CHAPTER 9

P C and Ren ate a quick breakfast, gathered the things they would need, and went on their way. They put on suntan lotion and floppy hats to protect themselves from the sun. It was another bright and beautiful day as they walked along the shore of the beach.

They were quiet as they walked through the day.

Tired of the silence, Ren finally spoke. "So, you're not into thrills?"

PC smiled at Ren. "Well, I have a different version of thrill than you do."

"And that is?"

"Well," PC said, "I look at it as something interesting to do. I'll give it a try. If I like it, I'll keep doing it."

"And if you don't?" Ren asked.

"If I don't, then I can say I tried it and if I never did it again, it wouldn't bother me."

"Like the Army?" Ren said with a curious look.

"The Army," PC laughed. "The Army was more of an adventure. After I left the Middle East, I felt it was time to do something else interesting."

"So, what do you do now?" Ren asked.

"Kind of in between jobs now. Living off my small pension from the military. I do some day trading, which I'm rather good at. It keeps me afloat. Do some security work on the side."

PC looked around for a spot where they could grab some lunch. "Not too many beachgoers here. Let's stop and have some lunch by that sign we just passed."

"Okay," Ren said as they headed away from the wet shore and onto the dry sandy beach.

They ate their sandwiches and drank the bottled water they'd brought from their hideout. Ren pulled out PC's binoculars from his backpack and scanned the horizon.

"What are you looking at?" PC asked.

"Just seeing what we have up ahead. How many miles do you think we covered so far?"

"I'm guessing twenty miles."

Ren dropped the binoculars down. She stared into the distance in the direction they were going, then put the binoculars back up to her face. "Hey, um, are there any clothing-optional beaches along the way?"

"Not that I know of. Been a long time since I've been to the beach on Long Island. Things can change. Why?"

Ren stood up and pointed at the sign that stated: 'Clothing Optional Beach Ahead.' "We're headed right into this."

PC stared at her and the sign. He stood up, took the binoculars from her hand, and scanned what was ahead. "Oh boy, I guess we're going to tiptoe through the tulips."

"Did Lambert tell you about that?" Ren said with a smirk as she put her hands on her hips.

"Eh, no. Must have slipped his mind. Curious if we find him there." PC scanned some more with the binoculars.

"I hope you're enjoying the view," Ren said sarcastically.

"Huh, what? No! I'm trying to figure out where we are."

"Uh-huh," Ren said with her arms folded.

PC said, "We're heading for Robert Moses State Park. I can see the Pencil up ahead."

"Pencil?" Ren said. "You mean we're almost there?"

"No, I wish we were, but we're going to head in the direction of the Pencil to see if we can find anything interesting. Come on, pick up your things, and let's get moving."

"But what about the nudists?" Ren asked.

"What about them? Look, they are just naturalists standing around buck naked, and they're harmless. Just smile a lot. The people on the beach seem oblivious to us, anyhow. I'm sure that's not the first person you've seen without clothes on. Come on, let's go." And off they went.

As they came closer to the bathing nudists, Ren stepped closer towards PC to the point where she was leaning on him.

"Hey!" PC said, "Just relax. Like I said, they're just a bunch of people walking around with their clothes off."

Ren stopped leaning on PC. "It's not that. It's a whole new experience for me."

"Another thrill," PC laughed.

Ren laughed too. "I don't know if I call it a thrill, but it is different. Just hope I don't meet anyone I know."

"What makes you think that?"

"Well, we ran into that guy Kevin I work with."

PC shrugged.

"That would be a horrible sight."

A voice called out. "Ren? Ren! Over here, Ren." Both Ren and PC froze where they stood. Ren closed her eyes tight and tensed up. "Oh, no. Tell me that's not him."

"Do I have to look?" PC said.

Ren elbowed him in the side. "YES! I certainly don't want to."

"What makes you think I do?" PC asked. He looked over his shoulder and back again. "Oh God, yes, it's him."

She stood tensely by PC with her eyes still closed. "Does he have anything on?"

PC looked over again. "Yeah, he does."

"Oh, thank God," Ren said, opening her eyes and relaxing.

"He's wearing a floppy hat but that's about it."

Ren elbowed PC, closed her eyes again, and tensed up. "You told me he was wearing clothes!"

"No, I said he was wearing something and that is a hat. You can wear a hat, you know."

Kevin was now in front of Ren and PC. Ren opened her eyes quickly and put her face into PC's arm. "Oh, my lord," she said to herself.

"What's wrong, Ren?" Kevin asked.

PC put his arm around her. "Uh, she's a bit under the weather. You know, not used to being out in the sun all day. All those years being landlocked, you know." PC wanted to laugh, but looked away instead.

"Why aren't you dressed like everybody else?" Kevin spread out his arms to the other nude bathers.

"Well, it is clothing optional, and we opted to keep our clothes on."

Ren shook her head against PC's shoulder. "Yes, we opted to keep our clothes on."

"Oh, okay," Kevin said. "You don't know what you are missing, though."

PC nodded his head. "Yeah, well, we'll take that into consideration. Hey, we must go. We're meeting some friends near the Pencil."

Ren, still with her head against PC's arm, nodded her head. "Yes, meeting friends."

"Oh, okay. Hey, good to see you both again. What don't you come over and meet the family?"

Ren squeezed PC's arm. PC started moving.

"Maybe next time. See ya my friend," he said, and off they went with Ren still holding onto PC's arm, gasping for air.

"Oh my god, that was horrible! Is he gone?"

PC looked quickly. "Yeah, he's walking the other way. Not much better looking from the backside, either."

PC looked at Ren. "Okay?"

"I think so." She let go of his arm. "Oh, man, please. Let's not do that again.

"Yeah, I'm not too fond of seeing that again, either. At least we'll be walking through this soon. I don't think there's any more clothing-optional beaches where were going."

"Why do we keep running into him?"

PC shrugged his shoulders. "I don't know. Must be some connection you have with him."

Ren slapped PC on the arm and gave him a brazen look. "I only work with the guy, not married to him, thank God. Not sure how his wife puts up with him."

"What about you, speaking of marriage?"

Ren let out a grunt. "Long time ago. Got married when I was young, had a daughter, and got divorced."

"Oh," PC said. "Sorry to hear that."

"Don't be. I was too young and should never have done it. Glad I had my daughter, though. She's the best kid in the world."

"Where is she?"

"Oh, in Indiana. She did what her mother did, had a baby young. She's married, though. She's happy and so am I."

"Except when Kevin shows up," PC said with a smile.

"Just when I was feeling better." She grinned back.

"Thanks."

"Eh, what are friends for." Ren changed the subject. "Why do you want to go to the, what did you call it, the Robert Moses Water Tower?"

"Yes, the Pencil. We must get off the beach for a bit and walk on along the parkway to get to the state park. I want to head toward Fire Island and get to the lighthouse. I have this feeling. It may be nothing, but we will be able to get to it without any issues."

"Didn't Lambert say stay on the beach?"

"Yes, but he said we would see openings when we couldn't see the boardwalk."

Ren looked at him curiously. "What is it that you are looking for?"

PC looked straight ahead. "I'll know when we get there.

CHAPTER 10

"Hey, why can't we just keep walking straight? It seems we can only walk in one direction and can't detour along the boardwalk," Ren said.

PC walked with his head down in thought. "Well, this is going to come to an end, and we'd have to swim across. I have a feeling the boardwalk won't be there. So, I'm thinking we should take a detour so we can get on the parkway and walk. We must walk over a bridge at Captree State Park to get back on the beach. Hopefully, it will have that opening."

"And if not?" Ren looked up at PC.

He shrugged. "Then, we swim. Hope you can swim."

Ren stared straight ahead. "Like a fish."

PC smiled. "Hopefully, it won't come to that.

Ren looked behind her, then in front. "Looks like we're done with the nudists."

PC glanced back. "Yes, looks like we're done with them." He adjusted his hat and sunglasses.

"Have you ever done that before?" Ren asked.

"What's that?"

"Do what we just saw behind us."

"No. Curious, but no, never," PC said quickly. "You?"

"No, no, never," Ren said emphatically.

"Apparently, your friend Kevin has."

Ren shook her head. "I don't know. This isn't real, so I don't know if he does that in real life. I don't think he's ever been to a beach, he's so white from not being in the sun; plus the fact that he lives in a landlocked state."

PC looked Ren up and down. "Well, looks like you spent some time in the sun."

"Well, yeah, I travel. I always like to be near the ocean and spend some time in the sun." She turned her head. "This is such a pretty beach." She gazed at the ocean. "And the waves. I love a beach with waves. The sound of the ocean is so relaxing. I'm not sure what I'm doing here, but it beats what I was doing back in Indiana. I don't want to get stuck here, but for now It's a..."

"A thrill?" PC smiled at Ren.

She studied the sand. "Yeah." She turned to him. "Don't you find this to be thrilling?"

PC lowered his head. "Like I said, more of a challenge to get home. This was home once. I grew up here. I've been away for a long time now. I still like to come back and visit, see old friends, see old places I used to know, and hang out. Go by my old high school, which helped mold the character I am today. I always come back to rediscover myself when I get lost in life."

"Does it help?" Ren said.

PC looked thoughtfully at Ren.

"Yes; yes, it does. Kind of resets my compass for me so I can remember who I am."

PC pulled out his binoculars to look ahead. He saw their rings flashing, as did Ren.

"What's up?" Ren said.

"I don't know. Nothing around us that looks like trouble."

He continued to scan the beach with the binoculars. Then he spotted what he wanted to see. "Okay, great. There is an opening for us to detour on the highway. Like I said, we'll have to walk across or it's swim."

Ren took the binoculars from PC and scanned the area. "Looks good, not too far. I don't see any trouble brewing." She pulled the binoculars away from her eyes. "Wonder why rings are flashing. We are near our safe hideaway; could that be it?"

PC shrugged his shoulders. "I guess. Let's head over to the safe place, rest, and fuel up. Sun's beating hard on us today."

PC and Ren headed across the sand to their hideaway and sat inside to get away from the sun. Ren savaged through their supplies and found some higher SPF suntan lotion. Both put some on and put it in their bag for the trek on the beach.

PC grabbed his AAI, threw it over his shoulder, picked up the two 9mm pistols with shoulder holsters he'd found, and gave one to Ren. "Here, strap this on for back up."

She pointed to the AAI. "Are you going to carry two cannons now?"

"Yeah, for back up. So I can spread out more ammo if need to. Besides, this is light-weight."

Ren strapped on her shoulder holster. She stood up. "Ready to go," she said with a smile.

"Okay, let's get going."

Both popped out of the boardwalk and put the boards back up so no one would go in. They headed back toward the shore to make the walk easier. When they were close to the parkway, they went across the sand and made their way along the road.

"Wow," Ren said, "I didn't think we'd be able to get off the beach. Nice to walk on something hard." She looked down at her ring. "Looks like the ring has stopped flashing. Maybe it only flashes near our hideaway."

"Yeah, most likely," PC said with some reservations.

"You seem unsure about something?"

"Well, I'm just concerned that if we run into trouble, we're not going to have our hideaway. We are off the beaten path, but we'll see where this takes us."

"Are you afraid we won't be able to get over the bridge?" Ren asked.

"I just have this feeling someone will be waiting for us there."

"These soldiers that keep appearing?"

"Yeah," PC said, "and they seem to be getting more and more armed. Since we started, we've gone from just being shot at with regular rifles, to mortars, to a half-track."

Ren looked up at PC. "So, the more encounters we have with them, the more armed they become."

"Exactly, Ren."

"What do you think they'll have next?"

"Something big, like an eighty-eight."

"Eighty-eight?" Ren asked.

"It's a big gun. A cannon, to put it in plain English. Seems like we have been coming across these World War II soldiers and the armor they used in the day. Nothing compared to today, but still lethal."

Ren looked down deep in thought and rubbed her chin. "You don't suppose they're sifting through our minds, do you?"

PC looked at Ren. "What do you mean?"

"Well, let me ask you. Are you a World War II buff?"

"Oh yeah," PC said. "Very much so. Interesting period. What are you getting at?"

"What I'm getting at is, they're in your head and pulling out what you know and using it, so it appears in front of us. Like Kevin; he keeps appearing."

"But why does Kevin keep appearing? I mean, the guy must really annoy the shit out of you."

"He does!" Ren said, "and that's why he keeps appearing!"

"But Kevin is harmless. What they're taking from me, these guys are not harmless. They want to take us out."

PC threw his arm in front of Ren to stop her.

"Did you hear something?" Ren glanced up, concerned.

A streak in the sky whistled toward them. PC grabbed Ren and pulled her into a nearby ditch on the side of the road. About fifty feet behind them, there was a tremendous explosion covering PC and Ren with dirt and sand. Both erected themselves, still sitting on their butts, coughing, and dusting themselves off.

"I suppose that was your eighty-eight?" Ren said.

PC pulled out his binoculars, still coughing. He looked ahead. Everything became quiet.

"What's going on?" Ren tried to stand up, but PC pulled her down.

"Stay down!" He said and continued to look through the binoculars. "Something is coming down the road." He put the binoculars down, checked the distance, then put the binoculars back up.

"It's another half-track coming our way. But this one has a machine gun on top of it. They probably think they got us and are sending out the half-track to check."

Ren looked at PC. "What do we do?"

PC checked for cover. "See the brush over there? I want you to play dead. I'm going to hide in the brush. I'll take out the soldier manning the machine gun. If they come to check to see if you're dead, hide the nine-millimeter pistol I gave you underneath and take whoever comes out of the vehicle."

"But I can take them out with my rifle."

"No, you won't have enough time. The pistol will be quicker."

PC looked at Ren seriously. "Are you okay doing this?"

Ren glanced to the half-track and back.

"Yeah, yeah, I can do this." Ren looked down the highway.

"You better get moving, they're getting closer." PC put his hand on her shoulder and crawled into the brush to set himself up.

Ren took a deep breath. "Okay, another thrill." She pulled out the nine-millimeter and lay face down with her left arm out and her right tucked under her body to hide the pistol.

PC moved through the brush. He wanted to be behind them when they pulled up to Ren. Stopping behind some shrubs, he lined up his M82 and looked through the scope to see if Ren was ready.

He waited as the half-track came down the road toward Ren. PC was nervous leaving Ren to do this, but he felt she could handle the situation. She seemed like a noticeably confident person who wasn't afraid of anything.

The half-track stopped on the highway next to Ren. Two soldiers got out, both armed with rifles. The soldier on top of the half-track pointed his machine gun at Ren. One soldier approached Ren and flipped her over. As she rolled, Ren presented the soldier with her pistol and took both soldiers out with two quick shots. They fell to the ground. Ren then pointed her pistol at the soldier on top of the half-track. But one quick shot from PC in the brush, and the soldier went down. Ren pulled out her rifle as two other soldiers came out of the half-track, and Ren took them down with two shots. She stayed low in the ditch, fearing the eighty-eight would lob another shell at them.

PC popped his head out of the brush. "You, okay?"

"Yeah, I'm good." She put her rifle in her left hand as she holstered her nine-millimeter. PC came low out of the brush.

"Hey, do you notice something?" Ren asked.

PC looked around. "The half-track and soldiers, they haven't disappeared."

"Winner, winner, chicken dinner," Ren said.

PC squinted. "I have an idea."

Ren raised an eyebrow. "I hope you're not thinking of taking this metal box and driving it down the road."

"That's exactly what I am thinking."

"But we don't know what is ahead of us. They can take us out quick."

"If it's just soldiers we run into, that machine gun on top will take them out quickly."

"What about the eighty-eight?" Ren asked.

"Well," PC pulled out his binoculars, "they're not firing on us, and I'm not seeing it." He put the binoculars down. "But that doesn't mean it's not out there. Could be miles away."

"What's your plan?" Ren folded her arms.

Drive that down the road. Right now, doesn't look like soldiers know what is going on here. If we run into troops, we'll go right through them."

"I'll take the machine gun," Ren said.

PC grimaced. "I'd rather you drive."

"No, I can handle myself on top. Besides, I don't want to drive that oversized eggbeater."

PC smiled. "Okay."

He picked up one of the soldiers' helmets.

"Put this on and lay low so the only thing they can see is your helmet and eyes. Don't wait for them to fire. Just take them down."

"Okay." She tried to hide a grin.

PC smiled again. "You're enjoying this, aren't you?"

Ren gave a half smile, put on the helmet, and said, "Sort of."

"Okay, let's do this." PC headed for the driver's side, opened the door, and got in. Ren climbed up top, positioned the machine gun, and lay low like PC had said.

The half-track started and lurched forward. Ren held on to the machine gun handles and steadied herself. The half-track moved down the road.

PC was looking through the small window provided. Half-tracks were used to scout the forward front, back in the day. He felt that's what these guys were doing, and he should be expecting them back.

As they rode, Ren heard a whizzing noise. An eighty-eight shell hit just beside the half-track. The percussion of the explosion lifted the half-track up and onto its side. Ren held on as long as she could, but went flying onto the road and into the ditch.

The hit to the ground knocked the wind out of her ,and she stood silent to gain her breath back. She rolled over to look down the road. Her eyesight was still fuzzy, but she realized soldiers were running down the road toward them.

Ren pulled off her backpack and grabbed her rifle. She got behind the half-track and looked up toward the driver's door. "PC!" she yelled. "Are you all right? More soldiers are coming!" She listened to see if he was answering. She saw PC kick the driver's door, and it came flying open, making a loud bang as it hit the side of the vehicle. He slowly climbed out and fell to the ground. Ren went running over. "Are you all right? Oh, my god, you have a cut on your head."

PC touched his temple. "Worry about that later."

Bullets ricocheted off the vehicle. "Shit, get behind the half-track." Both ran to the back as the bullets flew.

Ren held her rifle close to her as both leaned against the half-track.

"What do we do now?" Ren asked.

PC looked around the corner of the half-track as a spray of bullets ricocheted off the metal beast. "Ren, come around me. I want you to let loose like you did on the beach, to get their attention. Shoot off about ten rounds and duck back behind this bucket."

Ren grabbed PC's arm. "What are you going to do?!"

"I'm going to get up to the machine gun and cut these guys down. Can you do this?"

Ren looked at PC, surprised. "Of course." And she smiled.

PC smiled back. "Okay, on three. One, two, three!"

Ren jumped from the back of the half-track, rifle butt up against her right side of her stomach, and let loose ten rapid rounds. The first few shots deflected off the road to force the soldiers to slow down. She managed to take down three soldiers and ducked back behind the half-track. Shots were returned by the soldiers, and they deflected off the half-track. Suddenly, she heard the machine gun going off. She sat close to the vehicle until the shooting stopped. Silence.

Ren looked around and slowly stuck her head around the corner. All soldiers were down. "PC!" she called out. "Are you there?"

"Yeah, I'm here. You in one piece?"

"Yeah!" she yelled out. She pulled her head back and went to the other side of the half-track to find PC.

He got down from the machine gun and looked at Ren. "That was a bitch with this vehicle on its side, trying to shoot."

"But you made it work," Ren said.

He touched his cut forehead. "Yeah, I did." He glanced around. "Come on. Let's get our stuff and get moving."

They heard an artillery shell in the air. Both looked at each other and said together, "Eighty-eight!" and dove into the ditch as the shell hit near the half-track, which flew over them into the brush.

Both looked up to see the half-track behind them burning in the brush. They grabbed their backpacks. "Come on!" PC said.

"Where are we going?!"

"Back to the beach." He grabbed Ren's arm. "We're going for a swim!"

"Ohhhh, shit!" Ren said as both ran toward the ocean.

CHAPTER 11

Safely in their hideaway, Ren tended to PC's head wound. She cleaned up the cut and applied a bandage to his forehead. "There. How does that feel?"

PC felt the bandage. "Okay. My head is killing me. Do we have any aspirin in the first aid kit? Getting tossed around in that half-track didn't help."

Ren went scrounging through the first aid bag and found some aspirin. "Here, take these," she said. PC opened the small packet and popped the pills in his mouth. Ren handed him a bottle of water to wash the pills down.

"Okay, what is plan B?"

PC looked at Ren. "We need to find a boat."

Ren cocked her head. "No swimming?"

"No, no swimming. Some of these lifeguard stands have boats close by. They use them if someone is drowning, or the undertow takes a swimmer out too far. We need to find one.

"Okay," Ren said. "Let's get going."

"Let's do this first," PC said. "Let me rest a little bit. Being tossed around in the tin can rattled my cage. Just need a little rest and we'll be on our way. Cool?"

"Cool," Ren said. "While you rest, I can scout around and see if I can find a boat."

PC was going to say no, but realized she was very capable and would be all right out by herself. He nodded his head. "Okay. Just be careful out there and bring your rifle. If you see the beachgoers disappear, you know trouble is around."

"I'll be all right." She smiled back at PC. "Get some rest. I'll be back."

She grabbed her rifle and the binoculars along with her hat and sunglasses, walked out from underneath the boardwalk, and put the boards back up.

She walked toward the shore, stopped to see what was ahead of her, and began her walk. Beachgoers were around her, sitting on a blanket in the sand or running back and forth to the ocean. It was hard to see much in front of her with all the people in the way.

The beachgoers started to thin out as she walked near the shore. She had gone a couple of miles before she spotted what she was looking for. "A boat?" She pulled up her binoculars to confirm. "Yes! A boat."

She lowered the binoculars, walked toward it, and noticed the lifeguard stand next to the boat. And someone was sitting in the Lifeguard stand. "Must be Lambert," she said to herself as she got closer. "Oh yeah, it's him."

She stopped in front of the lifeguard stand and looked up.

Lambert looked down at Ren. "That was foolish of the both of you to go offshore. You both barely made it out alive. Both of you could have been killed, and the world would change for the worse."

"We were trying to avoid going across water. PC thought crossing the bridge would have been easier." Ren eyed the boat. "Can we use this boat to get across?"

"Yes, that is why it is here. We knew the bridge would have been trouble for you and that you needed to get to the Fire Island side."

"Why didn't you warn us of the bridge?"

Lambert looked down at Ren with scorn. "You were warned."

"You never told us to stay away from the bridge."

"I told you to stay on the path of the beach and you would be safe."

"But the beach isn't exactly safe, either. We've been attacked here, too."

"Yes, what you run into on the beach is mild compared to the bridge. Look what happened. They were shooting an eighty-eight at you." Lambert leaned back into the stand. "Could have taken you right out."

Ren lowered her eyes, then looked back at Lambert. "Okay, point made. She could tell by the color of the sky that it was getting late. "Okay, Lambert, we'll be back tomorrow to pick up the boat. I need to head back now." She turned to walk away.

"Remember what I told you," Lambert said.

Ren stopped in her tracks and looked back at Lambert. "Stay on the beach." She started walking away. "Don't worry I'll make sure." She turned back to Lambert but, just like that, he was gone. She eyed the empty stand. Shook her head and continued her walk.

By the time Ren made it back, it was dark out. She opened the boardwalk panels and entered. PC was out like a light. She checked to make sure he was breathing. She was feeling grungy and felt it was time to clean up. Going in the ocean to wash up wasn't her ideal thing to do, but there was no other choice. As PC slept, she stripped her clothes off until she was bare naked. She found towels and soap, along with shampoo with their supplies. She stuck her head out to see if anyone was around. "Nope," she said and ran for the ocean.

CHAPTER 12

P C woke up to the sound of rain. He squinted his eyes toward the dark.

"Yes, it's raining out," Ren said.

PC looked over to see Ren drying her hair with a towel wrapped around her head and another wrapped around her body. He looked back outside.

"Yeah, I hear it." He watched Ren as she sat in the light of the lantern. She took the towel off her head and began brushing her hair.

"You looked refreshed."

Her lips turned up. "Yeah, I used the ocean bathtub outside to clean up. Feel pretty refreshed, except fresh water would have been better."

"Ah, saltwater bath," PC said. That's what I must do."

"What about your cut and how's your head? Saltwater is just going to aggravate the cut."

He touched his head and winced some. "Yeah, well, I'll have to rough the hair and clean the rest of me. I'll have to redress the wound when I get back. It will be soaked from this rain. My head's not hurting anymore, just the wound."

He stood up and looked at Ren. "Can you turn around, please, while I get undressed?" He raised a playful brow.

She eyed him curiously, then spun around.

He stripped his cloth off, grabbed a towel, and wrapped it around his waist. "Okay, I'm good."

Ren still didn't move. "I hope you're covered."

PC gave her a smirk. "Yes, I am. I wouldn't want to flash you."

She spun around.

"Where's the soap?"

She flipped him a bar.

He smiled and said in his best Arnold Schwarzenegger, "I'll be back," and went through the entrance onto the beach.

Ren chuckled under her breath, "I'm sure you will."

Ren looked around to see what she could cook up. She rummaged through the supplies and found some beef stroganoff with noodles in a freeze-dried bag.

"Hmm, sounds interesting. Just add water. Cool." She prepared the meal and waited for PC to get back.

As he walked in, with the towel wrapped around him and the bar of soap in his hand, he could smell the dinner.

"Ah, smells good. What are we having?"

She smiled. "Oh, some beef stroganoff I whipped up."

"Cool. Uh, could you turn around again? Please?"

She spun around so he could get dressed.

He dressed quickly, turned around and said, "Okay, I'm good. Let's eat, been a long day."

"Yes, it has," Ren said.

Both PC and Ren scarfed down their meals and downed the bottled water they had.

Both relaxed for a few minutes until Ren said, "Okay, I did find us a boat."

PC sat up. "How far?"

"A couple of miles from here. I also ran into Lambert. He was not happy with us. Told me we need to stay on the path."

PC leaned up against the post with his arms folded. "Yeah, well, I'm not surprised."

"Why didn't we just keep walking on the beach?"

"Well, I knew we would need to get across. Swimming wasn't an option for me. I knew if we got across the bridge, it would have been easier for us. I realized later, after we got the crap kicked out of us, most of the lifeguard stands have a boat nearby."

"Where are we headed to next?" Ren asked.

"Next will be at Robert Moses State Park. Pleasant beach. Immensely popular on Long Island. From there, we continue our walkabout and head to Fire Island."

"You know," Ren said, "I'm thinking we're going to be vulnerable in that boat. We're going to be out in the open. Anyone can pick us off."

PC looked at Ren. "You're right, we can be picked off. But then again, we're out in the open on the beach with truly little cover, also. We've almost been picked off already, being out in the open." He sighed. "This is the best option for us. But I will bring us some help."

Ren looked at him.

"We'll bring the machine gun with us on the boat in case someone comes after us."

Ren sighed. "Well, guess it's better than nothing."

"When it gets light, we'll go do some scouting and check the boat."

Ren noticed PC's bandage was wet from the ocean. "Here," she said, "Let me change that bandage out. I can see it's wet. The salt water must be stinging the wound."

PC felt his head. "Yeah, it does kind of sting."

Ren pulled out the first aid kit, pulled off the bandage, cleaned the wound, and put a fresh bandage on.

"There, you're good as new," Ren said.

"Thank you." PC felt the bandage on his forehead, nodding in approval.

"Let's get some rest, and we'll go out in the morning."

Both popped into their sleeping bags, turned out the lights, and went to sleep as soon as their heads hit the pillows.

Morning came quickly. The rain had stopped, but it was still overcast. PC and Ren got up, had breakfast, resupplied their backpacks, and headed out to the beach. PC looked up at the sky. "Guess we're in for a shitty day."

Ren nodded. "Yeah, not looking too good for an enjoyable day." She started walking. "Follow me and I'll take us to the boat."

Both walked toward the shore, then turned heading east.

They walked together, moving quietly. The wind was light, and the temperature was comfortable.

"What do you plan to do when we get out of this craziness?" PC asked.

"Eventually, I'm going to start traveling. I've been waiting to get to a certain financial goal, and I'm almost there." Ren became quiet.

PC noticed her mood darken. "What is it?"

"Since my last cat passed away, it's more possible to travel."

PC looked at her. He could see her eyes tearing up. "What was your kitty's name?"

"Spotford. Spotford McDermott."

"What happened to him?"

She sniffled. "Oh, he had kidney disease, and it rapidly progressed, the last week of his life." A tear slid down. "It absolutely broke my heart. But I know I did the right thing, putting him down. I sat beside him, looking at him, and crying." She began to sob. "He reached his paw out and put it on my hand. He was always like that. I'll miss him forever." The tears began to flow now. PC stopped and let her gather herself. Ren wiped the tears from her eyes. "I'm sorry," she said.

"No, don't be," PC said. You did the right thing. I know what it's like to lose a pet. It's the worst feeling in the world. Especially when you must put the animal to sleep." PC looked at Ren. "This sounds like it happened recently with you."

She wiped the tears from her eyes. "Just after, I was pulled to here."

"Let me tell you something. You'll meet, what—Spotford McDermott, right? You will meet him again one day."

Ren looked up at PC.

"He's waiting for you in kitty heaven. Trust me, he'll be waiting for you."

Ren smiled and gave PC a hug. "Thank you. Come on," she cleared the tears from her eyes. "Let's keep moving. Not much further."

CHAPTER 13

PC and Ren came to the boat. PC walked around it, making sure it was seaworthy. He looked inside. "Two sets of oars. Great," he said. "Everything looks good." He studied the ocean. "It's low tide right now. When it's high tide, that's when we'll go."

Ren grabbed the binoculars from PC. She looked out into the ocean. "Hard to tell with this haziness." She put the binoculars down and looked at PC. "How far do you think we have to row?"

"Maybe a mile. Not too bad. If we hit the tide right, it will take us right to our destination." He turned to Ren. "Can you row a boat?"

"No, I have no idea," she said directly.

"I will do the rowing. If we get into any kind of trouble, you will man the machine gun."

Ren glanced at him.

"Well, you did so well before, and it gave you such a thrill. It's going to be rough rowing the boat. If you want to row and I..."

Ren cut him off. "I can do it; I can do it."

PC smiled at her. "Okay, case closed. Let's head back to camp and get the machine gun. It's going to be a while before we can set sail."

They headed back to camp. PC grabbed the machine gun and handed his M82 to Ren. "Here," he said. "Carry this for me."

She looked at the big gun. "You want me to carry this cannon?"

"Just till we get to the boat. It's not that heavy."

She took it awkwardly, and it didn't seem as bad as she'd thought.

PC put the LM1 over his shoulder. "Come on, let's get going. Grab the first aid kit, also."

Ren grabbed the kit, and off they went.

They made it back to the boat quickly as it began to rain. "Oh great," Ren said. "Now what do we do"

PC moved the boat over to the lifeguard stand and turned it over slightly so they could shelter themselves from the rain. They sat underneath facing the ocean.

"We have some time before we move out. Hopefully, it will stop raining."

"And if it doesn't?" Ren asked.

"Well, we'll get wet. It will make good cover—if the ocean is not rough. I don't want us to be dragged out to sea."

Suddenly, PC and Ren's rings started flashing. Both looked down at their rings, then at each other. They peered out in both directions.

"I don't see anything, do you?" PC asked.

Ren was looking down the shore. "No, not seeing anything. Wait—do you hear that?"

PC listened carefully. "Hard to hear with the rain falling." He listened some more. Then a sound caught his ear. His eyes widened.

"What is it?" Ren asked.

PC waved his hand at her so he could hear the rumbling. "Shit."

"What?"

PC looked nervously at Ren, pulled out the binoculars, and looked down the beach. "It's a tank."

"A tank!" She grabbed the binoculars and looked for herself. "Crap. Okay, now what?"

"Well, we can't let them find us."

"Well, yeah, that's a given," she said with her smirky tone. "There's nowhere to run and hide; we're pretty much out in the open."

"Well, yes, I kind of figured that out," PC said, returning the smirk. He scanned the area quickly to see what he could improvise. Nothing.

"We're sitting ducks," he said under his breath.

Ren lowered the binoculars. "I just see the tank; no soldiers."

PC got behind Ren as she looked again through the binoculars. "No support; hmmm," PC frowned pensively. "I have an idea, and it's the only idea."

Ren put the binoculars down. "What?"

It's raining; we'll just turn the boat over. They'll think it was turned over so the boat wouldn't get full of water."

Ren said sarcastically, "Is that the best you can come up with?"

"It's pouring rain; I doubt these guys are going to stop and check out an upside-down boat."

"And if they do?"

PC sighed. "Then, I'll just make it up as I go along." He smiled at her.

"Oh boy," she said as she pulled the binoculars back up to her eyes. "They're getting closer."

The two pulled the boat down over themselves, but left enough space so they could see outside.

Both watched from the bottom of the boat and dug out some sand to get a better view.

The tank moved slowly by them about fifty yards out.

"Wow, what kind of tank is that?" Ren asked.

"Looks like a tiger tank. Pretty fierce tank for its time."

"Shit, it's stopping," Ren said. "Someone is getting out."

A soldier dressed in black with the SS insignia on his collar popped out of the tank with a machine gun in his hand. He stood there and looked at the boat.

PC grabbed Ren's arm. "Quick, take your rifle. I'm going to pull the boat up, and I want you to take him out. Quickly!"

She nodded.

"Okay." PC put his hands on the rim of the boat to lift. He looked at Ren. "Ready?"

She nodded her head.

"On three. One, two, three!" he lifted the boat, and Ren took him down with one shot.

"Got him!" she yelled out.

PC lifted the boat up upright, grabbed his LSAT rifle, and ran straight for the tank. The tank turret swiveled toward the boat. PC yelled to Ren, "Get away from the boat!"

Ren jumped up and ran as fast as she could.

PC ran by the dead soldier who carried a potato masher hand grenade that the Nazi's used back in World War II. He grabbed it without stopping.

The turret was still turning toward the boat. PC jumped on top of the tank, pulled the pin, opened the lid to the tank, and dropped the grenade. A muffled sound came out of the tank. Everything stopped.

PC looked around for Ren. She stood about twenty-five feet from the boat and started walking toward the tank.

PC jumped off the tank and jogged toward Ren. They met in the middle. Okay?" PC said.

She nodded her head. "Okay."

They looked toward the tank, but it had disappeared, along with the dead soldier.

"Gone again," Ren said.

"Yeah, again." They stood silent for a moment. "Let's get back underneath the boat and away from this rain."

"I'm all for that," Ren said, and they walked back to the boat.

CHAPTER 14

Night had fallen. PC stuck his hand out from underneath the boat. "Rain has stopped." He popped his head out. "Okay, I think it's time for us to move; the tide is up."

They pulled the boat upright, got behind it, and pushed it toward the shoreline. They put all their gear onboard and PC placed the machine gun at the bow of the boat. Ren jumped in.

"Listen," PC said, "When you man the machine gun, you need to keep your ears and eyes open. You handled this rather good before, so I know you can handle this again."

She smiled. "Thanks for the vote of confidence."

They got to the ocean and pushed. Once the boat got deep enough into the water, both jumped in. PC took control of the oars and Ren took the position at the bow with the machine gun.

The water calmed down once they made it past the breakers. Ren looked around. "How come the ocean has calmed down?"

PC looked around as he rowed. "Keep your voice down," he said in a faint voice. The tide has gone slack."

"Is that a good thing?"

"It's a good thing and a bad thing."

"How so?"

"It's quiet. Someone can hear us on shore rowing and take a shot at us. Wasn't expecting the tide to go slack so fast." They rowed on in silence for the next half hour.

"How much farther do you think we have to go?" Ren whispered.

"I'm trying to take the shortest way, so we don't have to row far. Do you see any beach in front of you yet?"

Ren strained her eyes. "Hard to see anything in this dark."

PC stopped rowing and pulled out a compass. Turned around and pointed it toward Ren.

"Well, we're still going south, so we're on the right track." He put the compass back in his pocket and continued rowing.

"Do you need me to take over rowing?"

"No, I'm good," PC said, still in a whisper. "Just keep looking forward." He thought of something that would help Ren. "Hey, look in my bag. There should be some night vision goggles in there. Put them on so you can see what is in front of you."

Ren turned around and rummaged through his bag. "How come you didn't tell me that before?" She pulled out the goggles.

He shrugged his shoulders. "I just thought of it.

Ren threw him a look and put on the goggles. She looked forward again. "Wow," she said. "You can see a whole lot with these."

"How far do you think we are from shore?" PC said.

"About five hundred yards."

"See any movement on shore?"

She looked some more. "Still too far away."

They kept silent as they paddled closer to shore, with Ren keeping a close eye out.

"Uh oh," she said.

PC turned. "What?"

"Saw some movement on shore, straight ahead."

"What is it?"

Ren struggled to focus. "Crap. It's Nazi friends again. And they have a mortar lined up."

"How many?"

"I'd say about fifteen or twenty soldiers. One of them has some sort of bazooka. Weird looking. Looks like some kind of cyclone attached."

The soldier took aim toward them as another soldier began to load.

PC eyes went wide. "Panzerfaust." He looked at Ren. "It's an anti-tank weapon that's going to blow us out of the water. Start shooting!" he yelled.

"Crap!" Ren immediately got behind the machine gun and cut loose. Her fire took down the soldier with the Panzerfaust. A mortar was fired and missed them by a few feet as it exploded in the water, getting them wet.

PC turned around. "What the hell!" He grabbed his LSAT, stood up, and returned fire. Ren kept up her shooting, taking down more soldiers. Shots were returned and PC had to duck. Ren kept low but kept firing away.

PC looked around and continued to row, keeping low. He kept straight on course. He didn't want to turn the boat and give them an easy target. Another mortar hit the water with an explosion closer to the boat with more water splashing on them. PC knew they were getting closer, and the next shot might hit them. Ren kept firing. The soldiers got off one more mortar shot before Ren took them out and managed to hit the ammo, which created a large explosion, taking out the rest of the solders and lighting up the sky.

PC saw the last mortar go off. He ran to the front of the boat and grabbed Ren as both went headfirst into the ocean. The mortar hit the back of the boat but did not explode. Both PC and Ren popped their heads out of the water, grabbed onto the boat and looked inside.

"What the hell happened?" Ren asked.

PC climbed back in as did Ren, and they went to the back of the boat. "Holy shit," PC said. He looked at Ren. "That mortar hit us but didn't explode. It went right through the bottom of the boat." Ren looked over and noticed water pouring in.

"Shit," she said. "Were going down like the Titanic."

PC jumped behind the oars. "We haven't hit an iceberg yet, but we need to get to shore fast! Check to see if anyone else is out there."

She scanned the beach. "I don't see anything. Looks like we're good."

She eyed the bottom of the boat. It was about a quarter full of water. She looked out. "Were almost to the shore."

It was getting harder for PC to row with the boat now half full. PC stopped rowing and pulled one of the oars out. He put the oar in the water and it hit sand. He pulled the oar back in and threw it into the sinking boat.

"There's only three feet of water, we can walk the rest of the way in. Thank God. Quick, grab everything."

Both PC and Ren picked up their bags. Ren grabbed the machine gun and her own personal weapon, and both jumped in the water. They sloshed their way to shore and hit the sand together, dropping everything they had. Both lay on their backs looking up at the sky. PC watched as the boat sank halfway into the ocean. The current had picked up, and the waves overtook the boat; it sank to the sandy bottom.

"Are you good?" Ren smiled at PC.

"Good." PC stood up and looked around. Nothing. All the solders had disappeared. He reached his hand out to Ren. "Come on, let's find our hideaway."

She reached out her hand, and PC pulled her up. They picked up their things and headed for the boardwalk in the distance.

CHAPTER 15

P C awakened to Ren sitting nearby with just a towel wrapped around her, brushing her hair.

"Good morning," she said to PC.

"Good morning," he said with a groggy voice. He examined her. "I guess you've been bathing again in the ocean; or is that a new wardrobe?"

"Yep." She smiled at him, brushing her hair. "Hey, we need to put a new bandage on you. How is your head?"

He touched it with his fingers. "Feeling better. Doesn't hurt so much. Let me clean myself up some before we do that." He looked outside between the boardwalk boards. "Still dark out. Good." He stood up with a groan. "I'll be right back."

"Oh, I found some fresh clothes for us." She picked up a pile and dropped it in front of them. PC bent down to see what was available.

"Well, I see we have 'his and hers' Shorts. Good, it's getting warmer out so that will be good for us."

"And long pants also, plus some raincoats for those rainy days."

"That's good," PC said. "Course, we could have used that last night." He stood back up. "Let me go clean myself up before the sun comes up, while you get dressed."

He grabbed the shorts and a clean white shirt. He looked at the shirt's writing.

"Anything wrong?" Ren asked.

PC stared at the shirt. "No."

She eyed him curiously. "What does the shirt say?"

He looked at Ren and smiled. "Tampa Bay Rays."

He threw the shirt over his shoulder along with the shorts, socks, and underwear, and grabbed a towel and soap. "I'll be back." He walked out to the beach.

PC walked to the shore, stripped his clothes off, and ran into the ocean. It was a little chilly, but tolerable when he got used to the ocean temperature. He quickly soaped himself up. He realized he hadn't brought any shampoo, so he just washed his hair with plain soap. He quickly submerged underwater, then back up. *Not the first time I've roughed it, after roughing it in the Army in the middle of nowhere.*

He came out of the water and dried himself off. He put on his fresh clothes and headed back to the hideout.

As he walked back, he noticed something was in front of him. He looked closely and realized what was there. "A Lifeguard stand," he said out loud to himself, with Lambert sitting on top still wearing his sunglasses.

PC walked up to him, pointing to the sunglasses. "Don't you ever take those off?"

Lambert laughed. "My friend, where I am now, these sunglasses are needed."

"It's pitch dark out here."

"True," Lambert said, "but I am not here physically. I'm just a hologram to you."

PC wasn't sure if he believed him. He saw a seashell sticking out of the sand. He picked it up without taking his eyes off Lambert.

"Go ahead," Lambert said. Throw the object in your hand. At me."

PC launched it and watched it go straight through Lambert. "Holy shit." PC looked to his left and saw Ren standing there.

She moved forward until she was next to PC. "You threw that right through him," she said. "Lambert, if you're not here, then, where are you?"

"I'm in the dimension you should be in. It's hard to explain," Lambert said as the smile left his face. "A lot of energy is being used just to stay in contact with you. We had to cut ourselves short so our enemies cannot track us."

"Enemies? PC asked. "What enemies?"

"What I can tell you is that there are certain people trying to change the outcome of things."

"The outcome of what things?" PC asked, tilting his head.

"I cannot go any further with what I've told you. Therefore, it is so important that you get to the destination I have spoken to you about. If you get back, things will go back to normal. Right now, our enemies are aware of the both of you and therefore soldiers from the past have been trying to stop your trek."

"But how are they doing this? How do they know we are here?" Ren asked.

"Again, I am unable to explain at this time." Lambert looked around. "I must go. They're trying to track us. Be safe, and I will be in contact again."

And just like that, he was gone.

Both stood looking at each other.

"The plot thickens," PC said. "Come on." He grabbed Ren's arm. "Let's grabbed some breakfast and get ready for the day."

She stood there as he tried to pull her.

"Hey, come on." He stood in front of Ren. "We'll work this out. We've done good so far. Come on."

Ren slowly followed him back to the hideaway.

CHAPTER 16

It rained most of the day, so heavily that, though PC and Ren tried to travel, they finally retreated back to the hideaway, going over their travels and resting.

Everything seemed quiet outside. No soldiers approached the hideaway.

They had dinner that night and Ren fell asleep after their meal. She woke up and noticed it was dark out. PC was not in the hideaway. She looked outside. It has stopped raining and there was a full moon outside. She saw PC sitting near the shoreline. It was warm and humid outside for a summer night. She was in a pair of jean shorts and short sleeve shirt. She decided to take her shirt off since she had a sports bra on. She figured it was nothing he hadn't seen before. She walked toward the shore in her bare feet.

She found PC there, sitting in his shorts with no shirt on, with a fishing pole, bait, and bucket.

"Hey there," she said to PC. "Where did you get the fishing pole?"

He looked up at her, noticing she didn't have a shirt on, but didn't mention it. "Oh, I found it out here. Nobody's around so I thought I'd do a little fishing."

She sat down next to him. "Did you fish a lot when you lived on Long Island?"

He nodded his head and smiled. "Oh yes, quite a bit growing up. Me, my father, and brother. We used to go to the docks here at Jones Beach and fish a lot. We had a couple of other places we fished at. Our neighbor used to have a boat, and he would take us out occasionally. Used to have freshwater lakes near the home I grew up in. Did a lot of that also." He sighed. "Certainly was fun growing up as a kid on Long Island."

Ren listened, smiling. "Do you still fish? I mean, do you fish in Florida?"

"No, little to none." He put his head down.

She looked at him curiously. "How come?"

He gazed out at the ocean. "When my father died, I just lost interest in fishing. It was not fun without him."

"What about your brother?"

He laughed. "He moved to Ohio. He went to school there, met a girl, got married, had two kids. He tried to move back, but his wife didn't like the fast pace of Long Island living. So, they moved back to Ohio."

She touched his shoulder. "That's sad, I'm sorry."

He patted her arm. "No, that's okay." He turned to her. "It's all a part of life. Nothing lasts forever."

She looked at him intently. "What about you? Is there someone in your life?"

"There was, but she is no longer with us."

She looked at him sadly.

"Her name was Carol. We met at Macy's where I used to work back in the day. She was the fitting room checker in West Sider. We knew each other for about two and a half years before we started dating. We broke up after a while, but we were still friends. We would go out every now and then. When nine-eleven happened, I joined the Army. We met at this park called Cow Meadow Park just before I was shipped out. We sat with our feet hanging off the dock." He laughed to himself. "I was in my Army uniform, all spiffed up."

Ren smiled.

"I was telling her good-bye and wasn't sure when I'd be back."

"So, then what happened?"

"We lost contact with each other. A friend of mine who I worked with at Macy's, Rich, had written me saying she had uterus cancer. By the time I got back to the states, she was gone."

Ren leaned her head on PC's shoulder. "So sad," she said. "That was some years ago, haven't you met anyone since?"

"I have, but it just never felt right."

Suddenly, the pole started pulling. Both looked up at it.

"Oh! You got something, you got something!" Ren yelled.

PC stood up holding the pole as it kept pulling. "Holy shit, this guy is strong." He staggered forward but dug himself in the sand.

"Hold on!" Ren yelled.

PC started reeling the line in, but the fish was still fighting him. He went forward some as the fish dragged him. Ren ran behind him, sat down in the sand, and put her arms around his waist to hold him still and dug her heels in the sand.

"I gotcha!" she said.

PC reeled in some more but it was still fighting him.

"What the hell do you have?" Ren screamed out.

"I don't know. I'm guessing it's a striper."

"What's a striper?"

"A stripe Bass!"

PC was finally starting to win the battle. "Okay, I'm good, you can let go of me now. Thanks for the help." The fish finally jumped in the air, close to the shore.

"Oh my God! Did you see that?" Ren yelled out.

PC kept reeling as he headed toward the water. The fish was close enough for him to grab. Ren followed him.

"Here," he handed her the pole. "Just hold on." She took the pole as he grabbed hold of the line and followed it to the water. He put his hand inside the fish gill and pulled it up. He grabbed the tail and brought the fish onto shore. "Yep, it's a striper. Must be thirty-six inches."

Ren stood there, amazed. "Wow, never saw a fish that big, let alone a Striper. What are we going to do with it?"

"Well, we already ate, and it will go bad between tonight and tomorrow, so, we'll send him back to make more stripe Bass."

PC removed the hook from the fish's mouth, put it in the water, held it by its tail, shook it slowly back and forth to get water in the fish's gills, and let it go.

He watched, grinning, as it swam off.

Ren walked up to him and put her arm around his waist. "Feeling better?"

"Yes, yes, I do."

CHAPTER 17

PC and Ren decided to have a day of rest after their fishing exploits from the previous evening. Ren cleaned her rifle while PC watched the beach from the inside the entrance of their hideaway. He scanned the beach to the right with the binoculars. He jerked to the left.

"Oh, shit," he said.

Ren stopped cleaning her gun. "What? What's going on?"

PC put the binoculars down. "We have company."

"Soldiers?" Ren asked.

"Yeah. Quite a few, also."

Ren put her rifle down and knelt behind PC, looking over his shoulder. "Yeah, a lot of them out there. What do you suppose they're doing?"

"It looks like they're searching for something. And the funny part is there are people on the beach, and they haven't disappeared like they normally do when the soldiers appear."

"Wait," Ren said. She grabbed the binoculars and looked down the beach. "Uh, did you notice that the beachgoers…" she lowered the binoculars, "Have no clothes on."

PC rubbed his chin, still looking down the beach. "Yeah, I kind of noticed that."

"I thought you said we were clear of the nude bathers."

"I thought we were. Remember, I haven't lived here in a long time, things change."

"What are we going to do?" Ren asked.

"Well, we can't stay here. We'll be like trapped rats." He thought for a moment and smiled. "I have an idea. Not sure if you're going to like it, though."

She gave him a look. "You're not saying we go out there and…"

PC finished the sentence for her. "...and join the bathers, yes."

She stared at him.

"Listen, we can't stay here. What we'll do is just mingle in with the rest of the bathers and make it look like we're part of the scenery. We can't go out there with weapons and if we start firing, we may take out some of the beachgoers, and the soldiers might take people out also."

"No weapons?" Ren asked.

"No weapons. I know it's a chance, but we can't stay here."

Ren glanced at PC, then outside. "Okay." She started stripping off her clothes.

PC followed suit. "There are some beach towels here, grab them and the suntan lotion so we don't burn our butts."

Ren grabbed the towels and her hat.

"No hat." PC pulled it off her head and threw it. "They may recognize us with the hats.

"Sunglasses?" Ren held hers up.

"Yeah, sunglasses are fine."

They pretended to be cool with each other, bare naked.

"Ready?"

"Ready as I'll ever be," she said with a half-smile.

They walked out of the hideaway and put the boards back up.

It was a sunny day, and PC wanted to get the suntan lotion on quickly. But he wanted to get into the crowd of the beachgoers first. "Just looked relaxed like you've done this before. Don't look tense and nervous."

She looked up at PC and smiled. "I'm relaxed."

PC took her hand. "Let's look like the happy couple."

The soldiers were getting closer.

"Don't look at them. The beachgoers are oblivious to the soldiers, so we must be, too. I know we're wearing sunglasses, but don't look directly at them. We may give ourselves away."

PC eyed Ren as some soldiers came walking past them. He said, "My, you are looking lovely today," he grinned.

Ren tried not to laugh. "Thank you, love. And you are looking quite lovely today yourself." The soldiers kept walking. She whispered, "Those guys look awfully rough-looking."

"They're SS. They were a rough crowd in their day."

"You know, I just thought of something," Ren said. "Our rings never went off."

PC looked at his finger and back at Ren. "You know, you're right. They never did go off." He looked around. "And the beachgoers never disappeared when the soldiers came. Something is wrong. Hopefully when we catch up to Lambert, we'll find something out."

PC noticed they were in the middle of the nudist beachgoers. "Let's park ourselves here," he said.

They spread out their beach towels next to each other.

"Let's put some more suntan lotion on before we sit." Ren put some in her hand and some in PC's. They worked the lotion on their bodies.

"Here," Ren said. "Put some on my back. And don't go below my back line," she snapped.

"Yes, Ma'am," he said as she turned around and he saluted her butt.

"I saw that," she said.

PC smiled has he put the lotion on her back. "There, you're done." She turned around. "Do my back for me." He handed her the bottle and turned around. "And don't go below my back line."

She smiled and put the lotion on his back. "There, you're done too." She smacked him on the ass.

"Hey."

Ren giggled.

PC gave her a smirk. "Smartass."

She giggled again. "Let's sit down and blend in."

Both sat down among the nudist beachgoers. Soldiers passed through them, but the beachgoers paid no attention.

They settled onto their towels. "Lay down on your side facing me," PC said.

"Oh, so you can get a good look at me?"

"Cut it out," he said, annoyed. "So, we can both watch each side of us to see what's going on. If we sit up and look around, we may give ourselves away."

"Okay," Ren said.

Both turned to their sides looking at each other.

"There just seems to be a lot of them walking around. Seems endless."

PC watched the soldiers going by. "Yea, they seem to just keep walking and casually looking around. Uh oh."

"What?"

"There looking at our hideaway."

"What are they doing?"

PC did his best not to look like he was watching the soldiers. "They're just looking."

He watched them try to look inside, but they gave up and walked away. "Wandering away now. They don't seem to be interested." He felt relieved.

"That wouldn't be good if they found our hideaway, especially with us wearing no clothes," Ren said.

"You got that right."

Ren whispered, "Hey, they seem to be getting more curious."

"Well, with a bunch of nude people walking around, wouldn't you?"

"That's not what I mean," she said curtly. "They seem to be checking everyone out. Got a plan B?"

PC thought quickly. "Yes, I do. Come on." He pulled Ren by the arm and grabbed her hand.

"What are we doing?"

"Going for a swim. I am guessing they won't bother us in the water. Looks like they're not paying much attention to the swimmers."

Ren shrugged her shoulders. "Okay. Sounds like fun." She smiled at PC.

PC gave her a sexy look.

"Well, you said to relax and act natural."

PC shook his head. "Come, my dear, and I'll teach you how to ride a wave." PC took her hand, and both ran into the water. The waves slowed them down as they got deeper. PC was waist-deep, Ren chest deep, since she was shorter than PC.

PC looked toward the shore. "They don't seem to be paying too much attention to us, or anyone else in the water."

They bounced up and down as the waves came in.

"Can't see our hideaway." PC moved behind Ren.

"What are you doing?" Ren asked.

"Don't worry, I'm not getting fresh. When the wave comes in, I'm going to lift you up with the wave; check if you can see our hideaway." PC put his hands on Ren's hips and lifted her up as the wave came by.

Ren shook her head. "Couldn't see anything. Too many beachgoers."

Another wave came in, and PC lifted her up again. This time Ren got a good look. She came back down. "They seem to be standing around it, but it looks like they're just talking among themselves.

"I hope they don't park themselves there permanently or we're in a world of shit."

"What do we do now?" Ren asked.

"Wait it out. Hopefully, they will move. Or disappear like they always do. They disappear at night, so we may have to wait till nightfall."

"What do we do till then?"

PC shook his shoulders. "Enjoy sitting with the other nude bathers."

Ren raised he brow at PC. "Hey, thought you were going to teach me how to ride a wave."

PC smiled. That's right, I did. Okay, let me show you. When a wave comes you just ride it in. Watch." PC waited for a wave and rode the wave toward the sand. He landed belly first on shore and rolled over. "Go ahead and try it."

Ren smiled. "Okay. Watch me." She waited for a wave to come in. She readied herself and swam as the wave crashed around her. She glided in and hit the shore next to PC. PC laughed as she hit the beach. She rolled over. "That was fun!"

She got up and ran back out to the water. PC sat in shallow water watching her as he smiled. She rode another wave in, but the wave overtook her, and she came tumbling in and rolled up next to PC.

He laughed. "Having fun?"

She rolled over next to PC. "That was a blast!"

PC felt his head wound stinging and realized the bandage was wet, but he had to wait until they made it back to the hideaway to put a fresh bandage on. He didn't say anything to Ren.

They sat next to each other as the ocean came in and hit their feet and legs. They were quiet for a few minutes as they listened to the ocean. Ren spoke. "You never did tell me your last name."

PC looked at her.

"You do have a last name?"

"Of course."

She gave him and anxious look. "And?"

"Sebastian."

Ren looked at him and nodded her head slowly. "Sebastian. PC Sebastian." She kept nodding her head.

"What, you don't like my last name?"

"Oh no, I do like it! It has a nice ring to it. PC Sebastian." She smiled as she said it. "What does the PC stand for?"

He smiled.

They said together, "Almost anything."

Ren shook her head. "You think you can maybe one day tell me what it means?"

PC nodded his head. "Yeah, when we get out of this mess we're in."

"Promise?"

PC grinned. "Promise."

PC stood up and put his hand out to Ren. "Come on, let's get out of the water before we turn to prunes, and get some more suntan lotion on us."

Ren took his hand, and PC helped her stand up. They walked to the towels, dried themselves off, and put some suntan lotion on. They spread the towels out and sat down and observed the other nude bathers.

"You know" Ren said, "I've never been nude bathing before, but this is pretty liberating."

PC looked at Ren. "You like this?"

"Yeah, I do. I feel more at ease with myself, more relaxed and confident. Usually do when I take my clothes off. Don't you?"

"Well, if the soldiers weren't around I would. And by the way, what is your last name?"

Ren looked at PC. "Jenny."

PC slowly nodded his head. "Jenny. Ren Jenny."

Ren elbowed PC.

"No, no, I like it. It has a nice ring to it. Ren Jenny. You know, Paul McCartney wrote a song named Jenny Ren."

"Really? Wow, I wonder if my mother named me after that song."

PC breathed in the salt air. "You haven't said much about your family."

Jen pulled her knees under her chin and wrapped her arms around her legs. "Yeah, well, my mother has some issues."

"What kind?"

She looked at PC. "Mental." She scanned the beach watching the soldiers pass. "Unfortunately, my brother inherited her issues also. It saddens me that he is that way." She laughed. "My mother, before I was brought here, I had texted me. I asked how she was doing, and about an hour later she texted me back saying she was dying."

"Was she?"

"No," Ren said sharply. "When she's off her medication this is how she gets."

She became silent for a moment. PC watched her body movements to see if she was uncomfortable with the subject.

"We don't have to talk about it if you don't want to."

"No, no, it's okay," Ren said brightly. "I'm comfortable talking to you about it."

PC observed the soldiers. "Any other siblings?"

"I have a sister, but she is out of her mind. Not like my mother, but just does crazy shit. One day, some guy cut her off. She chased after him and when she caught up to him at the traffic light, she got out of the car. This guy had his window rolled down. She grabbed him and beat the living daylights out of him, and she's only about five-foot-one."

PC smiled, amused.

"She got arrested and had her picture in the local newspaper."

"Anyone else?"

"I have another brother." She looked at PC. "He's normal, though."

"Like you?" PC smiled.

"Good answer. Yeah, like me."

PC kept one eye on the soldiers. They seemed to just be moving through. He scanned the area. "Hey, have you noticed there are a lot of middle-aged fat people on this beach?"

Ren looked around. "Yeah, you're right." "Not too many young people here." She smiled and looked at PC. "We're the best-looking couple, body-wise."

Both laughed.

The soldiers seemed to be fading into the distance. PC looked to see if any more were on the way. "Hey, let's start creeping back to our hideaway so we can get some clothes on and something to eat."

"Let's hang out a little longer," Ren said.

"What?"

"Yeah, what's the rush? Let's just enjoy."

PC looked at Ren with a blank face. "You didn't even want to do this, now you want to stay?"

"Yeah, I'm enjoying this."

PC rolled his eyes. "Alright, we have time. Not like we're on a time schedule here. Actually, we are, but we have plenty of time."

They sat on the blanket watching the scenery. After a while, PC looked up into the sky. "Starting to cloud up some."

The beachgoers slowly started leaving as the clouds became thicker. PC stood up. "Come on, we'd better go so we don't get caught up in the rain." PC put his hand out and pulled Ren up. They grabbed the towels and headed back.

When they made it to the hideaway, PC stopped.

"What's the matter?" Ren asked.

PC looked at the boardwalk wall. "The wall—it's sealed." He walked over, feeling around, and tried to pull on the boards.

"Are you sure we're in the right place?" Ren asked.

"Yes, of course it is. This is the place." He kept pulling on the boards. He looked around to double-check that it really was the right spot. PC looked at Ren. "Were screwed."

CHAPTER 18

Ren wrapped her beach towel around her body as she looked up to the sky. "It's starting to rain," she said. PC checked through the gaps between the boards to see if he could see anything. He stood up and saw Ren wrapped up in her towel, so he did the same. He looked up to the sky and put his hand out. A few drops came down.

"Great; now it's going to rain." He put his hands on his hips and looked around the beach. "Everyone's gone except us."

"Look, over there," Ren said, pointing her finger toward what looked like something shimmering, trying to appear.

"What is that?" PC rubbed his chin.

"It looks like a lifeguard stand, doesn't it?" Ren turned to PC.

"Yes, yes it does. Come on." PC and Ren trotted over to where the Lifeguard stand was trying to form. They stood in front, ten feet away. PC noticed that Lambert was sitting on it, fading in and out.

What's going on?" Ren asked.

"He's trying to contact us, but something is interfering."

Lambert looked down at them.

"Can you hear us?" PC said.

Lambert tried to speak. Some words came out but not in complete sentences. "Stay—hideout—things—normal soon," and then Lambert and the lifeguard stand disappeared.

"Did you understand any of that?" Ren said.

PC slowly repeated what he said. "Stay, hideout, things normal soon. Yes, he's saying stay by the hideout, things will be normal soon."

Ren put her hands on her hips and looked at PC. "Well, I don't know if you call any of this normal. Sitting on a beach with no clothes, and it's beginning to rain." As if on cue, the rain came down steadily.

"Come on," PC said. "Let's go back to the hideout." Both walked toward the boardwalk.

Suddenly, Ren saw something in the distance. "Hey, look over there. Looks like someone left the beach umbrella and what looks like a cooler behind. Let's check it out."

They walked over to the location. PC opened the cooler.

Ren checked out the umbrella. "We can bring this back to the hideout and sit under it."

"Well, we're soaked anyhow, so I guess it can't hurt us." PC went through the cooler.

"Anything to eat?" Ren asked.

PC threw out a half-eaten sandwich. "Won't be eating that. Something for the seagulls." He pulled out two bottles of water. "Here, I'm sure you're thirsty since we haven't had any water in a while."

"Oh, thank you!" Ren grabbed the bottle, twisted the top off, and took a big gulp. "Any food?"

"Yes. Chicken and roast beef sandwiches." He closed the lid, picked up the cooler, and handed it to Ren. "Here, you carry this, and I'll take the umbrella." PC kept the umbrella open and picked up the blanket that was there as they walked back to the hideaway.

When they made it back to the hideaway, Ren spread the blanket out in the corner of the boardwalk wall. PC put up the beach umbrella and angled it to keep them dry from the rain.

They sat down, and PC opened the cooler. "What do you like, chicken or roast beef?"

"Roast beef," she said.

PC handed the roast beef sandwich to her, and he took the chicken. They ate their sandwiches and washed them down with bottled water. Both leaned up against the boardwalk wall and relaxed.

"Being in the sun all day can make you tired," Ren said.

PC laughed. "The sun can beat the hell out of you in Florida. Very potent in the south. Thank God we're here instead of there. We'd be dead already."

They sat in silence for a while, watching the rain with Ren's head leaned against his arm.

"You asleep?" PC asked.

Ren popped her head up. "Just resting my eyes."

PC smiled. "That's okay, you can rest them."

They sat in silence again when suddenly, PC said, "Hey, what about you?"

"What about me?" she said with her eyes still closed and her head on PC's arm.

"Well, you're such a pretty girl, there's got to be someone in your life."

Ren looked up at PC. "Are you saying that because you saw me naked?"

PC looked down at her. "No! Well, yes, I mean no! Well, you're an attractive woman. Women like you don't walk around free. They're usually an arm trophy for some gorilla."

She started laughing. "Is that what you think of me? Arm trophy?"

"No, not at all. You're attractive, interesting, intriguing, and a bit of a mystery."

She leaned her head back on his arm. "What I like about going home at night is that I don't have to come home to anybody. I hope that answers your question."

PC decided to let it go, and watched the rain as night fell, until both fell asleep against each other to the sound of rain.

CHAPTER 19

P C awoke when he heard a sudden thud. He jumped, as did Ren.

"What was that?" Ren asked.

PC moved Ren softly off him as he crawled on the sand to investigate. It was dark and he couldn't see much. It was still raining out, and the sand stuck to his legs and hands as he crawled. He was feeling around when he touched something wooden. He turned toward the boardwalk wall and reached out. He couldn't feel the wall and realized there was a space. He smiled and looked behind him. "Ren, come to me. The hideaway is back."

"Oh, thank God." Ren crawled toward him.

PC glanced inside.

"Can you see anything?"

"No, not really. I'm going to go in and see if I can find our lantern. Wait here." PC crawled in.

Ren knelt, straining to see something. "Anything?"

"Not yet. Wait." With a flick of a lantern, the hideaway was lit.

Ren crawled in quickly. "Back in business."

"That we are." PC looked outside. "Still dark out."

"What time do you think it is?"

"I don't know. My watch is around here somewhere. Ah, just where I left it."

PC picked up his watch from the top of a cooler. "It's three in the morning."

"How long do you think we were out there?"

PC scratched his head. "I'm going to say about nine hours."

Ren scratched her head also, as she was feeling dirty. "Well, I'd like to clean up before we go back to sleep."

"Clean up?" PC looked at her funny.

"Yeah, it's raining out. Fresh water. Shower in the rain, you know." She smiled.

PC scratched his head again. "Yeah, good idea. Soap and shampoo are over there."

"Aren't you coming with me?" She gave him a long stare.

"Well, I figured you want to shower by yourself."

She gave a wry smile. "We just spent the whole day walking around butt naked. I think at this point we can be open-minded."

PC stared at her now. "You're right. Let's go. Might as well leave the towels in here for now since they'll get soaked in the rain."

Ren removed her towel and threw it to the side as PC watched her walk out, bare and all. He blinked several times and heard her say, "Are you coming?"

"Coming," he said, as he dropped his towel and walked out in the rain.

It was raining steadily, so there was no problem soaping up and rinsing off. They went back to the hideaway and dried off. PC put on a pair of shorts and his Rays shirt, as did Ren.

"Let's get some sleep," PC said. We need to make plans for the morning."

They both crawled into their sleeping bags and passed out quickly.

The next morning, Ren woke up and saw PC looking out the entrance with the binoculars. Ren crawled up to PC, to the top of his back, put her arms on his shoulders, and looked out. "What's up?"

He put the binoculars down. "Our friends are back." PC handed the binoculars to Ren.

She looked eastward down the beach. "Wow. There's a lot of them."

"Waiting for us, no doubt."

Ren scanned the beach. "I don't see any beachgoers this time. Just soldiers."

"Yeah, my ring woke me up earlier and I've been watching them ever since. Our rings are working again. Look to the west now."

Ren turned toward the west. "Damn. They've got us trapped now."

"That they do." PC rubbed his chin.

Ren put the binoculars down. "They do not seem to be advancing. Just sitting there. Waiting for us. We need a plan." She looked down inside the boardwalk. We could go down the inside of this boardwalk."

PC rubbed the side of his face.

Ren looked at PC. "Well?"

"I'm thinking."

Ren looked at him blankly. "You don't think it's a good idea?"

PC took the binoculars from Ren and looked down the coastline. "Were trapped. And we cannot go out naked like we did yesterday since there are no nude bathers. In fact, there are no bathers at all. Certainly, we cannot charge them." He put the binoculars down and checked underneath the boardwalk. "I like your idea; this boardwalk seems to be consistent. It should have ended miles ago, but it keeps in front of us all the time."

Ren looked down the rest of the inside of the boardwalk.

"We can walk right by the soldiers, and they won't even know it.

PC smiled and tapped his nose. "Exactly."

"We don't know what is even down there."

"I know, but it's either that or be trapped like rats on a sinking ship."

Ren nodded her head slowly. "Okay. Let's do it."

PC and Ren got up, packed their backpacks, picked up their weapons, and started down the inside of the boardwalk.

"Let me grab one more thing." He picked up a gigantic gun.

"What is that?" Ren said.

"A Halo Rocket Launcher."

Ren raised an eyebrow.

"Just in case. Let's go and let's be quiet."

Both started down the inside of the boardwalk covered mostly with sand and some garbage dropped by the beachgoers. PC slowly moved along with Ren trailing him, looking through the slots to see where the soldiers were.

"Are we clear of the soldiers yet?" Ren looked through the slot also.

"No. Seems we'll be walking for a bit." PC tried to look at an angle but could not see anything.

PC and Ren walked another two miles. It was hot on the beach, and they were getting overheated.

PC noticed that Ren was soaked with sweat. "Let's stop here and take a break; get some water in our bodies." Both sat up against the wall and drank thirstily. PC pulled out two towels and gave one to Ren. "Here, wipe yourself down."

Ren wiped her face and arms down. "How much farther, do you think?"

PC looked through one of the slots. "I do not know. Does not seem to be getting any better out there. Soldiers everywhere. Hold it." Something caught PC's attention.

"What is it?" Ren asked.

"There is a tank out there. A big Tiger Tank." PC put his hand up to Ren, motioning her to stay quiet. One of the soldiers was looking in their direction under the boardwalk. He started speaking German, but talking to someone above them. A voice answered, above them on the boardwalk. Ren looked up, holding her rifle in an upward position.

Footsteps clamored from above. PC slowly took his M82, lay down in the sand, and positioned himself to fire if necessary.

The walking stopped. PC could not see much. The soldier knelt on one knee and peeked down through the cracks. PC aimed and waited. The soldier got up and walked to the rail, speaking to the other soldier on the beach. The soldier walked away.

Ren looked through a crack to see what the other soldiers were doing. She saw the turret move on the tank. Ren's eyes lit up. "Oh shit."

"What?" PC moved next to Ren to see what was going on. "Crap! Come on! Before they blow the shit out of us."

Both started running as fast as possible underneath the boardwalk. The tank took aim. PC and Ren were about twenty yards away when a big explosion knocked them both off their feet and into the sand. PC rolled over to see where Ren was and found her right beside him. "Okay?" PC asked.

"Okay."

PC looked back to where they had been and saw a big hole in the boardwalk wall. He grabbed the rocket launcher and ran toward the hole.

"Where are you going?" Ren yelled. "Keep going! I will catch up to you."

PC had both his M80 and his machine gun strapped over his shoulder behind his back and carried the rocket launcher. He stopped quickly to look through cracks in the boardwalk wall to see what the tank and soldiers were doing. The turret of the tank was moving toward where Ren was running.

"Shit!" He ran toward the hole that the tank had shot through. He dropped both of his rifles and looked through the hole. The tank took aim at where Ren was running. PC yelled down the boardwalk, "Ren! Get down!"

One of the soldiers saw PC and pointed toward him. PC had already taken aim at the tank when the tank blew a second hole in the boardwalk. PC screamed as he shot the rocket at the tank and blew the turret clean off, killing the soldiers around it. He threw the launcher down, strapped his M80 behind him, and grabbed his machine gun. There were still soldiers on the beach. PC sprayed the soldiers. One by one, they went down. "You bastards!" he yelled at them. "You killed Ren!"

He walked toward them as they went down. A half-track headed toward PC with a machine gun mounted on top. He quickly dove in front of the tank to avoid the bullet spray from the half-track. He dropped his machine gun and pulled out his M80. He climbed up on the turretless tank, lay down, and took aim at the driver. One shot pierced the armor of the half-track, and it came to a halt. The soldier on top still fired at PC, peppering the tank with the spray of bullets. PC let another shot go and took out the soldier manning the machine gun. But it was not over.

Ren popped her head out of the second hole the tank had shot open. Frazzled, she staggered out onto the beach and fell onto the sand. She opened her eyes and looked around. Her vision was blurry, so she wiped her eyes, only to see soldiers coming from both directions. Still dazed, she got up and ran, staggering toward the tank.

PC ran toward the half-track. He saw the soldiers coming too and wanted to cut them down. He jumped on top of the half-track and dumped the dead soldier over the side. He swung the gun around and started mowing down the soldiers.

Ren made it to the tank and saw PC. She looked behind her. The soldiers were coming fast. She noticed the tank had a machine gun.

"Right," she said to herself and jumped up on the tank. It had a small hatch in the gunner seat. She pushed the dead soldier aside. She closed the lid. At first, she was not sure how to fire the gun.

"Crap, how do you fire this thing?" She grabbed the trigger and started firing. It startled her, and she let go. "Oh! So that's how you do it."

She took aim and started mowing down the soldiers. They went down two, three, four at a time.

PC was also mowing them down, not knowing Ren was still alive and protecting his back. PC stopped shooting as Ren continued to fire. He turned around and noticed shots being fired from the tank. *Who is in that tank?* he thought to himself. Finally, the shooting stopped.

Exhausted, PC climbed from the half-track. At the same time, Ren popped the lid off the tank and jumped out. As she hit the ground, she looked around. They turned slowly as their eyes met.

"Ren."

"PC."

Both smiled as they ran toward each other. They hugged and held on for a good minute.

PC looked at Ren. "Okay?"

With dirt and sand covering her body, she smiled. "Okay. You okay?"

He smiled back. "Knowing you're alive, yes, okay." They held on to each other until they both caught their breath. PC looked around. "Look, everything is gone.

Ren looked around. "I'm not surprised."

CHAPTER 20

PC and Ren made their way to the boardwalk wall and sat down in the sand. Ren was still holding onto PC. She had been shaken up by her close call. The percussion of the explosion had sent her airborne, hitting the wall and going forward.

They fell asleep still holding on to each other. PC woke up and found it was dark. He looked at his watch, catching the moonlight for the time. It was just after midnight. Sand was still on Ren's face and most of her clothing.

"You two took a beating, I see."

PC pulled out his nine-millimeter Taurus and pointed to the man in front of him. He looked closer and realized who it was. "Lambert." He lowered his gun. "Not in your lifeguard stand, I see." PC holstered his weapon. Lambert squatted down. "No, not this time." He looked at Ren. "Is she okay?"

PC looked over at Ren, who was still holding on to him.

"She was shaken up rather good from an explosion. I'm sure she was sent airborne from an eighty-eight gun on that Tiger." PC stroked her hair. "She'll be okay. She's a tough girl. Just traumatized now."

"And you?" Lambert said. PC looked up at him with a glare. "I've seen plenty of action. I've seen guys blown to bits. I've seen women and children get killed, maimed. Am I alright, you ask?"

Lambert shook his head. "Point taken." Lambert stood up and looked around the beach with his back to PC and Ren. "The soldiers won't bother you for now, but they will be back. You shouldn't see the heavy armament anymore."

"How long before they come back?"

Lambert turned around. "A few days or so. It will give you time to get you closer to your destination. Go to the Fire Island and find the lighthouse. We're trying to set up a portal so we can get you home sooner. Not sure if this is going to work."

PC sighed. "Can we at least rest up some? This girl just went through a traumatic experience by almost being blown up."

"Yes. But don't rest for too long. We need to get the world back in order, and you're the only two who can do it." Lambert looked up and smiled. "Ah, my time is up here. Remember, don't rest up too long. Get as much distance in as possible. Remember what I said. Go to the Fire Island Lighthouse. The portal is still a work in progress. Hopefully, it will be working when you get there." And like that, he was gone.

Ren's head popped up. "What?! Who's there?" She looked around and then at PC. "Who is here? Who are you talking to?" Ren still clung to PC., seeming agitated.

"Easy, easy. It's okay. It was Lambert. He's gone now."

She lay her head back down on PC and took a deep breath and sighed.

"How are you doing?"

"I'm okay. Really, I am."

"Nobody is okay when they almost get blown up. It rattles the best of them. Even soldiers."

She looked up at PC. "Really?"

He nodded his head. "Really."

She put her head back down.

"Have you seen all the civilians in Ukraine on the news? See how rattled they are? They are not used to that sort of thing. Neither are you. God bless them. Hopefully, they will survive the horrible tragedy."

She looked up again. "How about you? You should be used to it. You've seen war."

He stared blindly into the ocean and said with a blank face, "I'll never get used to it." PC snapped out of it. "You look dirty there, girl."

She looked at herself. "Yeah, I am pretty raunchy."

Suddenly, lights went on behind the boardwalk.

"Well," PC said, "Looks like our hideaway has found us."

"Can you get a couple of towels and soap, and I'll meet you at the ocean? I got to clean up here," Ren said." She touched his forehead wound. "We need to put a new bandage on."

"No problem. You go ahead, and I'll get what we need."

PC went inside the hideaway and grabbed two towels, some bottled water, soap, and a blanket so they could sit on the beach. He looked through the cooler and saw two more sandwiches left. PC smelled them. "Still good," he said to himself and made his way to the ocean.

There was enough moonlight for PC to see Ren in the ocean. He found her clothes on the beach. He spread out the blanket as she came out of the water to him.

"Do you have the soap?" she asked. He looked at her in the moonlight. "Soap?" she repeated

"Oh, yeah." He handed the soap to her quickly. She walked back to the ocean to bathe herself. PC spread out the blanket, sat down, and opened the foil on one of the sandwiches. He smelled it again.

"Chicken," he said to himself and took a bite.

Ren came back from the ocean with soap in hand. PC handed her the towel. "Water is nice tonight. Don't you want to clean up?

"Maybe later," he said with a mouth full of food.

Ren wrapped herself in the towel and sat down on the blanket with PC. He handed her a sandwich. "Feeling better?"

She took the sandwich. "Oh yes, much better." She opened the foil and bit into the sandwich. "Chicken. Tastes good." PC handed her a bottle of water, and she drank down a big gulp.

"Lambert says we should be okay for a bit; we won't be seeing any of the big armor we have come up against. I want us to take it easy for a day. We'll keep moving and just enjoy the sights and recharge our batteries. How does that sound?"

With a mouth full of food, Ren nodded. "Sounds like a plan." Both finished their sandwiches and drank down the water.

"What do we do now? PC asked.

"Let's sleep out tonight, enjoy the relaxation of the ocean. Great way to unwind. It is relaxing," Ren said as she took a deep breath of the ocean air and closed her eyes. "You know, when this is all over, I think I'm going to move somewhere where there is an ocean. It's so relaxing. Besides, I'm tired of being landlocked.

"You should go to Clearwater Beach in Florida and watch the sunsets."

"Oh, that would be so nice to see." She lay back on the blanket and looked up at the stars. "Are the stars pretty in Florida, like New York?"

PC lay back on the blanket next to Ren. "Not as pretty. Florida is a tourist state, and it's lit up like a Christmas tree. Now here, where we are, it's pretty much pitch black so you get a better view of the stars."

"They're so nice," she said as she faded to sleep. PC was not far behind and fell asleep too.

CHAPTER 21

The sun was just coming up when Ren awoke. She sat up and stretched her body as she yawned. She looked to her left to see that PC was not there. She looked toward the ocean and saw him coming out.

"Good morning," he said to Ren as he picked up the towel to dry himself off.

Ren smiled and looked him up and down. "Feeling better?"

"Feeling great." He wiped himself down and wrapped the towel around his waist. He sat down next to Ren, took a deep breath, and exhaled. "Such a nice day."

"What's our plan?" Ren asked.

"Well, Lambert said we can rest a bit, but how do you feel?"

"I'm feeling good. I feel we should move on. I don't need to rest."

PC examined her. "Are you sure? I am concerned about you. Not everyone goes through what you just did. It's very traumatic. It can scare you. Ever hear of PTSD? I've seen people who never recover."

Ren leaned her head on his shoulder. "I appreciate your concern. But really, I'm fine. I needed to process what happened and just chill out for a bit. I have my energy back, and my head is clear."

PC turned her so Ren was facing him and looked her in the eyes. "Are you sure?"

Ren nodded. "Yes, sure, and confident."

PC relaxed his grip on her. "Okay. Let's go to the hideaway, get some clothes on, have something to eat, and get what we'll need."

Ren smiled. "Sounds good. But I do want to put a new bandage on your head."

They got up and headed for the hideaway. About an hour later, they came out with their backpacks, floppy hats on, and weapons ready and loaded, wearing shorts and shirts. Covered in suntan lotion, they headed for the shore to continue their trek.

They walked in silence for a bit as beachgoers started appearing on the beach.

"What's our next stop?" Ren asked.

"Well, we'll be going to Fire Island, and I want to make it to the lighthouse. Lambert told me there might be a portal there to get us home sooner."

Ren's eyes widened. "Really?! Why didn't you tell me this sooner?"

"He told me quickly before he did his disappearing act, and I didn't want to get your hopes up too soon, because he said he wasn't sure that would work."

Ren walked with her head down in silence, then popped it up again. "If this works, we won't see each other again."

PC looked at her sadly. "I don't know what is going to happen, if we're going to end up in the same spot, or separated, or end up somewhere else."

"Like?"

"Like another wrong dimension. Let's just see what happens."

Ren looked down and walked in silence again. "Do me a favor?"

"What's that?"

"In case we don't end up together, give me your phone number."

PC stopped and looked at Ren.

"Really, so we can stay in contact."

PC slowly nodded at Ren. he took his backpack off, pulled out his wallet, and handed her a business card. "Here you go."

"You have a business card?"

"Yeah. I told you I do security on the side."

Ren looked at the card. "Yeah, you did say that, but I didn't know you did it privately." She looked at the card and smiled. "Sprintfire Security. I like it." She looked up from the card. "Just you, or do you have other employees?"

PC started walking, and Ren followed. "No, just me."

"Do you have another card and something to write with?"

PC stopped again, reached into his backpack, and pulled out a pen and another business card from his wallet. She grabbed the pen and wrote on the back. "What are you writing?"

She looked up, smiled, and gave PC the card.

He looked down at the card. "Your phone number, I presume."

She nodded her head.

"Okay." He grinned and put the number in his wallet. "But don't count your chickens yet. We don't know what we'll be running up against when we reach the lighthouse." He pulled his binoculars out of his backpack, stopped, and scanned the area. "We have about three or four miles maybe to go before we make it to the lighthouse." He searched again. "And looks like we're going to walk through the clothing-optional people again."

"Again?"

"Yeah; should be the last time we see them. I don't think there's any more of that once we pass through Fire Island."

"Well, you sure seemed to enjoy their company."

PC shot a look at Ren. "Me!? You're the one who keeps taking your clothes off."

"Well, so did you."

"Well, yes, I did. But I was thinking like a soldier."

"By taking your clothes off?"

"No!" he said, somewhat annoyed. "It's called adapting and improvising. I was more interested in staying alive. And it did work, by the way."

Ren started laughing. "You call that improvising?"

He stopped and looked at Ren. "And what would you have done?"

Ren put her hands on her hip, glancing from the sand to PC. "I probably would have done the same thing."

PC looked around. "Come on. Let's take a break for a bit, then we'll get back on our trek."

"Okay."

They walked onto the dry sand and sat down, looking out into the ocean, sipping water out of their water bottles as they absorbed the sound of the ocean.

"So, where are you planning on moving?"

Ren looked at PC. "Moving?"

"Yes, moving. You told me you want to move near the ocean. Have any state in mind?"

Ren gazed out into the ocean. "I don't know yet. You have the East Coast, the Pacific Coast. I don't know. Still thinking about it." Ren looked around. I might take up fishing."

PC looked at Ren. "Really."

"Yeah. I enjoyed watching you the other day when you caught that fish. I want to try it, fishing, that is."

PC smiled and looked out at the waves. "That fish would have dragged you into the ocean, but I love your determination to learn. I think you'll enjoy it. It can be boring at times, but, as they say, if you don't catch anything, it is still a good day."

They relaxed for another few minutes and then PC said, "Let's get going."

Ren nodded and they returned to their trek.

They passed through the clothing-optional beachgoers who paid no attention to them. Both PC and Ren noticed a volleyball game being played in the sand.

"That's got to hurt," Ren said. "Does that hurt?"

PC shrugged his shoulders. "I don't know. I never played naked volleyball before. But I'm sure it would hurt. Must hurt for a woman to be bouncing those boobs up and down."

Ren shrugged her shoulders. "I guess." She smiled at PC. I never played naked volleyball before."

PC smiled back at her.

"How much further, do you think?"

PC looked ahead as the lighthouse was getting closer. "I'm guessing a few more miles now." PC looked behind him. "Looks like we're done with our new bather friends."

Ren chuckled. "Too bad. I'll miss them."

PC started laughing. "This has been an interesting adventure."

CHAPTER 22

PC and Ren began their walk up the boardwalk toward the house connected to the lighthouse.

"I'm guessing we have to go through the house to get inside the lighthouse," PC said.

Ren turned to PC. "Why wouldn't they have a door on the lighthouse?"

"In case of flooding from a storm, I guess."

As they walked up the boardwalk, they came to a house on the left with a red roof.

"What's this house for?" Ren asked.

"I don't know, let's take a gander."

PC and Ren made a left turn on the boardwalk and headed for the house. PC turned the doorknob, but it was locked.

Ren looked through the window. "Looks like a boathouse."

PC walked over and looked through the window behind Ren. "Yeah, you're right. It's a boathouse." PC looked over his shoulder. "Come on, let's head for the house." They walked back up the ramp and turned back on the boardwalk.

"Hey," Ren said, "What do we do if it's locked?"

"Well, we'll figure that out when we get there."

They walked up the long boardwalk and made it to the front door with the big red roof. PC knocked on the door. Ren looked through the glass side light windows, putting her hands up toward her face to reflect the glare.

"No answer," PC said.

Ren turned the doorknob. The door opened. PC and Ren looked at each other with surprise. Ren slowly opened the door. She peered inside, looking side to side. PC stood behind Ren, leaned forward, and looked around.

"Hello," Ren said. "Anyone home?"

Silence. Both stepped inside. PC said, "I guess nobody is home."

Both relaxed as PC closed the door. He took off his backpack, as did Ren.

"Come on," PC waved. "Let's walk this way. It should lead us to the lighthouse."

Both started walking with weapons in hand.

They walked across the house and found a door. PC opened it and looked inside.

"What's there?" Ren asked.

"Nothing, just an empty room. But there is another door."

They walked through the small room, and PC opened the second door.

"Hmm. Just another connecting room. This should lead us to the lighthouse."

They walked through the connecting room. PC opened the next door. They both walked in and looked up at the spiral staircase.

"Looks like we're in the lighthouse," PC said.

"Okay, now what? We're here, and we haven't exactly been transferred back home."

PC shrugged his shoulders. "I don't know. Lambert just said to go to the lighthouse, and we may be able to get back home. He didn't give me any specific instructions."

"Wait." Ren held her hand up as she listened.

"What? I don't hear anything."

"SHHH! Listen." A meow was heard from above. "Were not alone. We have a cat in here." Ren looked up. "Only way is up."

She walked up the winding staircase of the lighthouse. The meow became louder.

PC watched as she went up. "Anything up there?"

Ren continued up the winding staircase and came upon a cat sitting there, looking at Ren. "Oh, my God. It can't be!" She knelt next to the cat and put her hand out. The cat put his paw on hers. A tear came to Ren's face. "Spotford! Oh, my baby." She picked up the cat and came down the stairs.

PC was waiting at the bottom. "What did you find?"

Ren came down the steps in tears. "It's him! It's him!

"Who?"

"This is Spotford McDermott. The cat I was telling you about that I lost."

"Wait a minute, didn't you tell me he died?"

"Yes, yes, he did. But this is him. I know it is. It's the way he put his paw on my hand. He always did that to reassure me. Oh my God, I can't believe this."

She sat on the steps as tears slid down her cheeks.

PC rubbed his hand on his face, not sure what to say. He looked up, then back at Ren. "I'm going to look around. I'll leave you to together while you..." he stopped in mid-sentence as he noticed Ren was engrossed with her cat. He smiled and said, "I'll be right back." Ren never looked up.

PC went out the door. He wanted to check out the rest of the house, but first, he wanted to check the grounds to make sure they were safe.

PC made his way to the front door. He noticed the kitchen as he passed it and made a note to check if any food was available, and maybe they could do some cooking. Been awhile, he thought to himself, since he had a good, cooked meal.

He made it to the front door and opened it. In front of him was a soldier. The soldier came right at PC and knocked him down on his back. The soldier tried to aim his gun at PC, but PC, still on his back, managed to swivel his body around and had enough leverage to take the soldier's legs out from underneath him with his rifle. The soldier hit the wall and fell on top of PC. PC let out a groan and grabbed the soldier by his chest, rolled him over, and slammed his head up against the wall. Both men lost their weapons as they both stood up. PC drove himself into the soldier, and the soldier hit the wall again. PC pulled out his nine-millimeter, but the soldier had a potato masher in his hand and knocked the gun away with it. PC grabbed the hand holding the weapon and hit it on the wall until the soldier dropped it. The soldier had a second potato masher hooked to his waist, and PC knocked it to the floor. The front door opened with more soldiers on the way. PC grabbed the soldier and ran toward the door, flinging the soldier up against the door and slamming it shut, stopping them from getting in. They pushed back at the door. PC had his forearm up against the soldier's throat, holding him up against the door, trying to stop the other soldiers from coming in. PC, realizing he couldn't hold them off forever, screamed, "Ren! Ren! Get up here!"

Ren was still inside the lighthouse with Spotford when she heard the commotion. "Uh oh. That doesn't sound good." She put the cat down on the steps and picked up her rifle. "Stay here," she said. "Mommy will be right back."

Ren ran to the front door and saw PC barely holding on as soldiers outside were pushing back.

PC had his forearm up against the soldier's throat still. He looked back at Ren and pointed to the potato masher. "Give it to me!" He held his left outstretched arm out with his hand open. "Now!"

Ren ran for the potato masher and put it in PC's hand. The door began to slide open more with the solders pushing from outside. PC looked at Ren. "Pull the pin! pull the pin!" She ran up and yanked the pin out. He threw it through the open crack in the door, low at their feet and said, "Happy trails." He closed his eyes and held on to dear life. The explosion knocked him and the soldier backward as the door blew open. Ren landed on her back from the percussion of the explosion.

PC was down on his back. The soldier stood up first and grabbed the nine-millimeter and aimed it at PC. Ren sat up, quickly, her rifle still in hand, and fired three rapid shots into the soldier. He hit the ground flat on his back. She crawled over to PC, who was out cold. She stood up and looked outside to see three dead soldiers. She quickly closed the door and locked it. She turned around to notice the soldier was gone.

PC began to move and groan. Ren ran over to him, putting down her rifle and tending to him.

"Hey, hey. I'm here. Can you hear me?"

PC looked up at Ren. Ren put her hand on his chest as she looked around for wounds.

"I'm okay." He put his hand on hers. "Just got the wind knocked out of me."

Ren sat him up against the wall, concerned.

He looked around, then at Ren. "What a day, huh, kid?"

CHAPTER 23

R en helped PC to his feet. She looked at his forehead. "Oh, that blast opened up your head wound again. She touched it.

PC winced. "Yeah, lucky me."

"Let me get the first aid kit."

"No, no, we'll do that later. I want to check the perimeter outside. There might be more of them out there."

"Let me fix your head first."

PC touched his forehead. "I'm okay." PC looked at Ren and smiled. "Just a flesh wound."

She sneered at him. "You been watching too much English humor."

PC walked towards the door and stopped. "Come here." Ren walked over to him. "I want you to lock the door behind me. I'll bang hard three times to let me in. Okay?"

Ren nodded her head. "Be careful."

PC opened the door slowly and looked both ways. He scooted out the door and heard Ren lock it.

Ren stood looking at the door and her eyes widened. "Oh! Spotford!" She turned, picked up her rifle, and ran back to the lighthouse.

She opened the door and looked around. "Spotford?" She called again. "Spotford?"

She looked up the spiral staircase and started up the steps, calling his name. "Spotford, where are you?" She made it all the way to the top and Spotford was nowhere to be found.

She sat on the steps and started crying. "Oh Spotford. I lost you again."

As soon as PC had walked out the door, he'd noticed the scene had changed. "Hey, where the hell am I?" He looked around. The ocean was gone, and he was on a stage inside a small stadium. "I'm not in Kansas anymore." He lowered his rifle. "I know this place." He moved forward. "This is the Jones Beach Theatre. How the hell did I end up here? It's miles away."

He looked around the empty stadium and noticed a young blonde woman sitting in the first row. He started toward her slowly. He slung his rifle over his shoulder as not to scare her.

As he got closer, he recognized her. She smiled at him. PC stopped at the steps and gazed at her. "Carol?"

Her blue eyes gleamed. "Hello, PC. How are you, my old friend? Please come sit next to me."

He sat there frozen, not knowing what to do.

"It's okay. Really."

He came up the steps and stopped in front of her.

"Sit. Please," she continued to smile.

He took his rifle off his shoulder, leaned it against the wall, and sat down. He looked at her, not knowing what to say. He wanted to touch her but was afraid.

"It's okay," Carol said. She put her hand on his. He took it and held her soft hand.

"What are you doing here? You're... you're..." he glanced away, then back at her. "You're supposed to have passed."

She nodded her head. "Yes, I have passed."

He put his other hand underneath hers and squeezed it.

"But you look and feel so real."

"In this world, I am."

Carol looked at the wound on PC's head with concern. "Your head. What did you do?"

"Oh, well," he touched his head and winced. "Just a flesh wound."

Carol smiled at PC. "Just a flesh wound. You've been watching Monty Python again."

He smiled. "One of my favorites. You're the second person who has said that today."

Carol put her hand on the wound and held it there for several seconds.

"Really Carol, I'm okay."

"Shh." She slowly took her hand off.

"There; feel better?"

PC put his hand on his forehead, and his wound was gone. "Yeah, yeah, I do." "What did you do?"

"Just a little magic on your flesh wound." She smiled.

PC smiled back. "No, really, how did you do that?"

"You're in a different world, my old friend. Different things happen."

"Different strokes for different folks, huh?"

Carol grinned. "And you listen to too much music."

They laughed together until their voices trailed off. "Why are you here, Carol?"

"We never got to say goodbye, and it's been on your mind for so long. I've come to ease your pain. So, I've been granted this time to come see you."

"Rich told me you were sick. I'm sorry I couldn't come see you. I was in the middle of Iraq, and they weren't going to let me go."

"I know, I know. You were serving your country. I understand."

PC turned toward the stage. "I'm sorry things didn't work out for us."

Carol put her hand on his face and moved his head to face her.

"We were both young and confused emotionally. It was best that we went our separate ways to find ourselves. You found your way in the military, and I found my husband and had three beautiful kids.

"Rich also told me your husband passed away nine years after you. I'm sorry."

She smiled. "No reason for you to be sorry. We're together again."

Suddenly, a person appeared on stage calling Carol's name.

PC looked at Carol. "I'm guessing that is your husband."

"Yes, it is. It's time for me to go." Carol put her hands on PC. "I'm glad we got see each other."

"Will I ever see you again?"

She nodded her head. "One day we will. But for now, live your life and take care of your friend." She put her hand on his face again. "She needs you."

"Friend? Do you mean Ren? How do you know about her?" Carol just smiled as she stood up.

"She's a good person. Watch over her." Carol kissed PC on the cheek.

PC hugged her. "Thanks for checking on me." He released his embrace.

Carol walked down the steps and up to the stage. She took her husband's hand, stopped, and turned to PC. She waved at him. They began to walk toward the back of the stage and they disappeared.

PC stood there with his mouth open. He sat down on the stadium seat and looked blankly at the stage for quite some time.

Finally, he stood up, picked up his weapon, and said, "I have to get back to Ren." He looked around. "Shit, where's the entrance to the lighthouse?"

He slowly walked toward the stage, looking around. "The stage. That's where I came from."

He walked up on the stage and scanned the area. He eyed the back of the stage to get his bearings and headed there. He stopped when he realized he was at the front door of the lighthouse. PC turned the door handle, and it was locked. He banged on the door three times. He waited. No answer. He banged three more times. Nothing. He went to bang again, and Ren opened the door.

"Where have you been?" She pulled PC inside, closed the door, and locked it. "Are you okay?"

Distracted, PC answered, "What? Oh, yeah, great. Never felt better."

Ren looked at him curiously. "You look like someone from your past came to haunt you."

PC put his back up against the wall and slumped down to the floor. "Yeah, I guess you can say that."

Ren walked over to PC and sat down next to him. "Yeah, I know the feeling."

CHAPTER 24

They sat up against the wall, their minds far away. Ren snapped out of it when she noticed PC's unmarred forehead. "Your wound. What happened to it? It's healed." Ren touched PC's head. "It's completely healed. How the hell?"

PC touched his head. "Yeah, wish I could explain that."

"Wounds just don't heal that quickly."

PC got up quickly and said, "Come on, let's go."

"Go? Shouldn't we stay here awhile?"

"No, no, too much weird shit going on here. We need to move on. Lambert was wrong. There is no portal here for us to go home. We'll continue our trek to the Montauk Lighthouse. It's our only way home." PC looked at Ren. "Where is Spotford?"

Tears came to her eyes. "I don't know." She wiped her face. "When you left, I went back to find him, but he was gone. Just like that, into thin air."

"Did you look around the house for him?"

"I left him in the lighthouse and closed the door. He couldn't have gotten out."

Tears streamed down Ren's face. PC walked toward her and hugged her. She leaned her face onto his shirt.

"He must have meant a lot to you—Spotford."

He could feel her nodding her head.

She cried some more before she let go of PC and said, "I'm okay now."

"Are you sure?"

"Yeah. Really, I am. I just had to get it out of me. I'll be okay." She wiped tears from her eyes once more.

PC nodded his head. "Okay." He looked around. "Let's gather our things and get back on the beach."

Once they picked up their backpack and weapons, they left the lighthouse and made their way to the beach from the boardwalk. Both were silent for most of the day as they walked along the shoreline.

Ren broke the silence. "What happened to you back there?"

PC continued to look ahead. "Hopefully, we'll pick up our hideaway soon."

Ren jumped in front of PC and halted his walking. "What happened to you back there?" She repeated with an aggravated tone.

PC stared blankly and sat in the sand. "Here, sit."

She sat down next to him. "What happened? Talk to me, please."

PC looked out into the ocean. "Remember the girl I told you about that I had dated, and she passed when I was overseas?"

"Yes, yes, I do. She appeared to you. Like, Spotford appeared to me?"

"Exactly."

"What did she say?"

"She knew I felt sick about never getting to see her before she departed this world. So, she came to ease my guilt." He continued to look out at the ocean. "It's a shocking thing when someone from your past comes to talk with you and tell you good-bye. I'm still in shock over this. In one sense, it's a relief, not feeling guilty about not being there in the end." He looked at Ren. "That's why Spotford came to you. He knew you felt bad when he departed and wanted you to know he was all right and not to feel bad." PC stared at the waves.

Ren followed his gaze. "They're both in a better place now."

"Yes, yes they are." They sat in silence, leaning on each other.

"Finally, Ren said, "We should go now. The sun is starting to go down."

PC looked up at the sun. "Yeah, we better get going. Hopefully, we'll find the hideaway soon.

They both got up, wiped the sand off themselves, and continued their trek. By the time the sun was down, the boardwalk appeared, and they headed toward it.

They found the hideaway, went inside, closed the opening, turned on the lights, and cooked up a meal. They chatted for a while, and both dozed off in their sleeping bags.

Ren woke up as dawn was about to break. She decided she needed a cleaning. She took her clothes off, picked up a towel and soap, wrapped the towel around her body, and looked at PC. She was going to wake him, but left him to sleep since he'd had a long day yesterday.

She opened the boards, slipped out, and put the boards back up. As she turned around, she stopped dead in her tracks. "Where's the ocean? It's like someone pushed the ocean back, like it's draining."

Ren went back to the hideaway and shook PC awake.

"Hey, hey, get up. The ocean is gone."

"What, what, what!" He looked at Ren. "What's wrong? Why are you waking me up?"

She pointed outside. "The ocean. It's gone."

PC was still trying to wake up. "Gone? What do you mean it's gone? Oceans just don't disappear.

Ren pulled at his arm to get him up. "Come take a look."

Ren pulled up PC and went out the entrance. She dragged him a few feet, and they both stopped.

PC was wide awake now. "Holy shit."

"What? What is it? What's happening?"

PC took a few more steps toward the now-empty shore. "We have to get out of here."

"What is it? Tell me?!"

He looked at Ren. "It's a hurricane. When a hurricane is going to hit, the ocean will surge back, then surge forward as the storm arrives. We must get the hell out of here.

"Hurricane?" I never experienced one before."

"Well, you're going to, now. Come on."

PC grabbed her hand and started heading for the hideaway.

"Wait, wait, wait!" She pulled back on PC's arm, and they stopped. Where are we going?"

"Back to the lighthouse. It's the safest place to be."

"But that has to be ten miles away."

"The more we talk, the longer it's going to take. Come on, let's go!"

CHAPTER 25

The wind was picking up as PC and Ren walked along the shore back to the Lighthouse.

"That's not a good sign," PC said. He looked up on the beach and noticed the hideaway was gone. *Well, so much for going back*, he thought to himself.

"It's getting rough out here," Ren said. "How much further, do you think?"

"We've been walking for a while. I'm guessing another seven miles."

Ren looked out into the distance. "Can't even see the lighthouse yet." She looked toward the ocean. "The ocean is starting to creep back. Not good, huh?"

"No, not good, Ren. If things get bad, we'll have to move onto the beach, and it will probably slow us down, along with the wind and rain that might be hitting us."

PC scanned the area. "I doubt we'll have any issues with soldiers for a bit.

Ren shuddered. "I hope they're not waiting for us at the lighthouse."

PC frowned. "I hope not, either."

"What if they are there? What then?"

PC shrugged his shoulders. "I don't know, we'll just make it up as we go along."

Ren shook her head. "God, you watch too much TV."

PC smiled. "I go to the movies a lot."

The wind picked up, and PC and Ren struggled to move forward. The ocean was creeping back more. Waves were getting bigger.

Wham!

Someone rushed by them and almost knocked them down. PC and Ren spun their rifles off their shoulders as another person ran by them, toward the ocean with surfboards in hand.

Ren stared. "Surfers? In this weather?"

"Oh yeah. Best time to do it." They lowered their rifles.

Ren tilted her head and smiled. "Looks like a cool thing to do. Might have to try it one day."

"Yeah, well, not today. Come on, it's getting worse out here."

They pushed along as the waves came closer and closer to them. The wind was roaring along with the rain. PC leaned into Ren's ear and shouted over the wind, "We'd better move away from the ocean or we'll be swallowed up by the waves."

Just as he said that, a rogue wave came in and knocked them off their feet.

PC rose to his knees and pulled Ren up to her knees. He yelled, "Are you alright?"

She nodded her head. "Yeah. Don't get this kind of weather where I come from."

PC stood her up, and they headed toward the beach. It was more of a struggle to walk on the soft sand.

"How much further do you think?" Ren yelled at PC.

"I don't know. I'm guessing another mile. It's hard to see anything out here. I'm hoping we don't pass the lighthouse. Let's move in closer so we don't miss our target. We should run into the boardwalk of the lighthouse."

They moved closer still, toward the beach. The weather was getting worse. The wind was howling. It was like trying to walk in a blizzard. The rain hurt their faces. They tried to keep their heads down to protect themselves from the stinging rain.

Finally, Ren collapsed. PC went down on his knees. "Ren! Come on!"

"I'm exhausted. I need a break."

We can't take a break. It's getting worse out here. We're almost there! Please!"

"Okay. Okay," she said. "I can do this." Ren stood up. They took a few more steps and tripped and fell. They hit something hard.

PC banged on the ground and looked up. "Hey, it's the boardwalk. He looked straight and could barely make out the lighthouse and its beacon.

PC picked up Ren, put her arm around his shoulder, and his arm around her waist. "We're here. Just a little bit further.

"Thank God," she said.

They slowly made their way to the lighthouse, up the boardwalk, and then to the front door. "Okay?" PC asked.

She nodded her head and took her arm off him. "Okay." She gathered herself. "It's dark inside. Or maybe the electricity's out and we have some of our friends inside."

PC nodded his head. "We shall see."

They took off their backpacks, their rifles in hand. PC slowly opened the door. He pointed to Ren. "Grab my flashlight out of my bag."

Ren reached over and rummaged through his bag. She shook her head. "I've seen better messes in handbags."

PC rolled his eyes. "Come on, come on, dispense with pleasantries till later."

Ren found the flashlight and handed it to PC.

"Thank you." He pushed the door further open. He turned on the flashlight and scanned the house. He put his rifle down and pulled out his nine-millimeter.

Ren, with rifle in hand, stopped and grabbed PC's arm. "Is that a good idea, leaving your rifle behind?"

PC looked at her. "That's why I have you here, Annie Oakley. You will be my wingman. Or woman. Besides, I do rather good with a nine-millimeter." He turned his head and continued the slow walk, scanning the house with Ren right behind him.

"Annie Oakley," she said under her breath, shaking her head.

They slowly moved through the house with no incident. They made their way upstairs and found nothing. They even checked the basement, where they found, oddly, a washing machine and dryer.

Finally, they settled down and relaxed.

Ren looked around for some lights and found some in the kitchen, flicking them on as PC turned on the other lights around the house. "I'm surprised the lights are working in a storm like this."

He glanced down at himself and Ren. "We need to get out of these wet clothes and dry them. Let's see if we can find anything to wear. I'll get our backpacks from outside."

"Okay. I'll look upstairs."

Ren headed up the steps. She went into the first bedroom and noticed a queen-size bed.

"Oh, wow," she said out loud. "This is where I'm sleeping tonight."

She looked around and saw the closet. Ren walked over to it and found two white terrycloth robes. She took one robe, held it in front of her, smiled, and said, "His and hers."

She put her hand on it and felt the softness.

"Oh, this is nice." Still dripping wet, she stripped off her clothes and put on the robe.

"Oh, that's so much better." She pulled the other robe out of the closet and ran down the steps like a little kid to find PC.

"PC? Hey, where are you?"

PC came out of the kitchen. "Right here." He pointed toward the couch. "Backpacks are by the couch." He saw the white robe she was wearing. "Oh, well, I see you found something dry."

She beamed at him. "Yes, and something for you." She handed him the robe. PC checked it out and smiled. "Ahh, his and hers."

"Come on," she said, "You need to get out of those wet clothes. I'll see if the washer-dryer in the basement works."

"Hopefully," PC said.

PC stripped off his clothes and put on the robe. "This does feel nice. Hopefully, the owner won't be home tonight."

"Give me your clothes and I'll get mine. I will go to the basement and clean them."

PC picked up his clothes and handed them to her.

As she was walking up the stairs, she said, "What are you doing in the kitchen?

"Fixing us dinner."

"What are you making?

"Um, it's a surprise."

"Can't wait," her voice echoed down the hall.

PC opened the refrigerator and looked inside.

"Hmm. Chop meat, American cheese, and beer. Hmmm. Well, at least we have beer." He looked in all the cabinets and found a can of beans and a bag of hamburger buns. "Burgers, beans, and beer. How can you go wrong?" He laughed.

Suddenly, he heard a noise at the front door. PC peered from the kitchen. He figured it must just be the wind howling. He then noticed the handle jiggling. "Shit, that's not the wind doing that," he said to himself. He picked up his nine-millimeter and moved quickly away from the sidelight windows to the door and stood up against the wall with his gun at his side. The doorknob continued to jiggle. Someone was trying to pry open the door.

He felt his foot touch something in the corner. He looked down and noticed the potato masher that had been left in the corner when they'd been at the house earlier. He slowly picked up the potato masher and held it low in his left hand, with the nine-millimeter in the right. He heard some talking. Soldiers, he thought to himself. "Damn, I hate these guys," he said under his breath.

The door slowly began to open. When it was just wide enough, PC pulled the pin, threw the potato masher down toward their feet, and slammed the door, quickly locking it. A muffled sound came from the outside.

He looked through the sidelights of the door, which hadn't blown out from the explosion, and saw three soldiers dead on the ground. PC opened the door, and like that, they were gone.

He looked around both sides to see if anyone else was lurking. PC closed the door, deadbolted it, took a chair, and propped it underneath the doorknob.

Ren came bounding into the room. "What the hell was that sound I just heard?"

"Oh, just the wind. Probably something banged up against the house."

She looked at PC with a deer-in-the-headlights look. He smiled back. "Okay," she said, giving PC a weird look, still not sure if she believed him. "Is dinner ready?"

"Not yet. Still working on it."

"And what gourmet meal are you making us?" she gave him a little smile.

"Eh, cheeseburgers, beans, and beer."

"And I bet you slaved over a hot stove."

"I did. Eh, rather, I will. Come to the kitchen while I prepare the meal."

She smiled and walked into the kitchen with him.

CHAPTER 26

PC and Ren ate their 'gourmet' dinner, spoke for a while about the different things they did in their personal lives, then retired for the night.

Ren went upstairs to sleep in bed while PC stayed on the couch with a nine-millimeter in hand to make sure no one got into the house while they slept.

The next day, Ren came down the stairs and saw PC sleeping on the couch with the nine-millimeter. She walked over to him, knelt, and rubbed his shoulder lightly to wake him. "Hey, hey, sleepy head, are you awake?"

PC opened his eyes and looked at Ren. "Good morning." He smiled at her.

"Why didn't you sleep in the other bed last night?"

He stretched his body to wake up. "I was just guarding the fort last night, so no one got in while we slept."

She looked at the door and saw the chair propped up against the door handle. "Is that why you have the chair up against the door?"

PC grinned at her as he finished stretching. "Winner, winner, chicken dinner."

She hit him on the shoulder, and he laughed.

"And what was that noise last night when I was in the basement? That was no debris hitting the house."

"That? Oh, yeah, I did not want to alarm you, but we had visitors, and I let them know they weren't welcome, with a potato masher."

"You could have told me." She hit him in the shoulder again. "After all we been through."

"You're right, we have been through a lot, but it was quick and painless. Well, maybe not for the soldiers, it was not," he grinned.

She rolled her eyes. "Okay," she stood up, walked to the window, and looked outside. "Looks like the storm has passed. Sun is coming up."

PC stood up and looked out the window with her. "Yeah, looks good. We should be hitting the trail soon. Let us eat something quick and get our things together."

"Why don't you get a shower, and I will take care of breakfast. I had my shower last night."

"Okay," PC said. "Sounds like a plan." He went upstairs to shower while Ren scrounged around the kitchen for breakfast. She found some instant oatmeal and decided this would do.

PC came into the kitchen, dressed, his wet hair slicked back, and feeling refreshed.

Ren handed him the bowl of oatmeal. "Breakfast is served."

"Ahh, breakfast of champions." He took the bowl and was handed a spoon.

"I'm going upstairs to get dressed and get my things together while you eat." She picked up the bowl of oatmeal on the counter, smiled, and disappeared into the living room.

PC finished his oatmeal, went into the living room, and took a quick peek outside to make sure no soldiers were lingering around. He gathered his things and was ready to go. He then walked around the house, looking out the windows to make sure there were no unfriendly outsiders. He grabbed his three weapons—both rifles and nine-millimeter—and was ready to go.

Ren came bounding down the stairs, dressed, with her rifle and backpack in hand. She stopped at the foot of the stairs. "Ready?"

"Ready when you are, my dear."

A loud blast shook the house.

"What was that?" Ren asked, startled.

"Shit." PC ran to the window and looked outside with Ren looking over his shoulder. As he scanned the outside, another explosion followed, shaking the house again. The next explosion hit closer to the house, and both were knocked off their feet.

PC fell on top of Ren. "Crap," he got up and pulled Ren to her feet. "Okay?"

Ren nodded her head. "Yeah, okay."

"Come on, grab your things. We need to get the hell out of here. They're bombing us."

They grabbed their things frantically and headed for the front door, when another explosion rocked the house.

"Where are we going to go?" Ren said.

"We cannot stay here. We'll be sitting targets." PC opened the front door as another explosion came closer to the house and knocked them to the ground. PC picked up Ren.

"I'm okay, I'm okay," Ren said.

"They're zeroing in on the house; we must get away." They made their way running down the boardwalk as another bomb hit the house and knocked them off their feet again. Both got up quickly. "Quick, over to the boathouse."

More explosions hit around the house as they ran over to the boathouse. They hid against the side as the bombs kept coming. PC pulled out his binoculars and scanned the area. Both sat on the ground.

"What are you looking for?" Ren asked.

"Looking for spotters."

"Spotters?"

"Yea. Someone must be calling this in. We're not dealing with state-of-the-art technology here with these fellows." PC continued to scan the area and saw what he was looking for. "Found them." He handed the binoculars to Ren.

"Where are they?"

"Up on the sand dune." He pointed. "Over to the left."

Ren looked with the binoculars as PC readied his sniper rifle.

"I see them, Two of them."

PC put on his noise-blocking headphones to silence the noise of the rifle. "You'd better put yours on, too."

Ren pulled her headphones from her backpack and put them on.

PC lay in the sniper position. Ren lay on his back and took the binoculars, locating the spotters again. PC scanned the area with his scope and found his target.

PC turned his head and pulled the left headphone down, as did Ren, so they could hear.

"Ren keep still for a moment." They both covered their ear again.

"Okay." She watched the spotters with the binoculars. One of the soldiers pointed toward them as the other soldier spoke on the radio. She tapped PC several times on his shoulders to warn him. "Uh oh, PC?"

"I know, they spotted us. Stay still." He gave a thumbs-up to her.

PC zeroed in on the radio operator. He exhaled as he slowly pulled the trigger. A loud gunshot went off. But by the time the soldiers heard it, the radio operator was down. The other soldier stood up to run but PC put a bullet in his back.

Ren slapped PC on the shoulder. "Wow! Nice shooting, Tex!" Ren kept looking with the binoculars.

"Thanks. You want to get off me now. I do not know why I let you park yourself on me."

Ren rolled off PC's back.

PC stood up and pulled Ren up. "Come on. They spotted us. They're going to zero in on us." They picked up their backpacks and pulled off the earmuffs as they ran down the boardwalk away from the boathouse. Suddenly, they heard a noise in the sky. "Get down!" PC yelled as they hit the floor of the boardwalk, followed by a loud explosion. Wood debris fell all around them, some hitting them. They rolled over to see that the boat shed had been blown up.

"Holy Shit!" Ren said.

PC pulled Ren up. "Keep moving, keep moving!"

"Where are we going?!"

"Beach!"

"Beach!?" We're sitting ducks on the beach!"

"We're sitting ducks here, too. Come on!"

They continued down the boardwalk, and they ran on the beach. Bombs continued to rain around them. They zig-zagged so the soldiers could not get a target on them.

Ren pulled on PC's arm to stop him. "Wait, wait! Over there! It's our hideaway!"

PC looked over and noticed. "Shit, come on!"

Both were already out of breath from running. Explosions were getting closer and closer to them. PC grabbed Ren's hand. "We're almost there! Good?!"

"Yeah, good." She gasped for air.

They finally reached the hideaway and fell to the ground inside, breathing heavily. The bombing had stopped. PC stood with his head between his legs, still catching his breath. "Still liking this adventure, my dear?"

Ren pulled herself up. With a deadpan look, she said, "Yes, yes I do."

CHAPTER 27

PC scanned the beach with his binoculars. "Nothing," he said to Ren. "Nothing out there. Disappeared again. Which is good for us."

Ren peered out the entrance with her rifle in hand. "How long do you think we should stay here?"

PC put the binoculars down. "I do not know. We need to think what we'll do next. Wait a minute." PC pulled the binoculars back up to his eyes.

Ren readied with her Winchester. "What do you see?"

"I don't believe this. Take a look."

Ren took the binoculars and looked out towards the beach. "Beachgoers." She looked at PC. "I'll be damned." She put the binoculars back to her eyes. "They're coming in droves."

"This might be a good thing," PC said. "The soldiers are not going to bomb the beach with all the beachgoers there. What we can do is mingle among them. They will not find us."

"Yeah, but they were looking through the crowd last time, and we had to strip to fit in among the nudists."

"Hmm, yes, true," PC scratched his head. "We can do the same again, only this time with our clothes on. You know, look like beachgoers. We'll have to leave the guns behind, maybe take one backpack and pack our nine millimeters in it. This hideaway follows us anyhow, so we can get our things later." PC looked around. "Hopefully, we have some bathing suits. They thought of everything else."

"I'll look around," Ren said, and hunted through the containers that were laying around the supplies.

PC continued searching to see if any soldiers were lurking. Suddenly, something landed on PC's head. He put the binoculars down and grabbed it.

"I found these swimming trunks for you," Ren said and tossed a beach towel at him. "I found something too; a nice T-back." She proceeded to take off her clothes. PC looked at her as she was stripping. "Come on, get in your trunks."

PC shook his head and said, "When in Rome," and proceeded to undress.

They had their bathing suits on and towels in hand. PC picked up his backpack and put their nine-millimeters into it. They put on some T-shirts, floppy hats, and sunglasses. Ren found and took the blanket. "Now we look like beachgoers."

PC smiled at Ren. "Ready?"

"Ready," Ren said.

They boarded up the hideaway and glanced around. PC said, "Wow, quite a crowd. We'll mingle in fine with this crowd. Come, let us head toward the shore and walk along there."

They headed for the shore, PC with the backpack on, both towels over their shoulders, while Ren carried the folded blanket. They walked along the shore without any issues and saw no soldiers among the crowd. Both relaxed some, but PC still had one eye on guard, scanning the crowd for possible soldiers.

They walked awhile without any soldiers present. The beach was wall-to-wall beach-goers. PC said, "I just realized why it is so crowded."

"And that is?" Ren said.

"It is the fourth of July. Everybody goes to the beach on the fourth."

They stopped in their tracks, and Ren's eyes widened. "Hold it a second. It was June fourth when this whole thing started." She shook her head. "We've been out here for a month now. Oh, my God."

"Time flies when you're having fun," came a familiar voice.

PC and Ren looked over and saw the lifeguard stand with Lambert on top in his usual position, arms spread out behind the stand with his mirrored sunglasses.

They approached him. PC growled, "Where the hell you been?"

Lambert grinned, "Keeping you safe." He waved both arms at the beach crowd. "No one will bother you with this crowd. We made sure of that."

"Have we truly been on this beach for a month now"? Ren asked.

"In this dimension, yes. When you make it home, it will be like you never left. A day will not have passed."

"Well, that's interesting," PC said. He looked around. "And how long is this crowd going to last? People go home, you know."

Lambert put his trademark cheek-dimpling smile on his face." Ahh, not this crowd. They will not be leaving.

"How so?" PC eyed him curiously.

"We made this dimension like a loop starting today. The sun will never go down, and the people will never leave, so you will be well-protected."

"And how did you do that?" PC realized he wouldn't get a straight answer from him, shook his head at Lambert, and waved his hand. "Never mind, I don't want to know."

PC and Ren looked at each other.

"Won't they get tired and hungry?" Ren asked.

Not this crowd, my friend." He leaned back in the lifeguard stand. "You will be safe. Hopefully for the duration of your trip."

"Hopefully?" PC looked at Ren again.

"Listen," Ren said, grabbing PC's arm. "Remember, he is trying to help us. This is better than nothing. If it lasts till we get to our destination, great. If not, it's alright. We've been in and out of trouble since we got here." PC shook his head. "Come on, either we'll make it, or not."

PC sighed and put his hand on Ren's arm. "Okay." He looked back at Lambert. "Okay, we appreciate what you are doing."

Lambert smiled down at them. "Terrific." He disappeared from the lifeguard stand. PC and Ren smirked at each other.

"Guy always makes dramatic exists, doesn't he?" Ren laughed.

PC looked at the empty lifeguard stand. "Yeah, he does. Come on."

As they moved back toward the shore, Ren grabbed PC's arm. "Hey, wait a minute." She looked up toward the boardwalk.

"What—do you see—soldiers?"

"No, hot dog stand."

"Hot dog stand? Where?"

"Up on the boardwalk. Right above our hideaway."

PC looked toward the boardwalk. "Yeah, you're right. It is a hot dog stand."

Ren's lips spread. "Let's go get some hot dogs. Do you have any money?"

"Well, yeah, I do. My wallet came with me in this world."

Ren grabbed his hand. "Come on."

They walked up to the boardwalk and the stairs to reach the hot dog vendor—an elderly gentleman sitting on a stool next to the stand.

"Well, hello there, young ones. What can I get you today?"

Ren smiled back at him. "Hi there. Can we have two hot dogs and two bottled waters? Oh," she looked at PC. "Mustard?"

He nodded his head. "Mustard on both."

"Certainly. Do you want any toppings on your dogs?"

Ren looked at PC with a sour face, and he shook his head. "No, just mustard please on both."

"Okay."

He handed Ren the water as he prepared the hot dogs and rolls, added mustard, and put them on a paper holder. "That will be twelve dollars even, folks."

Ren elbowed PC. "Pay the man."

"Oh, yeah." He took his backpack off and pulled out his wallet, which was fat with cash.

Ren's eyes got wide. "You always carry that much money on you?"

PC handed the man fifteen dollars and looked at Ren.

"Yes, yes, I do." He smiled at the old man and said, "Keep the change."

"Well, thank you, young man. You folks enjoy this wonderful day."

"Thank you. We will," Ren answered, her white teeth flashing.

Both walked away back onto the beach.

"Let's park it over here in this spot."

"Okay," Ren said. She spread out the blanket as both sat down. Ren handed PC a bottle of water and a hot dog. PC dropped his backpack and proceeded to take a bite. "Not a bad dog," he said.

"How come you carry so much money on you?" Ren's hand covered a mouthful of hot dog.

PC swallowed a bite. "Well, you never know when you're going to need money in a situation."

Ren nodded. "Like now."

He smiled and winked at her. "Exactly."

"Yeah, but so much? Looks like you have a several hundred dollars with you."

PC bit into his hot dog and said with a muffled voice, "More like a couple of thousand."

Ren's eyes went wide. "Two thousand dollars! Who carries that much money?"

PC swallowed his hot dog and smiled at Ren. "Me." He took a swig of water to clear his throat. "You should have seen the face on my car dealer when I gave him four grand for repairs on my car."

"Don't you ever worry someone robbing you?"

"No. Someone did try that once when I was coming out of a 7-Eleven."

And? What happened?"

"You know, I'm not sure if he got hurt hitting the ground or from my foot getting tangled in his face."

Ren's face lit up with surprise. "You took him out with your foot?"

"Oh yeah, Army taught me well."

"Was he bigger then you?"

"Bigger than the both of us put together."

"How big?"

"Hmmm, about six-foot-five, probably two hundred and fifty pounds. Long blonde hair and beard, overalls. Typical redneck."

"After you took him down, what happened?"

PC took another swig of water. "Well, when I was in the store, I asked the counter person to call the cops. I'd seen him sitting outside waiting for me. He'd been harassing me out in the parking lot as I was walking in. When I went outside, he got in my face and pushed me. I turned and jumped up in the air, spun around with my leg straight out, and planted my foot in his face. I was wearing steel-toed shoes, by the way. When the cops showed up, they thought I was the aggressor. They threw me up against the car and asked me where the weapon was. I just pointed to my foot and said, 'Here, this is the weapon.'"

Ren was hanging on every word. "Then what happened? Did the cops arrest you?"

"No, some witnesses came to my rescue and told the cops what happened. They let me go. Had to go to court and everything, but he spent some time in jail."

Ren finished her hot dog, pulled her legs up, and wrapped her arms around her legs. "Wow! You've had some interesting things happen to you."

PC laughed. "I don't know if I call that interesting."

"But—in your life. You have seen the world."

"Yeah, but not the way I wanted to. It was a time of war. It was more devastating than sightseeing."

"But there must have been times you enjoyed where you were."

"No, it was a sad situation. Germany was nice, enjoyed being there, but the rest was not pretty. One day I will get back to traveling on my terms and see the nuances of the world—not the destructive parts."

Ren rested her head on her knees. "You're an interesting person, PC, no matter what you say. I hope to do that one day, travel and see the world. Tired of the landlocked state I live in, the cold weather." She looked around the beach. "This is what I like. I like adventures." She beamed at PC.

PC smiled back. "Well, you're on quite an adventure now."

"Yes; not of my choosing, but it's been quite interesting not knowing what is going to happen next."

PC spotted a large figure coming toward them. "Uh oh."

"What? Do you see something?"

"Yeah, I do. Your friend is back."

She followed PS's gaze and spotted Kevin. "Oh, no." She put her legs down and pulled her shirt down to cover herself.

PC noticed this and laughed. "Don't want Kevin to see you in that nice bathing suit you're wearing?"

Ren hit PC on the arm. "Shut up."

PC laughed again.

Kevin came up to their blanket. "Well, hi there, again. How are you kids doing? Enjoying this nice weather?"

"Oh, yes, yes, we are. How are you, Kevin?" Ren asked.

PC tried his hardest not to laugh.

"Why don't you come over to where we are. We have lots of food and drink."

"Oh, that is extremely sweet of you, Kevin, but we just ate and will be moving on soon. We want to do some exploring on the beach. Isn't that right, dear?" She elbowed PC.

"Huh, oh, yes, we are going to hunt for seashells. Ren has a great collection." Ren shot PC a look. "Isn't that right, dear?"

Ren smiled back at PC and looked at Kevin. "Yes; yes, I do."

"Well, if you kids change your mind, we're right over there near the far lifeguard stand."

"Okay, thanks, Kevin. You enjoy yourself," PC said.

"Take care, kids." Kevin walked away.

PC and Ren looked at each other. "Well," PC said, "at least he had a bathing suit on."

They laughed.

"Seashells!"

"Well, it was the only thing I could think of. We are on a beach and a lot of people look for seashells." PC looked around. "Come on, let's start moving and put some space between us and Kevin."

Ren stood up quickly. "You don't have to tell me twice." They picked up the blanket, and Ren shook out the sand. PC picked up the backpack, stuffed their water bottles inside, and continued their trek.

CHAPTER 28

PC and Ren walked for the next three days. With the sun never going down, they traveled quite far, resting when they had to, bathing in the ocean, and eating to fuel back up, without any incidents. Both started relaxing, for the time being, knowing they were safe from the soldiers.

"Let's take a break."

"Okay," Ren said. She found an open spot among the beachgoers and spread the blanket out. Both sat down and sighed at the same time.

"We have made some good time up the beach. How much further, do you think?" Ren asked.

"Well, if we keep making good time without any interruptions," he looked around the surroundings. "... a few days or so."

"I'm not sure. With the sun up all the time, I've lost track of things." Ren scanned the beach.

"Hey, don't worry," PC said. We'll get out of here; I promise you I'll get us back home." Ren leaned her head on PC. "We'll make it?"

"Guarantee it," PC said.

Suddenly the sky went dark, their rings started flashing, the stars were out, and the beachgoers were gone. "Uh oh," Ren said. "What's happening?"

"Crap." PC reached for his backpack and pulled out both nine millimeters. "Here." He handed one to Ren. "Come on, let's go."

"The hideout?" Ren said.

"Yes, quick, before soldiers appear."

They picked up the blanket and walked quickly to the hideaway.

They heard the rumbling of a vehicle. It was coming from PC's left, and he looked over. A spotlight lit up on them. They both stopped, blinded by the glaring light.

PC went to one knee and aimed at the light, yelling at Ren, "Keep moving! Go! I'll catch up to you! Go!"

Ren ran.

PC took aim with his nine-millimeter and fired three shots. He heard glass breaking, and it went dark. PC bolted toward Ren.

Ren was at the hideaway pulling down the planks to get in.

"I'm right behind you!" PC screamed out.

She pulled the last plank out and jumped inside with PC following. "What happened out there?"

"I shot out the spotlight." PC wiped the sand off himself.

"With that little gun? How did you learn to shoot like that?"

PC looked up at Ren. "Arcade. As a kid, of course."

Ren gave him an exasperated look.

"Really, I did." PC grabbed his sniper rifle and aimed it out the opening, scoping the area.

"Anything?" Ren lay on PC's back to look.

"Not yet. I am guessing it was a half-track carrying that light doing reconnaissance." PC continued to scope the area and spotted what he was looking for. "Ahh, there we go."

"What; what do you see?"

I was right; it is a half-track and they're beating feet out of here."

PC scoped to see if he could get a shot off and saw he had an angle to take out the track. "I'm going to give them a sending-off present."

"Wait!" Ren yelled. She crawled off PC and reached into his backpack, pulling out both headphones. She put hers on, climbed back on top of PC, and put his on. "Fire away."

"Thanks," he said. PC still had an angle. He aimed carefully, exhaled, and slowly pulled the trigger. The shot hit the track of the vehicle and stopped it dead. As soldiers climbed out, PC took them down one at a time.

"Done and done?" Ren asked, still lying on PC's back.

"Done and done, my dear."

"Wow, what a rush." Ren rolled off PC's back.

"Is that why you park yourself on my back when I'm shooting?"

She nodded her head. "I don't know what it is, but I get a rush seeing you do that. It's weird, I know. I can't explain it."

PC looked at Ren. "You know, I once told you I find you very interesting and a bit of a mystery, which is probably why I find you so intriguing."

Ren smiled at PC.

"You're alright Ren, no matter what Kevin says about you."

Her smile disappeared from her face. "Keven can kiss my German Irish ass."

Both started laughing.

PC turned his attention back to the beach and scoped around.

Ren sat down next to him this time. "Anyone else out there?"

"Looks clear. Half-track has disappeared, of course."

"Of course," Ren repeated. "Should we stay here for the night?"

PC continued scoping. "Yeah, we should stay, wait for daylight, and see if we can get back on track."

He put his rifle down and looked at Ren. "Hopefully, we'll have a crowd of beachgoers and we can mingle through them."

Ren stood up. "Sounds like a plan." She pulled her shirt off and stood there in her T-back bathing suite.

PC looked her up and down. "Do you always walk around like that?"

Ren looked at him. "What, like this?" Does it bother you?"

"Well, no, it doesn't."

"It's very natural for me." She smiled back at PC. "And besides, we been together for how long now? And you have seen me naked on the beach. I've seen you naked on the beach."

PC just looked at her. "And we seen Kevin naked on the beach."

Ren rolled her eyes and held her stomach. "Oh, please, don't remind me."

"Okay, I will leave it alone. You're right, I should be used to it, and it doesn't bother me." He changed the subject. "Are you hungry?"

She nodded her head. "I can eat."

"Great. Let us see what we have."

CHAPTER 29

Ren woke up in her sleeping bag, stretched, and looked to see where PC was. She found him lying down at the entrance with his sniper rifle and binoculars, scanning the beach.

"What's going on?" She stood up, put her shirt on, and lay down on top of him.

"Well, our friends are back but in force."

Ren looked outside over PC's head. "Wow! A lot of armor out there. They seem very interested in us."

PC kept looking through the binoculars. "Well, I do not think they want us to go home."

"Why? What did we do to upset them?"

"My guess is, if we go back, things in the universe will go back to normal. Someone out there is trying to stop us and wants to turn things to their advantage. That is my theory."

"You think?"

"Oh, I'd put money on it. That is why I have been so in your face with Lambert. He is not telling us something. He may have his reasons, but it is our lives on the line."

Ren put her chin on PC's head. "How are we going to get out of this?"

He put his binoculars down. "Don't know yet." He looked up at the cloudy sky. "Here comes the rain. Should slow them down. No beachgoers today." He scanned the area as Ren rested on top of his back. "Wait a minute..." PC focused near a half-track, where some soldiers and officers were talking among themselves.

"You see something," Ren said.

"Yeah, yeah, I do. There are officers out there and one looks familiar to me."

"An officer from history you remember?"

"No. An officer I know in the present."

"Present? How could that be? Those soldiers are from the past."

"You are correct, they are. But not this guy." PC kept looking, and it dawned on him. "Hey, I know who he is. Damn, what is he doing here in another uniform?"

"Who is he?"

"He is a general in the US Army. A lousy one-star general at that. At least, he was."

"In the US Army? What is he doing here? And in a different Army from the past!"

"It is a particularly good question, my dear. I bet you Lambert could tell us."

"What happened to the general?"

"The president had him removed. Just as well, he was a lousy officer."

"Why did the president remove him?"

"According to the rumor mill, corruption. I heard he was selling our technology to our enemies, but they were never able to prove it."

Ren snorted and said, "dirtbag."

"That he is, and a lot of other things."

PC watched as the officers continued to talk. "Even has a riding crop in his hand. Like a true Nazi."

He watched as two soldiers appeared carrying a long wooden box. "Well, well, what do we have here, hmm."

Ren tried to focus in on what PC was seeing. "What are they doing?"

"Two soldiers have a long box, and they are putting it in front of the officers."

The soldiers opened the box, and the general pulled out a rifle.

"Holy shit."

"What? What is happening?"

"He's equipped these soldiers with modern technology. They have the same sniper rifle as I do."

Ren lifted her head and strained to look at the beach. "Oh, no. That's not good."

"No, no it's not." PC watched as the officers admired the rifle and the general put it back in the box.

"Quick," PC said, "get our headphones."

Ren crawled off PC and grabbed both headphones from the backpack. She climbed again onto PC's back. "What are you going to do?"

"I'm going to put a few holes in the box and damage the rifle so they can't use it."

Ren slipped the headphones on PC and put on hers, watching.

"Hang on, Ren."

Ren put her left hand on his shoulder and put the binoculars up to her face with her right.

PC aimed at the wooden box as the officers stood behind it. He took aim where he thought the vital part of the gun would be. "Say goodnight," he said under his breath as he exhaled and gently pulled the trigger. The bullet ripped through the box, and PC sent out two more shots, leaving the box in shreds and the sniper rifle mangled.

The shots sent the officers reeling back as wood shrapnel hit them.

"How'd I do?" PC asked Ren as she looked through the binoculars.

"Oh, I'd say you made Swiss cheese out of that box, and the rifle. A definite fucktard."

She watched the officers as they managed to gather themselves. She looked at the general. She noticed a three-inch cut on his cheek. "You cut up the general surprisingly good." She handed PC the binoculars.

"Nice." He nodded his head. "That will leave a scar. Now he looks like a true Nazi with that gash on his face."

Suddenly, all the vehicles, armor, and soldiers disappeared, except the general. Through the binoculars, PC could see the general staring back at him in defiance, with the rain draining from his hat, then he disappeared.

"Gone again," Ren said.

"Yeah, which is a good thing. Funny how the general did not disappear right away. He just sat there knowing I was looking at him."

Ren looked outside, still on PC's back. "Raining harder now. Looks like we're not going anywhere today."

PC put the binoculars down. "Yeah, it's looking that way." Ren rolled off PC's back as he flipped into a sitting position.

They jumped to hear a voice coming from the back of the hideaway.

"You should have taken him out."

PC grabbed his other rifle and pointed it in the direction of the voice. Out of the dark, Lambert came walking out. PC lowered his rifle. "What is the general doing here, Lambert? In this dimension?

"He wants to take the two of you out."

"Why?" Ren asked, worried.

Lambert looked at Ren. "He doesn't want you to get back to your world."

"I knew it," PC said. "If I take him out, will it get us home faster?"

"Things won't change, but it will eliminate a threat."

"You need to level with us. What is going on?"

Lambert sighed and shook his head in agreement. "There are certain people in our government who are trying to change the outcome of certain events in our country."

"Who are these certain people? Can you give us names?"

"As you know, we had an election last year and the former President, President Jay, did not take the loss well. As I'm sure you have seen on the news, he felt the election was stolen from him, and we all know it wasn't, with all the safeguards we have for elections. Most in his party have dismissed what he is saying and have moved on. Some loyal rogue scientist found a way to manipulate history by changing the timelines."

"So how are you getting here in this dimension if they have the power to change things?" PC asked.

"One of his former colleagues came to us and let us know of his plans. He has access to the same technology, and he has been helping us slow and hopefully stop the ex-President from what he is doing. But it has not gone accordingly, and you two ended up here. Our man was trying to cancel what the rogue scientist was doing, which created a storm, as the best I can describe it, which brought you here. Bringing you back would put everything back to normal, which is what the former president does not want. He will go to jail if you come back. If you don't come back, he will run for president and win, and consolidate power, and we'll have a dictator on our hands. He is aware of the two of you, and bringing you home would not benefit him. Right now, he is winning the battle at home, convincing some of the public that the election has been stolen from him."

"So, they've been sending soldiers from the past to take us out, "Ren said.

"That is correct, young lady. They're dipping into a past dimension to bring these soldiers in. SS. The most vilified soldiers that ever were. We are not sure how he is doing this, but we've managed to push them back, on occasion. Then they figure a way around what we block."

"And how did this general get involved?" PC asked.

"Before Jay became president, President Barron fired this general for working with the enemy."

"But it was never proven. Yes, that part I know," PC said. "Rumors were swirling when I was in the military about that time. How did he get a hold of today's technology and give it to these soldiers?"

"We don't know," Lambert said. "We're not sure how he is getting into this dimension. We are looking for him as we speak to cut him off from giving today's technology to these soldiers of the past." Lambert looked at PC. "If you see him again, you must take him out. This way we can stop him from giving any technology out."

PC looked at Ren and sighed. "Okay, I'll do your dirty work for you if he reappears."

Ren thought deeply. "Do you think he will reappear again since PC injured him earlier?"

"Oh yes," Lambert said. "He has quite a large ego, and he likes to put on a show to attract attention, even if it's to soldiers of the past." Lambert looked outside as it rained. "You will be safe for a while. We shut them down for now, but they eventually will find a way around us, as I said, and be back at you."

Lambert stood straight with a faraway look in his eyes. "I must go now. Be safe." He disappeared.

CHAPTER 30

P C and Ren sat in silence for a few minutes, digesting what Lambert had told them.

Ren sighed. "Let's do some fishing."

PC stood up and looked outside at the rain. "Yes, let's go fishing." He disappeared into the hideaway and came walking out with a bucket and the fishing pole he had collected earlier. He stopped, pulled his shirt off, leaving him in his bathing suit. He looked at Ren. "Coming?"

Ren looked at him blankly and jumped to her feet. "Yes, yes, I will." She pulled off her shirt, still in her bathing suit.

"Can you grab the beach umbrella for me?"

Ren picked up the umbrella. "Got it."

"Let's go," They went out of the hideaway, put up the planks, and headed toward the beach.

Ren popped up the umbrella to protect them from the rain as they walked toward the shore. "Fishing good in bad weather?"

"Why not? Nothing we can do until the weather clears. Besides, Lambert said we'll be safe for a while, so might as well relax."

"By fishing?"

PC looked at Ren with a smile. "You have been landlocked too long, haven't you? Fishing is a relaxing hobby to do. Even if you do not catch anything, it's still a good day, like I've said."

"But you don't even have any bait."

PC put the bucket down and looked around. "I saw a dead fish when I was scanning the area earlier. We can use that for bait." He spotted it. "There it is!" He pointed toward the dead striped bass. He walked up to it and bent down. "Looks like someone bit you in half. Probably a shark." He picked up the dead fish and walked back toward Ren, who was placing the umbrella in the sand to sit under.

PC pulled a knife out from the bucket, cut a piece off the striper, put on the hook, and cast the line far into the water. He pulled the pole holder out of the bucket, put it into the sand, put the pole in the holder, and sat down next to Ren.

They sat in silence for a while until Ren spoke. "I've been thinking about what Lambert said."

"Yeah, looks like the fate of our country is in our hands when it comes to getting home and putting things back to normal."

Ren pulled her legs up, wrapped her arms around her legs, and leaned her head on PC's shoulder. "We're going through all this so one man... *one* man can stay in power." She looked up at PC. "Why is it, in the course of history, one person is in power and so many suffer?"

PC looked down at Ren. "I don't know, but many of those men were pushed out of power eventually. Most of the time at a great cost."

"The cost could be our lives," Ren said.

"The needs of the many outweigh the needs of the few."

"What? Where did you get that line from?"

PC looked at Ren and smiled. "Star Trek."

"Oh my God, I keep saying you watch too much TV."

PC laughed. "Well, in this case, the few—you and me—need to save the many from the one."

"Why do people want war?"

"People don't want war, they want peace. It's the politicians who want war."

"Do you believe that the former president is doing this, trying to change history so he can be back in power?"

"Well, Jay was never wrapped too tight to begin with, but I didn't think he would go that low and try to change history to get back into power."

"Oh, I don't know," Ren said. I voted for the guy."

PC shot a look at Ren. "You voted for that windbag?"

"Yes, I did. Twice."

PC shook his head.

"You voted for the other guy?"

"Yeah, I did. It was a better alternative than that fat windbag wanting to be king. He could have been good if he had surrounded himself with good people. He fired them and put in a bunch of yes men."

"Yeah, but he promised to put the country back together again."

"And he made things worse, just like most politicians do. He was a novice president and a failed businessman. I understand that people did not want the status quo in office, but this was a failed experiment, and we need to get home, so he will not be king. And besides, he is trying to kill us."

Ren leaned her head back on PC. "Guess you are right. He seemed like he was going to be good." She sighed, "Disappointed."

PC put his hand on her knee. "It is alright. I did not mean to lecture you. I usually do not talk about politics with people. Too volatile these days." He looked around the beach. Rain was steady but not hard. The area looked deserted, but he wanted to make sure. "Hey, Ren, I am going back to the hideaway and get the binoculars. I just want to make sure things are clear." He stood up. "I'll be right back."

She looked up at PC. "Okay. I might go ride some waves."

"Okay. Be careful, surf looks a little rough."

She smiled, "I will."

PC grinned back and headed to the hideaway.

Ren stood up and watched PC walk away. She took her top off, dropped it in the sand, and headed for the ocean.

PC came back a few minutes later with binoculars in hand, along with a blanket and towels to put under the beach umbrella so they wouldn't have to sit in the wet sand as the rain continued.

As he was spreading out the blanket, he found Ren's top. He picked it up and looked out to the ocean to see Ren riding the waves. He smiled and shook his head. "Crazy girl," he said under his breath. "Guess when you're landlocked all your life, you do those things. But, nice to look at though," he laughed.

PC finished spreading the blanket out, checked the fishing pole, and sat down on the blanket. Ren came in from the ocean, and PC handed her a towel.

"Oh, thanks." She wiped herself down.

PC held up her bikini top. "I think this is yours."

She took the top, threw it back at him, and sat down next to him, still wiping herself down.

"Thought you might be cold."

Ren elbowed him to the side. "No," she said sternly, "I am not cold. Not in this weather."

PC picked up the binoculars and, on his knees, scanned the beach on his left side, then scanned the right.

"Nothing," he said. "We're good."

He sat back down next to Ren.

"This is very relaxing, with the rain and the sound of the ocean hitting the shore," Ren said. "I wouldn't mind moving here to Long Island."

PC looked at Ren. "You would? Long Island is not a cheap place to live.

"Really?"

"Really. Cost of living is high. Housing, property taxes are off the chart."

Ren hugged her legs and put her chin on her knees. "Wow, I didn't know it was that expensive." She stared at the ocean for a bit. "Do you still have family here?"

"Yes, two of my sisters live on the Island and my brother just moved back. Another sister is in Saint Pete, Florida.

"Who do you stay with when you come to visit?"

"In my house."

Ren's head popped up. "You own a house here?"

"Yeah. When my parents passed, my siblings wanted to sell the house. I wanted to keep it. So, I bought it."

"Wow. You really are rich."

PC started laughing. "I wouldn't say that."

"Well, you walk around with two thousand dollars in your pocket."

"Doesn't mean I'm rich."

"Doesn't mean you're poor, either. No one walks around with that much cash in their pocket."

"Maybe, but I do." He smiled at Ren. "I am simply good with the stock market. That is where I make most of my money, and my little side business doing security, as I have told you. I am not rich, just extremely comfortable."

"Comfortable enough to own two houses? One on Long Island, the other in Florida."

"Well, just one house. I live in a condo in Florida."

"A condo?"

"Yes, on the beach."

"On the beach?" Ren looked away with her mouth still open.

PC was trying to hide his smile.

She looked back at him. "How many cars do you own?"

"Two."

"Two?

"Two." PC held up two fingers.

"What kind?"

"Well, in Florida, I drive a Cadillac XT5.

"Why?" she shot back.

"It is comfortable and has some power, so I can get by slow drivers, which are many in the state of Florida.

"Okay. And the other car?"

"It's a souped-up Challenger I keep here on Long Island."

"Why souped-up?"

"Well, there are a lot of fast drivers on Long Island."

Ren stared blankly with her mouth open. "Oh. Did not know that." She looked up and saw the fishing pole bending. "Oh! Look, look, you have a fish."

PC jumped up, grabbed the pole, and pulled back.

"Oh yeah, we got something here.

He held on tight as he walked behind Ren. He sat down behind her and put the pole in front of her.

"What are you doing?" she asked.

"Ever catch a fish before?"

"No, never."

He put the pole in front of her. "Well, you're going to catch your first fish. Grab the pole."

She hung on. "I don't want to be dragged into the water."

"You will not. I have a hold on you. Keep a tight grip on the pole; I have a hand on it, too. Start reeling in." PC put his left arm around her waist, holding on to the pole with his right.

"Oh my God." Ren reeled in the line with her free hand on the pole. "Damn, it's pulling hard."

"Keep reeling. I've got ya."

The fish pulled harder and PC held onto Ren. He wrapped his legs around her to keep her in place.

"Son of a bitch won't give up," Ren said.

"Come on, you're doing fine."

Suddenly, a striped bass just popped out of the ocean.

"Did you see that?" Ren yelled. He's a big bastard!"

After ten minutes of give and take, the fish came closer to the shore.

PC let go of Ren and grabbed the line. "Hang on while I pull him in." PC worked the line with his hands and brought in the exhausted striper. He put his hand in the gill and lifted him out of the water.

Ren stood up, smiling, and walked toward PC. "Wish we had a camera."

PC smiled. "Your first fish; and dinner tonight.

CHAPTER 31

After a tasty fish dinner and a good night's rest, PC and Ren woke up to sunny skies. PC scanned the beach with his binoculars to make sure it was safe to leave. Ren packed their backpacks for the continuing trek to their destination.

"Anything?" Ren said.

PC put the binoculars down. "Nothing. Looks good for us to get started."

A motorized noise from above caught their attention. They pulled out their rifles and remained quiet. The sound stopped. Footsteps could be heard walking down the steps. PC motioned for Ren to move to her right as PC moved to his left, rifles pointed at the entrance. They heard the person walking in the sand toward their entrance. The person stopped and called inside the hideaway. "Hello."

Both stood still, aiming their weapons at the entrance.

"It's okay, young ones; you can come out."

Ren moved toward PC and whispered, "That sounds like the old man with the hot dog stand."

PC looked at Ren. "You sure?"

"Yeah, I remember him calling us young ones."

PC looked at the entrance. "Stay behind me." He slowly made his way to the entrance, looked outside, and saw the old man standing there.

"It is okay. You can come out."

PC peered left and right to make sure no one was sitting in wait.

"I am by myself. No one is going to hurt you."

PC slowly came out, looked around some more. Nobody but the old man. He lowered his rifle. "Ren, it's okay. Come on out."

Ren popped her head out, looked around, and smiled at the old man. "Hello there." Ren stepped out.

"Who are you?" PC said.

"I am the Gatekeeper of this dimension."

"The Gatekeeper?" Ren asked.

"Yes. I guard over this dimension. I know you young ones do not belong here, and we mean no harm to you. We want you to get back to your dimension, so all dimensions are back to normal.

"So, you know what's going on," PC said.

The old man nodded his head with a smile.

"And Lambert—do you know him? Have you spoken to him?"

"We know he is guiding you home, but have no contact with him."

"Can you help us get home?" Ren asked.

The old man smiled at her. "I am here to help. Come with me."

They followed the old man up the steps to the boardwalk. There stood a red motorized Taurine Gulf car. He said, "This should quicken your trip."

PC and Ren glanced from each other to the car.

"This will work, "PC said.

Ren kept looking at PC.

"Really, it will. Beats walking."

Ren nodded her head quickly. "Yes! This is true!"

PC walked around the cart. "How far can we go in this?"

"As far as you like." The old man grinned at PC.

"You mean it is endless when it comes to fuel?"

"Like your weapons, yes."

"Speaking of weapons, Ren said, "can you do anything about the soldiers that come after us?"

The old man shook his head. "I am afraid I cannot do anything about them. The soldiers you see come from another dimension from the past that has collided with this dimension that you've collided with. We wish we could get rid of them, but we're hoping that your Lambert and his people will correct this. We do not want them here, either. But our hope is in you two. Once you get to your destination and enter the lighthouse, things will be back to normal in all dimensions.

"Lighthouse? You said lighthouse. We just enter the Montauk Lighthouse, and that will send us both home?"

The old man nodded his head knowingly.

"Wonder why Lambert held that back?" Ren said.

"Eventually, he would have told us," PC said. He turned to the old man. "We thank you and appreciate what you are doing for us."

The old man smiled. "We just want you to get home so life in all dimensions goes back to normal." He headed down the boardwalk. "Be safe, my young ones."

He disappeared. Ren and PC stared, astonished.

"Where did he go?" Ren asked.

"I don't know, but that was an interesting exit." PC looked at the car and walked around it, nodding his head, pleased. "This will do us fine. Get us to our destination."

"Yes, yes it will. Let's get started."

CHAPTER 32

PC and Ren zoomed down the beach shore in their Terraine Gulf car with the provisions needed to sustain them through the trip. Ren had the binoculars up, searching ahead for trouble as PC drove.

"Anything ahead of us, Ren?"

Ren put the binoculars down. "All clear so far. Do you expect we'll run into trouble?"

"I'm sure we will. But let's hope for the best."

Suddenly, an explosion hit in front of the vehicle. PC swerved right into the ocean and came back out.

"Looks like they found us!" Ren yelled out.

"Hang on, girl!"

PC made a quick left-hand turn onto the beach and floored it as another explosion hit behind them.

"What are you doing!?"

"Trying to keep us alive! I don't want them to zero in on us! Hang on!" PC spun the cart around and headed for the shore as another explosion hit behind them.

"Shit! Sucks being out in the open like this! Nowhere to hide!"

Ren scanned the beach for the source of fire. "There!" she yelled. "There; over there!"

PC shouted, "Where? What? What are you seeing?"

"Over there!" She pointed her left arm out. "Eleven o'clock. That's where they are shelling us!"

PC saw soldiers with mortars. "Hang on!" He grabbed his rifle and handed it to Ren. "Think you can shoot this?"

She looked it over. "I think so."

"You've done pretty good all this time. I know you can do this. Just put the butt of the rifle on your shoulder so you don't go flying."

She positioned it. "Ready."

"Hang on, I'm going straight at them. Just keep firing at them!" He spun the cart around, put the pedal to the metal, and sped toward the soldiers.

The enemy tried to drop more mortars but the target was getting too close. They started firing their rifles at PC and Ren.

Ren let loose, planting her feet to the bottom of the cart with the butt of the rifle on her shoulder so she wouldn't lose control shooting.

PC pulled his nine-millimeter just in case as he sped toward the soldiers. Ren's shooting took two down, and three soldiers started to run. PC pulled up his pistol and took the three soldiers out. He came to a screeching halt as Ren put the gun down. PC looked her up and down. "And you never fired a weapon like that? You're a natural."

She shrugged her shoulders. "It just comes natural to me."

PC nodded his head slowly and looked away. "Interesting." He got out of the cart and looked around. "Soldiers are gone. What a surprise." He surveyed the area and grabbed the binoculars to look around.

Ren got out of the cart. "Anything?"

PC continued to survey. "So far, nothing."

He climbed up on the sand dune and scanned from left to right. Wide-eyed, he lowered the binoculars.

"What? What do you see?" Ren climbed up the dune.

PC put the binoculars back to his eyes. "Well, I have some good news and bad news."

"What, tell me," Ren said pulling on his arm.

"The good news is I can see the lighthouse."

"That's great!" Her smile faded. "What's the bad news?"

PC handed her the binoculars. "It's surrounded by soldiers."

Ren took a long glance and said, "Oh." She looked at PC. "Shit. There's a lot of them, PC." She handed him back the binoculars. "A lot."

"Yeah. We have a problem, Houston." PC scanned the lighthouse area. "Damn. They turned it into a fortress." PC looked at Ren. "Let's get a closer look and see if there are any holes we can sneak through."

"Let's go right to them."

PC looked up at the sky, then to his watch. "We'll wait till it gets dark. Let us find the hideaway, get some rest, and think about what we're going to do. We'll hide our vehicle close by so we can access it."

"Any ideas?"

"Maybe some night maneuvers."

A smile came to Ren's face. "Night maneuvers. That sounds sexy. Cool!"

PC looked at Ren up and down. "Well, maybe not sexy, but it will be an adventure, which I know you like."

"Uh huh," Ren said with a smile.

PC rolled his eyes.

They found the hideaway and ate some dinner. PC was deep in thought about how to make it to the lighthouse. Ren was deep in the hideaway looking through the supplies and making a lot of noise, interrupting PC's thought process. "What are you doing, Ren? Certainly, making enough noise." The noise stopped, and she came out.

"I found what I was looking for." She smiled triumphantly.

"What do you have there?"

Black pants and shirt for you and me." She threw the shirt and pants at PC's head.

He pulled them off his head and looked at them. "Where did you find them?"

"Back there in the containers, of course."

PC looked at Ren blankly. "Of course."

"Have you any ideas about what we are going to do?"

PC wrapped his arms around his legs and rested his chin on top of his knees. "It is going to be tough. The lighthouse is on the high ground, so they have the high ground."

"Which is to their advantage. They will see us coming."

He looked at the clothes Ren threw at him and smiled at her. "You are natural at this. Incredibly good."

Ren curtsied for PC. "Thank you."

"They will have the roads covered, so that would be difficult to go through. But our best bet is to come up through the brush up the side road on the beach that leads to the lighthouse."

"How are we going to do that?"

"Well, when it gets dark enough, we'll put on the clothes you found and do some scouting."

Ren looked outside. "Looks dark enough, don't you think?"

PC turned around and looked. "Yeah, yeah, it does. But let's wait till it gets a little later, then we'll head out. Lull these guys to sleep with a dull evening. Better yet, let's wait a few days or so and really lull them to sleep."

"They'll get complacent!"

"Exactly, Ren." PC pointed his finger at her.

"But what will we do till then?"

"Well, we will go and scout tonight and keep checking up on them to see their movements, so we can predict what they are going to do."

"Sounds good. But what are we going to do during the day? We can't scout them during the day."

"We can keep a close eye on them from a distance. We have binoculars and guns with a scope," PC sighed, "and time." PC looked at his watch, then outside. "We'll leave at midnight. Let's get some rest before we go."

"Okay. Let's get into our clothes so we'll be ready."

"Okay, girl, let's do it."

They dressed in the black clothes. Both fell asleep for the next few hours as they waited for the stroke of midnight. PC's watch alarm rang fifteen minutes before midnight. He shook Ren, who lay asleep by his side.

"Hey, sleepyhead, are you awake?"

"I'm awake." She stood right up. "I'm ready, let's go."

PC was astonished at her eagerness and energy. He stood up and Ren handed him a pair of binoculars.

Ren said, "We'll need the night vision binoculars."

"You are quite one step ahead of me. Yes, yes, we will. Good thought."

They grabbed their rifles and headed out of the hideaway. Ren put the boards back on the opening as PC scouted the area with the night binoculars. She turned to PC. "Anything?"

"Quiet on the beach." He looked at Ren. "Let's head over to the road. We'll stick close to the brush, so no one sees us. Come on, let's go."

They began their walk off the beach.

PC and Ren came up to the highway and lay low in the brush. PC slowly stuck his head up. Tanks and half-tracks were moving up toward the lighthouse.

"Let's move back into the brush," PC said quietly to Ren.

They moved back slowly and low to the ground. It was quite dark out, and their black clothes blended in with the scenery.

They stopped in the middle of the brush and looked toward the highway.

"We're not going to get in this way, with the traffic." PC looked toward the lighthouse. "Wow."

"What, what do you see?" Ren asked.

"It's just crawling with soldiers." He glanced at Ren. "And a few artillery and machine gun nests. I don't know how we're going to get to this."

Ren said, "Why don't we go back toward the wooden fence we passed earlier. Lots of brush there. Let's see how far we get."

PC scanned the area. "Okay, let's give it a try and see what happens. What's the worst that can happen?"

"Be seen and get killed," Ren said with a straight face.

"Yeah, well, minor detail, come on, let's go, and keep your voice down." He tugged on Ren's arm.

"Minor detail." Ren snorted.

They made their way to the fence. Ren started to climb over the fence.

PC pulled her down immediately. "No, no, go underneath. Remember, always stay low."

Ren nodded her head, "Okay."

They crawled underneath the fence and through the brush, staying low. They stopped in the middle, and PC looked around. "They're not making this easy," PC said. "Place is crawling with guards."

"Can we go right?"

"It's high around there. They will see us coming."

Ren grabbed PC's arm. "Shh. I hear something."

They heard voices headed their way.

PC cocked his head to see which direction the voices came from. "Quick, over here, and stay down."

They moved to their left, where the brush was heavy, and hid.

PC watched as three guards spread out, combing the area. One guard stopped in front of them, just inches away. For a moment, Ren stopped breathing. The soldier continued following the others.

PC slowly stuck his head up scanned the area. "Soldiers to the left of us." He looked to his right. "Soldiers to the right of us." He scanned the beach. "And soldiers on the beach." He looked at Ren. "We're surrounded?"

"Yep, we're surrounded." Ren took the binoculars and looked around. "They're not moving."

"No, and they're not going to. They must know we're here. They're waiting for us to make a move. They built a fortress so we can't move or get into the lighthouse."

"But we're trapped here. When daylight comes, we may be dead ducks."

"Yeah, got to think this one out," PC said. "Meanwhile, we'll have to sit quietly for a while and see if they make any moves so we can escape."

Ren continued to scope the beach. "Wow, they're all over the place. Hey. Wait."

"What, what do you see?"

"That general we saw a few days back. He's on the beach."

PC grabbed the binoculars. "Where? Show me!"

"There, about one o'clock."

PC stared into the binoculars until he found the general. "Damn!" He looked at Ren. "And I left the sniper rifle back in the hideaway."

"Sucks to be you right now."

"Yeah, it does."

"It's too far to take him out with this. Crap."

"Do you think taking him out will make all the soldiers disappear?"

"That's my hunch. Kill the leader; the rest will follow." He glanced at Ren. "Anyhow, I will be doing Lambert's dirty work for him."

They heard some brush movement. Both stood still, weapons ready. Suddenly, out of the brush, they heard a meow.

"It's a cat," Ren said as it came out of the brush. She recognized the cat right away. "Spotford!" Ren said out loud.

"Not so loud!" PC whispered.

Zing!

Shots sprayed near them. PC pushed Ren to the ground as Spotford ran off.

"No, Spotford!"

"Stay down! We're being fired at!"

"But it's Spotford."

"I'm not going to die over a cat. He will be fine." PC looked around. "Shit, they're coming at us from all directions."

Ren scanned for Spotford. "What do we do?"

They pressed their backs against each other, sitting on the ground. PC said quietly, "You fire left, and I'll fire right."

"Then what?"

PC went silent as he kept looking around.

"Then what!?" Ren said forcefully.

"I don't know."

Ren turned to PC.

He shrugged his shoulders. "I don't know. I'm just making this up as we go along.

"Terrific."

"Never mind that, just start firing."

They stood up and started firing. Ren rapidly fired her Winchester and mowed seven soldiers down before they got a shot off. PC kept firing with his rifle and never stopped until he mowed down a half dozen soldiers.

They lowered their weapons and looked around. Silence.

"Come on," PC said as he pulled on Ren's arm. "Come on, let's get out of here."

They both stood up as more soldiers appeared from behind them and to their flank.

PC shouted to Ren as they were being shot at, "Go get the cart, and I'll keep you covered."

"What are you going to do?"

"Keep them at bay until you come. There are too many of them. Go, go, now!" PC fired as Ren stayed low and headed for the cart. When she cleared the brush, she ran at full speed. She saw two soldiers in front of her. They were stunned to see her coming straight for them. She fired right at them, and both went down.

She stopped in front of them and noticed they had two potato mashers each. She pulled them off the dead soldiers and stuffed them in her backpack. She heard PC firing away. More soldiers appeared, and she gunned them down as she ran. She grabbed some more potato mashers from dead soldiers and kept running.

There was some brush ahead, which she ducked behind. Just beyond that was the cart. But two soldiers guarded it. Ren looked around to see if any other soldiers were around. She stood up.

"Good evening, gentlemen." She shot both soldiers down.

PC was firing in a fury. He spun around as they came up his back. "Damn it! Ren, where are you?"

He mowed down the soldiers behind him, but more soldiers appeared in front of him and to his flank.

He was surrounded. He stopped firing as he lowered is weapon, defeated and shocked as they approached him.

Boom!

There was an explosion behind him, and soldiers went down. PC ducked as more explosions went off all around him. Then, everything was silent.

PC heard a motorized vehicle pull up. He popped his head up and saw Ren sitting in the cart.

"Are you coming, or what?"

He stared at the mayhem as he got into the cart. There was no movement. "Did you do all this?"

She smiled back at PC. "Nothing like a potato masher to do the job."

PC stood up and got in the passenger's seat. "Okay then, you can drive."

"Where are we going?"

They heard a whistle, and explosions detonated around them.

PC shouted, "Shit, the beach, hit the beach. We're going to have to retreat."

Ren put the pedal to the metal, and they spun off down toward the beach.

One after another, explosions boomed behind them as they sped along the shore. They drove two, three, four miles, bombs following them all the way. They drove another ten miles before the explosions sounded further and further away from them.

Finally, the bombing stopped. Ren slowed, but PC told her to keep driving.

"I want to get away as far as we can so they can't hit us."

They drove another ten miles before they stopped. Both got out of the vehicle and sat on the sand next to each other, exhausted.

"Well, that was fun," PC said.

Ren smiled wearily. "I got a kick out of it."

PC looked at Ren. "Well, I'm glad one of us did."

Ren put her head on PC's arm. "What do we do now?"

PC sighed. "Well, this is a definite setback. We must be twenty miles away from the lighthouse now." He stood up and surveyed the area.

"Anything?"

"No, not seeing anything." He looked at Ren. "We're safe now."

He sat back down in the sand with Ren, watching the ocean. PC looked at Ren. "Tired? hungry?"

She nodded her head. "I can eat, and I can sleep, too."

PC stood up and held out his hand. "Come on." She took his hand, and he pulled her up. "We'll drive back to the hideout, I'll hide the vehicle somewhere, and we'll sleep on what we'll do next."

"Okay." They got back in the cart and drove away.

CHAPTER 33

A voice woke PC up the next morning. He jumped up with the nine-millimeter in hand and saw that Ren was still sound asleep in her sleeping bag. Looked around the hideout. "Must be dreaming," he said to himself and lay back down.

"Hello," he heard again. He stood up and looked out on the beach. Standing there was the general.

"Well, I'll be damned." He slid over to Ren. "Ren, Ren, get up." She was out like a light. "Ren!" He shook her harder.

"What, what, what!" She pushed his arm away and looked at him with her hair in her face.

"Better tidy up yourself, we have company."

"Company?" Ren was still half asleep.

"Yeah." He put his pistol away and grabbed his sniper rifle.

Ren crawled over to the entrance and looked through one of the slots. "Holy shit!" She looked at PC. "Is that the general you scared?"

"Yeah, and about to scare him again." PC pulled down the planks and aimed the rifle at him.

"Wait, wait, wait!" She put a hand on the rifle. "Let's see what he has to say."

PC looked up. "What?"

"Let's hear what he has to say."

PC glared at her with silence.

"What do we have to lose?" We're stuck at the moment. It looks like they may have the upper hand on us."

"What do you think he has to offer us? He's certainly not going to let us go to the lighthouse."

"I know, but we've inflicted some pretty good damage on him. And he is coming to us. So, doesn't that make us the power of strength?"

"In war, yes."

"Well, aren't we at war?"

PC looked at her in silence.

"We have beaten the shit out of these guys; we beat them back ninety miles, and we almost made it. He must be afraid we're going to penetrate his wall. Look what he has out there. The ghost of an Army past. They don't have the technology we have, and we outsmarted him for ninety miles. Let's hear what he has to say."

PC didn't notice anyone else with the general. PC stood up. "Grab your rifle, Annie Oakley."

PC stood up and hid the nine-millimeter behind his back under his shirt. He paused for a second and went to the dark side of the hideout, where the containers were.

Ren heard some rumbling and strained to see what he was doing. He came walking out and had on a different shirt with something else underneath. "What are you doing?"

PC repositioned the piston behind his back. He didn't answer her question. "If something happens to me, I want you to put a bullet between the general's eyes. Got it?"

Ren glared at PC. "Nothing is going to happen to you."

He smiled at Ren. "I'll be back." He knocked off the remaining planks.

"Annie Oakley?"

PC stopped and looked at her. "It was a compliment."

Ren nodded her head and smirked. "Oh."

PC walked out of the hideaway, toward the general. He moved to his left so Ren could have a clear shot at him if necessary. Along the way, he searched for trouble.

"No need to look around, son. You're safe."

PC stopped in front of the general just slightly off to the left and about ten feet away. "Can't say I can trust you, General Jay."

The general smiled. "So, you know who I am. I'm pretty sure you are or were in the military. Some excellent combat skills you have."

"I was in the military for a short time, General. And I certainly heard a lot about you. General Dirt Bag, they used to call you. Betrayed your own country so you could fill your pockets."

The General laughed. "No one has ever proved a thing."

"What do you want, general?"

"A peace offering."

"A peace offering? And what would that be? Letting us go to our destination in peace?"

"I'm afraid I can't do that, son. I want to offer you to stay in this world."

"Stay in this world?"

"Yes, it's exactly like the world you were in. Everything is the same. You just have to blend back into society, and things will be fine."

"Maybe for us, but not from the dimension we belong in. We're in the wrong dimension, and we want to go home. It wasn't our idea to be here. If we stay here, you and that moron of an ex-president will turn this country into a dictatorship. What's been promised to you, General? What part of the country are you going to rule? Is that why you have these Nazi soldiers chasing us around? You want to turn the United States into Nazi Germany? Power and money, that's what it's all about. The more power, the more money. You politicians make me sick. And that is what you are, General! A sick politician like the rest of them."

The general looked at PC with disgust. "You know I can take you out with one shot. I have someone off in the distance who will fire when I signal, and we can end it all here. And I will get what I want." The general laughed. "Yes, yes, I am a politician. So, what will it be, soldier boy?"

"Well, I tell you what, General, you take your best shot at me. But I must warn you, if I go down, my partner will put a bullet right between your eyes, and I will send you back dead to our world."

The general smiled. A shot rang out behind the general, and PC went down from the force of the bullet hitting him.

"Oh my God!" Ren quickly took aim at the General. "You're going down, mother fucker!" Ren took aim and slowly exhaled as she fired one shot, putting the general down quickly. She watched him hit the sand.

Another shot rang out, ricocheting off one of the wooden planks. Something smacked Ren on the shoulder. She hit the ground thinking she'd been shot. Checking her wound, she realized it was just a scrape from a splintered plank.

She lay low, looking outside to see who was firing. She could not help but look at PC lying in the sand. She wanted so desperately to go out to him, but realized there was someone looking to shoot her dead.

Both bodies lay still. She feared PC was gone. She studied the general's body but saw no movement at all. Suddenly, about fifteen feet behind the general, she saw a mound of sand moving. She stared at the spot, and more sand moved, falling off the mound. "Sand doesn't move like that," she said to herself. She waited. The sand moved again. She cocked her gun and took aim. One shot rang out and hit the moving sand, which began to bleed red.

"Got ya, you bastard!" She came out of the hideaway and looked around cautiously, gun in hand, ready to fire. She slowly moved around and looked left to right and behind her. She picked up speed, and tears came to her eyes as she got closer to PC. She fell to her knees by his side and dropped her rifle.

"Oh my God! PC! PC! Please tell me you are alive?" Tears flowed, and she lay her face against his chest and sobbed.

"Okay, I'm alive."

She lifted her head and beamed. "You're alive?"

"Yeah, well, if I wasn't, we wouldn't be having this conversation."

Ren put her head back on his chest and cried for joy.

"It's okay, Ren. I'm still here." He put his arm on her back.

"I thought you were gone. I was so scared at the thought of you being gone." Ren wept until she'd cried herself out.

"Feel better?" PC said. He could feel her nodding her head.

She inhaled and let out a big exhale. "I think so."

"Okay, pull me up."

Ren grabbed PC's arms and pulled him to a sitting position on the sand. She felt around his chest. "You're not bleeding."

"No." He grimaced and pulled a smashed bullet slug from his chest. "Bulletproof vest," He dropped the slug in Ren's hand.

She looked at the slug with astonishment and then at PC. She put her hand on his chest where he'd pulled out the slug.

PC winced. "But hurts like hell."

"Are you sure you are okay?"

"Except for the soreness and most likely a bruise, I'm okay." PC noticed Ren's shoulder bleeding. He put his hand on her shoulder, his forehead creased with concern. "You're hurt."

"I'm okay. Just a flesh wound."

PC gave her a look. "And you tell me I watch too much TV."

They laughed, pulled each other up, and walked toward the general, holding each other. PC looked down at him. "Wow! You really did hit him between the eyes." He looked over at the bloody sand with an outline of a body. "How did you know he was there?"

"The sand kept moving. It's not exactly a windy day, and sand doesn't move by itself."

PC nodded his head slowly. "This is true."

Abruptly, both bodies disappeared.

"Won't they be surprised when he comes back dead." PC looked at Ren's shoulder. "Come on, let us get back to the hideaway and get you patched up."

CHAPTER 34

"Do you think the soldiers will be gone with the general gone?" Ren asked.

"I don't know. Only time will tell. My thought is, probably not. Maybe delay them some."

"When do you think we can move forward again?"

"Well, we have to rest our wounds and figure out our next plan of attack."

They made it back to the hideaway, banged up and bleeding. They crawled back inside. PC pulled out his first aid kit. "Okay," he said as he turned around, "You may want to..." he stopped midway through his sentence when he saw Ren sitting shirtless in her bra.

"May want to what?" She inspected her wound.

PC shook his head. "Nothing." He knelt, pulled out some peroxide, dabbled it on some cotton, and applied it to the wound. Ren never flinched. He cleaned the wound thoroughly to avoid infection, put a bandage on, and made sure it was on firmly. "Better?"

Ren smiled at PC. "Better." She picked up a clean shirt. "Thank you."

PC put the first aid kit away and sat down next to Ren. He took a deep sigh as Ren discarded the other shirt with a hole in it. She took a deep sigh too, and they leaned up against each other.

"What's our next plan?" Ren asked.

PC sighed again. "I'm not sure, my dear." He looked outside the entrance. "Problem is penetrating the barrier around the lighthouse. The lighthouse is on the high ground."

"So, they can see us coming, like you said."

"Exactly." He smiled at Ren.

Ren smiled back and smacked PC across the chest. PC winced in pain. Ren realized what she'd done. "Oh! Oh, shit! I'm sorry. I didn't mean that."

"It's okay. I know you meant it with love." He rubbed his chest.

"Hello, inside."

PC and Ren looked at each other. PC grabbed his nine-millimeter. "Quick, grab your nine-millimeter."

"Hello," the voice called again.

"Wait." Ren grabbed PC's arm. "That's the Gatekeeper again. I'm sure of it."

PC nodded his head. "Okay." He moved forward on his hands and knees, peeked outside, and saw the old man standing there.

"Hello." He smiled at PC. "You can come out, it's safe."

PC holstered his weapon and came out of the hideaway. He looked behind him, and Ren slipped out with him.

"I hope you young ones are okay. I saw the exchange on the beach. Are you okay, my dear? Did they damage you much?"

Ren put her hand on her shoulder. "Oh no, I'm okay. Just a scratch."

"And you, young man, it was smart of you to put that bulletproof vest on, or we wouldn't be having this conversation. How are you feeling?"

PC rubbed his chest. "Sore, but I'll live." PC looked around and sighed again. "I do not know how we're going to get inside that lighthouse. It's a fortress, and they have the high ground."

"I know, son, it's a difficult task. But don't give up."

"Can you help us?" Ren asked.

The Gatekeeper shook his head. "I cannot. If I tell you what to do, I could alter the course of the dimension. I can only help you in small ways, like supplying you with a vehicle."

"What other small ways can you help us?" PC asked.

"I want the both of you to go back to the beginning of your trek."

"What?" Ren's voice raised, perplexed. "Go back where we started? After all the traveling we've done, and you want us to go in reverse?"

PC put his hand out to Ren. "Hold on." He looked back at the Gatekeeper. "Go on, sir."

"Go to the gift shop on Field Four and you will find what you need to get the both of you home."

"What are we looking for?" PC asked.

"I cannot give you that information. Like I said, it could alter things. You will have to search the gift shop to locate the way home."

"But you can point us in the right direction."

He smiled and nodded his head. "Exactly."

PC looked around. "What about the soldiers?"

"They will stay put at the Lighthouse. They know they have the advantage over you, and the only way to get in is to get by them."

"Well," PC looked at Ren, "at least we won't get harassed."

Ren nodded her head.

The gatekeeper smiled at them. "Be safe young ones. Until we meet again," and he was gone in a mist.

PC and Ren stood there. "People seem to disappear quickly in this world," PC said.

"They certainly do." Ren shook her head. "Do we really have to go all the way back to start?"

"Looks that way if we want to get home."

"I'm not happy about this."

"Neither am I, but if it helps us get home, we'll do it."

Ren started walking toward the ocean.

PC called out to her. "Ren, where are you going?"

Ren pulled her shirt off and dropped it in the sand, continuing her walk to the ocean as she undid her bra. "Going for a swim. Are you coming?" She dropped her bra in the sand and continued walking.

"But what about your shoulder? The saltwater is going to irritate your wound."

"I won't get it wet. Are you coming, or not?" She dropped her shorts in the sand, completely naked now, and jogged toward the water.

As PC watched Ren go into the ocean, he scratched his head and said, "Certainly not a shy girl."

CHAPTER 35

PC stood about fifty yards from the hideaway with binoculars to his eyes, looking east. He lowered them and looked straight. Nothing, he said to himself. He turned west and looked down, as not to trip over the towel he'd brought Ren, or the clothes she'd scattered on the beach. He stood there for a moment, trying to focus in, looking for any type of movement.

"Nothing," he said out loud. PC felt a tap on his hip.

"Hey, what are you doing? How come you didn't come in the water?"

PC lowered his binoculars and saw Ren standing by him, naked and dripping wet.

"I wanted to make sure we were safe."

She picked up the towel. "Hey, thanks." She dried herself off.

"You're welcome."

"Gatekeeper says we're safe."

"I know. Just wanted to confirm what he was saying."

"Well, are we safe?" Ren wrapped the towel around herself and sat in the sand. PC followed suit.

"Everything is clear from what I can see." PC looked at Ren. "Did you keep your wound dry?" He touched her bandage. "Huh, dry. How did you manage to keep it dry?"

She smiled. "Oh, I only went up to my waist; maybe a little higher."

"Well, I'm glad you kept it dry. Stinging salt water on a wound isn't pretty."

They stared out at the ocean for a moment until Ren broke the silence. "We should wait till nightfall to leave."

"Yes, we will wait till night before we head back to our starting point."

Ren nodded her head slowly.

"I want to drive the terrain on the highway so we can make better time than on the beach."

"But didn't Lambert tell us to stay off the highway?"

"He did, but he's not here to help us. I'm making an executive decision."

"Plus, it would be pretty weird for a terrain vehicle to be on the highway in the middle of the day," Ren said.

PC looked at Ren with some surprise. "Exactly. And we don't want any cops pulling us over. It's not common in New York to be riding in a terrain car. In Florida, yes, New York, no."

"They really ride terrain golf cars in Florida?"

"Oh yeah, quite common in some areas. Of course, it must be road-ready."

"Road-ready? What's that?"

"Has to have headlights, signals, rearview mirrors, brake lights, and a tag. Just like a car."

"Oh. Do you think we can get away with it?"

PC nodded his head. "I think so. Highway is deserted at night."

"It will be interesting to see what we're going to find when we get to the gift shop."

PC shook his head. "Yes, it will. I'm not sure what we'll be looking for. We'll just have to scout the store and see what we can determine."

"And if we don't find anything?"

PC looked at Ren. "We'll find something. The Gatekeeper would not be sending us if there wasn't something there." He looked up at the sky. "Starting to get dark. Let's go back to the hideaway, grab something to eat, and get moving. Sound good?"

"Sounds good."

They stood up. Ren walked away and PC saw her clothes on the sand. He picked them up and caught up with Ren quickly. "Forgot something?" He held out her clothes.

Ren took the clothes. "Oh, yes, thanks."

PC rolled his eyes. "You're welcome."

CHAPTER 36

P C and Ren gathered what they would need for the trip back to ground zero.

"We'll just take our nine millimeters and leave the rifles behind." Ren raised a brow, curious. "We cannot drive around with big guns. If the cops see us, they will be like flies on shit with us."

"But everyone seems oblivious when we walk around with them," Ren said.

"True, but I have this feeling it is not a good idea."

Ren nodded her head. "Okay." She holstered her nine-millimeter on her hip and covered the holster with her shirt.

PC did the same. "Ready?"

"Ready as I'll ever be."

They picked up their backpacks and made their way out of the hideaway. PC put the boards up to cover the entrance. Jen put the backpacks in the cart. She sat down in the cart, and PC followed suit. He flipped the switch, and the cart came to life. He looked at Ren.

Ren pointed her arm out. "Engage, Number One."

PC gave her a half-smile. "Don't you ever tell me I watch too much TV again."

Ren laughed.

PC shook his head. "Let's go." The cart moved forward.

The cart went up and down over the brush. Ren grabbed hold of the bar so she wouldn't fall out. "Pretty rough," she said.

"It will smooth out shortly." PC continued slowly, not wanting to run into anything that could tip the cart. He switched the lights on. "Looks like we're running into fog."

"That's a good thing, isn't it? Make good cover, right?"

"Well, yes, but also makes it hard to see. Fog can be thick as pea soup in this part of the woods. Just don't want to run into anything."

They finally made it out of the brush. PC stopped on the edge of the highway and looked both ways to make sure no vehicles were coming. He drove across and made a quick left to the west side of the road.

"Where are we, exactly?" Ren asked.

"Montauk Highway."

"How much of a ride do we have?"

"Couple of hours. Maybe three. With the fog in the way, it may take us longer."

"I don't know how you can see with this fog."

"I can't. Even with the lights on, it's not helping."

They drove at a slow speed for a while without incident. The fog was getting worse as they drove.

"This is soup. You can cut it with a knife," Ren said.

"Yeah, we just have to be careful and drive safe."

They drove in silence for a while, with PC focusing on the road, and Ren doing the same.

Ren broke the silence. "So, how come you're still single?"

PC shot a surprised look. "Huh? What?"

"Why are you still free? You're quite a catch. How come no one has reeled you in?"

PC smiled at her. "Didn't we have this conversation?" He put his focus back on the road. "Well, I can ask you the same question."

"Come on now, don't try to turn it back at me." She slapped him on the arm.

PC wore a distant look. "After I left the military, I was just comfortable in my lifestyle. Really didn't want anybody in my life. Anyone who got close to me, I pushed away."

"Did you push Carol away?"

PC sighed deeply. "Yes." He looked at Ren. "Yes, I did. I had to. It was too painful for the both of us."

"Was she the love of your life?"

PC rubbed his chin. "She's the one who got away."

"Do you think you'll let anyone in your life?"

Her question pulled him back. He smiled at her. "I let you in."

"But not by choice," she said with a smile.

"What about you? A Pretty thing like you running around free. How come you're not an arm trophy for some gorilla?"

Ren hit PC in the arm again as he started laughing. "Second time you said that! I can't believe you said that again!" She gasped. "An arm trophy for some gorilla."

PC smiled. "Hard to find a girl like you, especially one who likes to take her clothes off."

Ren's smile faded.

PC noticed. "I'm sorry, Ren. I didn't mean to be..."

Ren cut him off. "No, no. That's not it." She took a big breath of air and exhaled. "I guess you can say I've attracted a lot of men in my life, especially in college." Her voice trailed off, and she looked down.

PC looked at her, and her gaze met his.

"I was sexually abused in college, and to deal with loss of control, I became a stripper."

PC's eyes widened.

"It was the most liberating thing I did for myself." She laughed to herself. "Helped me pay for college." She looked at PC. "It's like therapy, it gave me confidence in myself. It made me into the person I am." She leaned back in her seat. "That is why I am comfortable taking my clothes off. It doesn't bother me. I knew when I danced, no one would touch me because the security at the bar made sure. They used to walk me to my car after work." She glanced at PC. "I am comfortable with you and know no harm will come to me because you are protecting me."

"You seemed apprehensive when we first walked the beach naked."

"I was. I never did it in public, just in a bar, but it melted away quickly, and I soon felt that comfort level I used to have, being naked in front of people. I can understand being stuck on the taboo that we were all taught growing up, not to take your clothes off in front of people. But it doesn't bother me."

PC sat silent and kept his eyes straight ahead. He then turned his head toward Ren. "You don't do that for everyone, do you?"

"You mean take off my clothes off?" Ren started laughing. "No. No, I don't. It's..." she paused to find the right words. "It's therapeutic, like I said."

"Kind of like some old Army buddies I know. They have PTSD. They deal with it in different ways."

"Ren looked at PC, curious. "How so?"

"Well, one smokes pot to deal with it. Another buddy does one of the types of Karate. Uh, Shotokan, I think. And another, you'll like this, he makes dresses."

Ren gave PC a funny look. "Dresses?"

"Yes, and he is quite good at it. In fact, he is starting to become well known in the industry for that kind of work."

"Wow," Ren said.

"So, what you are telling me makes sense. You're dealing with something from your past, and this is how you deal with it. Relieve the mental pain."

Ren smiled at PC. "Thanks for understanding."

PC smiled back at her.

Suddenly, from behind, a roaring sound could be heard coming up on them fast. Ren looked back. She couldn't see what it was, but she yelled, "Look out!"

PC swerved to get out of the way, but they were partially sideswiped. The hit pushed them to the other side of the road. PC managed to keep the cart straight until his left front tire hit something projecting out of the ground. The cart flipped on its side and hit the ground.

Both had their safety belts on, and they lay silently. PC reached over to feel Ren. "Ren, Ren. Okay?"

She groaned, "What was that?"

"Had to be a truck, a pick-up. It was loud and hit us with force."

Ren felt her shoulder. "I think my shoulder is bleeding again."

"Shit. Okay, hang on. Let me get out of this position and get you out."

PC grabbed onto the bar of the cart so he wouldn't fall on Ren when he unbuckled his seat belt. He held on tight as he released the seat belt, grabbed the bar with his other hand, and pulled himself out. He sat on top of the car and said to Ren, "Okay, unbuckle yourself and reach up with both arms; I'll pull you up."

Ren did as he said and unbuckled herself. She turned herself to straighten out her body and reached up with both arms. She groaned as he pulled her out and placed her on top of the cart.

He looked at her. "Okay? You did some groaning on the way up."

She nodded her head quickly. "I'm good. Just a little shaken."

PC jumped off the cart, reached up, and pulled Ren down from her waist. He pulled her shirt collar down some to see her shoulder.

"Yeah, you are bleeding. Let's get you fixed up. But first, let's pull the cart down and assess the damage. Stand back."

Ren took a few steps back.

With little effort, PC pulled down the cart.

Ren stepped forward again. "Is it still ridable?"

PC checked the cart. "Well, from the looks of it, seems okay, with a few blemishes here and there." He got into the cart and turned the key. He smiled as the cart started right up. "Just like new."

Ren smiled at PC, holding her shoulder.

The smile on PC's face disappeared. "Let's look at that shoulder." He reached back in the cart and got out the first aid kit. "Here, come in front of the headlight so I can get a better look." Ren moved over to the light. PC sat on the ground as did Ren. PC rummaged through the first aid kit and found what he needed. When he looked up at Ren, she was shirtless. PC took it as normal and moved her bra strap down, removing the bandage. Ren winced as he cleaned the wound.

"Hurts more the second time around, huh? Sorry."

She smiled. "It's okay. You have a soft touch."

PC laughed. "That's what the guys I served with used to say."

Ren gave PC an inquisitive look. "I thought you were a sniper?"

"I was, but sometimes I doubled as a medic. Well, I wasn't officially a medic, but when someone got hurt, I'd be Johnny on the spot." He looked at Ren. "I don't like seeing people I'm with get hurt. I don't like seeing anyone get hurt."

"But you were a sniper. You killed people for a living."

"When it comes to war, it's kill or be killed, my dear." He finished cleaning the wound, then added some ointment and a fresh bandage.

"There, all fixed up." He pulled Ren's bra strap back up.

"Thank you," she said, and put her shirt back on. PC stood up and pulled Ren up by her hands.

They walked away from the vehicle to get their bearings. "Wonder where the hell we are," PC said. As the words came out of his mouth, PC fell forward first and disappeared into the fog, followed by Ren. Both hit the ground.

PC landed flat on his face and quickly rolled over with his butt on the ground. He held himself up with his arms straight and hands face down. He shook his head. "Shit." He looked around. "Ren? Are you okay?" He couldn't see her through the thick fog.

"Yeah, I think so. You?"

"Yeah, I'm good. Where are you?"

He got on his hands and knees, crawling to find Ren.

"Right here."

PC reached out and touched her leg. "There you are."

Ren was in a sitting position.

PC sat next to her. "Shoulder okay?"

"Oh yeah, I rolled the other way. What the hell did we fall off from?"

PC stood up and pulled Ren up by her arms. "I don't know. I've never seen such a bad fog before."

They both moved forward slowly. Ren's foot hit something hard. She stopped and grabbed PC arm. "Wait," she said. She tapped it with her foot. She lifted her foot. She let go of PC's arm and took a second step. She turned around and was almost as tall as PC. "Steps. We fell off steps.

PC took a step up and was taller than Ren again. "No..." he said.

"What?"

"I got a feeling where we are. Come on; walk slowly with me." He took Ren's hand, and they moved forward, feeling for the steps with their feet as they climbed up slowly until there were no more steps. They continued to walk carefully.

"Where do you think we are?" Ren asked.

"Well, do you remember the big tower, the Pencil, we passed earlier in our trek that I told you about?" PC put his arm out and moved slowly back and forth, feeling for something. His hand stopped as the palm of his hand hit something hard and wet.

"Yeah, I remember." Ren stopped with PC.

PC let go of Ren's hand and put his other hand out to feel what was out in front of him. He looked up but couldn't see much due to the fog. He looked at Ren. "Well, we're here at the Pencil."

"The what?"

"The Pencil, like I told you before. That's what they call this tower. We just about drove into it. The steps are what saved us from driving into it. Well, sort of."

"The Pencil? Why do they call it the Pencil?"

"Because it looks like a pencil!"

Ren looked up. "Yeah, well, can't see much, but if you say so." She strained to see PC. "Now what? It's hard to travel in this weather."

"Yeah, I know. Let's head back to the cart and figure it out." PC walked forward and disappeared in the fog.

"Wait, slow down or you're going to..." Suddenly, Ren heard a stumbling noise and heard PC hit the ground again. "Fall," she said as she put her hands on her hip. "Jerk." She called out, "Are you okay?"

"Yeah, and I heard that!"

She rolled her eyes and moved slowly with her arms out and feet shuffling so as not to trip on the steps.

"Give me an idea where you are. Oof!" She fell over PC and landed flat on her stomach.

"Right here." PC said in a sarcastic tone.

Ren sighed. "No shit."

PC pulled his legs out from hers, stood up, and pulled Ren up, rubbing her arms. "Okay?"

"Yeah, okay." She walked away from him.

"What?"

She turned around and walked back to him. "You could have told me where you were before I tripped over you."

"I did tell you."

"Yeah, after I fell over you."

"Well, I couldn't see you. It's foggy out, you know."

"Yeah, I know, but you could have told me sooner."

"Oh my God." PC threw his hands up and turned, taking a few steps away from Ren.

"You could have said something," Ren repeated.

PC turned around. "Yeah, and you didn't have to call me a jerk."

Ren placed her hands on her hips. "Well," she hesitated, "You are."

They stopped talking and glared at each other. PC looked around, then at Ren. "What's happening here?"

Ren folded her arms and looked away. "Our first fight."

PC's laugh faded when he heard something ricochet off the pencil. Instinctively, he grabbed Ren, and they hit the ground. Several more bullets whizzed by and hit the Pencil.

PC lay on top of Ren as the shots continued. Finally, there was silence. PC pulled his head up and looked around, but with the fog, he couldn't see anything.

Ren popped her head up. "What the hell was that?"

"Shh." PC listened intently, since his visibility was zero. "Somebody is shooting at us."

"I thought the caretaker said we would be safe."

"Yeah, well, guess he made a mistake on that."

"Soldiers, you think?"

"Maybe. I'm not sure. Unless they got a hold of some state-of-the-art weaponry the general may have given them. They didn't have that kind of weaponry back then."

"We need to get back to the cart," Ren said.

"I'm all for that, but where is it?"

"It's about ten steps this way," she pointed to her right.

PC's face twisted.

"Now how do you know that?"

Because I counted the steps as we approached the pencil."

PC stared, incredulous. "Seriously?"

"Yeah. Ten steps that way." She pointed right again.

PC pulled out his nine-millimeter. "Okay, stay low, don't stand."

"Well, how are we going to count steps if we're crawling?"

"Well, standing is not a good idea. We're just going to have to go by direction. Let's go."

Ren pulled out her nine-millimeter, and they crawled slowly on the ground. Ren was counting in her head; PC was listening for possible sounds. They had reached the ten-step mark. Ren stopped and was feeling around for the cart. Ren moved to her left, still on her hands and knees. PC kept one hand on her so he wouldn't lose her. "Here!" Ren put her hand on the tire. She smiled to herself. "Found it."

PC pushed her down as more shots passed over their heads. Lying on his side, PC took aim with both hands on his nine-millimeter and sprayed the location where the shots were coming from. Knowing his clip would not run out, he fired twenty rounds. Everything went silent. PC put his hand on Ren. "Okay?"

She nodded her head. "Okay."

"Quick, get in the cart."

Ren entered the cart on the driver's side and PC pushed her through so he could get behind the wheel. He started the cart one-handed, as they both held their nine-millimeters. PC gunned it and found his way to the highway and kept up the speed to get as far away as possible. He kept the lights off to keep things dark.

Ren asked, "Do you think the guy who tried to run us off the road was the same guy who shot at us?"

"I'm thinking so."

A white light came up behind them, fast. Ren spun around in her seat, held her nine-millimeter with both hands, and fired rapidly. She shot the lights out and continued firing.

They heard a screech and the crashing sound of a vehicle tumbling over and over.

Finally, the tumbling stopped.

Ren sat back down in her seat, looking over her shoulder then at PC. PC put his nine-millimeter back in its holster as Ren stared straight ahead. He took her hand as she squeezed his.

"Okay?" he asked.

Ren squeezed his hand once more. She finally looked at him. "Okay." She holstered her gun, still holding PC's hand. "Do you think we should go back and check?"

PC glanced at Ren and back to the road. "No, no, we shouldn't. We don't know what's back there that may be waiting for us," He noticed her worried expression. "Are you sure you are, okay?"

She smiled at PC. "Really, I'm okay. I think I just scared myself back there."

PC raised a brow. "How so?"

"My adrenaline. I never felt my adrenaline like that. It was like I was so focused, and I was going to take out what was chasing us. And it didn't even bother me. I just scared myself. I never felt like that before. Did you ever feel like that in war?"

PC continued to hold Ren's hand. "More times than I can count."

CHAPTER 37

PC and Ren made it to Field Four at Jones Beach. It was still dark out. They pulled in.

"This is a huge parking lot." Ren looked around. "No cars. A good thing."

"Yes, a good thing for us. No one to bother us."

PC drove to the back end of the parking lot, found a good spot to hide the terrain, and backed it in as far as he could into the trees so the brush would cover the vehicle. "No one will see us back here." He looked around. "Fog is still pretty thick."

They heard sirens screaming down the highway. They listened quietly until the sirens went by.

"Wonder where they're heading," Ren said.

PC had a feeling about where they were going. "Come on, grab your backpack."

"Where are we going?"

"Going to find some showers in the bathrooms so we can clean up. We don't look that good. Hope you brought a change of clothes."

"Yes, I did, and a bathing suit too, just in case."

"Okay good. Let's get moving." He looked at his watch. "Two in the morning, no one should be around."

They slipped on their packs and began the long walk across the parking lot.

"Where do you suppose those sirens were headed for? You don't think..."

"Yes, I do think they are headed where we just were."

"But there should be no sign of anything since it seems everything disappears when someone gets killed."

"Maybe, but I have this feeling it wasn't soldiers."

"Who do you suppose it was?"

"I don't know. Lambert needs to make an appearance. He's been MIA for a while now, and he needs to enlighten us."

They made it across the parking lot, up to the path toward the beach. They went under a tunnel, and above them was the Wantagh Parkway. Some more sirens screamed overhead as they walked through the tunnel.

"They seem to be in a hurry," Ren said.

"That, they are."

They came out of the tunnel, and a little further before they made a left onto the main walking area going to the beach. Ren looked at the tower that they'd walked around. "What is that for?"

PC looked. "That is known as the Jones Beach Tower. The symbol of Jones Beach. Used to be a water tower, but now it's just a symbol."

Ren nodded her head. "Interesting."

"Come on, let's go."

No one seemed to be around as they walked up the steps and onto the boardwalk.

"Here, to your right. I'm sure you will enjoy a freshwater shower instead of a saltwater bath."

"And how," Ren said. "Wait a minute...." She grabbed PC's arms and stopped him. "This is the Men's room."

"So? There's no one here." He smiled. "Never stopped you before."

"Point taken." They walked into the bathroom.

PC stopped as the lights were out. He felt along the wall till he found the light switch and flipped the lights on. It wasn't brightly lit, but they could see enough.

"Over there." He walked over and turned on the shower. "Good flow." He turned on the second shower. "Good flow here. Not hot, but it will do."

They took off their dirty clothes and jumped into their respective showers. Ren had brought a razor blade with her to shave her legs. PC had his razor to shave his face, along with shaving cream.

"Hey, Ren said, "can I borrow your shaving cream so I can shave my legs?"

"Just a minute."

He put some lather on his face, reached around the corner, and handed the shaving cream to Ren.

"Thanks! Man, starting to look like a hairy beast."

"Yeah, I know what you mean," PC said back.

As he was shaving, he felt his wet hair. "Damn, I'm starting to look like a hippy. Can't remember the last time I had a haircut."

"I think you look good with the way your hair is."

PC felt the length of his hair again. "You think so?"

"Yes, it looks good."

They cleaned and groomed themselves, dried, and put on some fresh clothes. PC tended to Ren's wound with a clean bandage. He put on a pair of white shorts with a white cut-off shirt. Ren slipped into some khaki shorts with a bikini top, put a white top over it, and slipped into some sandals.

Both put their floppy hats on and looked at each other. "We clean up pretty good, don't we?" Ren said, laughing with PC.

"Come on," PC said, "Let's gather our things and head out.

"To the hideaway?"

PC looked at his watch. "Yeah, I figure we can lay out at the hideaway. Sun won't be up for a few more hours, and hopefully burn this fog up. We can sleep for a while. How's that sound?"

Ren smiled. "Sounds good. Let's go."

They headed out with their backpacks. PC kept his hand close to his nine-millimeter. They walked to the deserted boardwalk and onto the beach. They found the hideaway, and PC pulled the boards down, crawled in, and grabbed the sleeping bags. They slipped in, lay down together, and passed out quickly.

CHAPTER 38

PC woke up feeling something on his body. He looked up to find Ren's arm across his chest and her body snuggled up against him. He looked at her with some surprise, then at his watch. Seven thirty, he said to himself. He looked at Ren again. "Oh, boy." He politely rubbed her hand. "Hey, hey, wake up. Hey."

Ren's eyes slowly opened. "Good morning," she said with a smile.

"Come on, time to make the donuts."

She looked at him curiously. "Donuts? What?"

PC shook his head. "Never mind. Come on, time to get up."

She freed herself of PC, stood up, yawned and stretched, saying, "What time is it?"

PC looked at his watch again. "Seven thirty."

Ren froze, still stretched out. "In the morning?"

"Well, it's certainly not the evening with the sun coming up." He looked around. "Sun's burning up the fog. Things will clear up soon enough."

"Is there somewhere we can get something to eat?"

PC stood up, deep thought. "Hey, the Jones Beach Restaurant is still here. Should be opening soon."

"Do you have any money?"

PC looked down at Ren with his hands on his hips. "Do I have any money."

Ren realized what she'd said. "Oops, sorry, I forgot how much money you carry."

PC reached down and grabbed Ren by the hands. "Come on!" He pulled her up. "Let's get some good food for once." They crawled out of the hideaway, put the planks back, and walked up the steps and onto the boardwalk. PC pulled his shirt down so no one would see his weapon. A few people were walking on the boardwalk. Ren slipped her hand into PC's.

PC looked down, then at her.

"So, we look like the happy couple, like we did when we mingled with the nudists." She smiled at PC.

PC gave her a long look. "Right."

"Come on, don't you think we would make a good couple?"

PC turned away. "In another world, maybe."

"What do you mean, in another world?" she snapped.

PC thought fast to get himself out of trouble. "Well, look at the world we're in. We have soldiers from the past chasing us. I've been shot, you were wounded, and we almost got run off the road last night. This is not the place for a romance."

"I really didn't think of it that way." She fell silent.

PC started feeling bad. He saw a bench and sat Ren down next to her.

"Listen, this has been some adventure for the both of us. But let's put this on the back burner for now and get out of the current situation we're in."

Ren looked him straight in the eyes.

"Okay? we'll talk about it when we get back to our world."

Ren nodded her head. "Okay. You're right. This is no place to start a romance. But I will say I'm comfortable with you, PC Sebastian. More comfortable than with any other person I've been with. And maybe one day you will tell me what PC stands for."

He smiled and said, "One day. One day."

Come on, let's get something to eat. I'm starving."

"Agreed."

They walked on. Ren took PC's hand again. PC looked at Ren.

"At least we can still look like the happy couple," Ren said, smiling.

PC smiled back. "Okay. Happy couple we are."

They strolled up to the entrance of the restaurant, and PC opened the door for Ren.

The hostess was waiting at the entrance. "Good morning to you both. Two in your party?"

"Yes, two," PC said.

Ren grinned.

"Okay, follow me, and I will take you to your table."

They followed the host, and she sat them by the windows and handed them menus. "The waitress will be right with you."

"Thank you," Ren said, and the host walked back to the front door entrance.

PC looked around. "Looks like we're their first customers."

Ren looked around. "Looks like it. Nice place."

The server greeted PC and Ren. "Good morning to you both. My name is Karen, and I will be your server for today. Can I get you any coffee?

"Yes, black for me," Ren said.

PC glanced from Ren to the server. "Yes, coffee for me, with creamer."

"Okay, I'll get you some coffee while you decide what you want." The server stepped away.

PC shot Ren a look. "Black coffee?"

"Yeah. Only way I'll have it. Can't wait. Haven't had any coffee since we landed here."

"An acquired taste, I guess."

Ren nodded her head slowly. "Yeah."

Both stared at the menu for a minute. Finally, Ren slammed down the menu, startling PC. "I've decided what I want."

PC shook his head. "So glad you did. What are you getting?"

"Two eggs over easy and some grits. What are you getting?"

PC perused the menu. "Hmmm, I think I'm going with the French toast."

"French Toast? That's a lot of carbs."

"That's okay, I've probably lost a good five pounds doing all the walking we have done."

"Yeah, you are right." Ren patted her stomach. I've lost some weight myself."

The server reappeared. "Have you decided what you want to order?"

"Yes, yes, we have. Ren?"

Ren looked back down at the menu. "Hmmm, I'll have the waffle with strawberries."

PC looked at Ren. "Changed your mind?"

She smiled. "Women's prerogative." She giggled.

"Right." He looked back at the server. I'll have the French toast."

The server took the menus, said the meals would be out shortly, and walked away.

PC glanced out the window and noticed the gift shop across from the restaurant. "Look," he pointed. "That's where we are going next. The gift shop."

Ren looked out the window. "Okay. I don't know what we're looking for."

PC shrugged his shoulders. "Neither do I, but we'll see what we can figure out." He craned his neck. "I wonder if they sell newspapers."

"Why don't you go look?" Ren said.

"I think I will." He smiled as he got up. "Be right back."

He scurried over to the gift shop. A minute later, he returned with a newspaper in his hand. He paused and frowned, eyeing the paper. He sat back down and read an article on the second page.

Ren saw the seriousness on his face. "What's wrong?"

He looked up at Ren. "Remember the sirens we heard last night?"

She frowned. "Yeah."

"They found a dead body near the Pencil. They found him with a sniper rifle."

"Oh, shit. The guy that was shooting at us."

PC nodded his head. "Exactly. And up the road they found a turned-over pick-up truck with two dead bodies in it."

Ren's face went white. "Why didn't they disappear like everyone else that has been killed?"

PC read on. "They identified one of two people killed. He was a mercenary."

"So, people from our world hired mercenaries to kill us."

"And they hired them from this world."

"Which is why they didn't disappear."

"Correct, my dear."

Ren picked up her coffee and took a sip as she watched the people passing by on the boardwalk.

PC grabbed his mug and read on.

"Do you think we're safe?" Ren planted her face in her hands.

PC put the paper down and looked around. He leaned over to Ren. "For the moment, I think we are. No one knows it's us, and they have no witnesses or clues, and it was dark, foggy, and no one was on the road last night."

Ren took PC's hand. "You know, I think this is the first time in this adventure I've been afraid."

PC held on to Ren's hand. "We'll be fine. I'm not going to let anyone hurt us."

The waitress showed up with their breakfast.

"Okay, who gets the waffles with strawberries, again?"

PC and Ren let go of their hands. "That would be me," Ren said.

The server put the plate of waffles down and then PC's French Toast. "Can I get you anything else?"

"No, we're good." PC nodded to the server. "Thank you." She bobbed her head pleasantly and walked away. A steward walked over and refilled their coffee cups.

"Okay, let's just relax and enjoy our meal." PC sighed happily. "We've been living in the sand for a while now. Good to have a meal."

She dug in. "Yes, let's enjoy."

CHAPTER 39

Ren put her utensils down and leaned back in her chair with her hand on her stomach. "Oh, that was good."

PC wiped his mouth with his napkin and looked up with surprise. "I guess you didn't like your meal. God, you wolfed that down, girl."

"I did not!

"Or you just eat fast?"

Ren looked insulted. "I never!"

PC laughed. "Well, after all these weeks on the beach, I guess you were a little famished?"

"Yes. Yes, I was."

PC laughed again. "Okay, we'll leave it at that."

PC pushed his plate forward and picked up his newspaper as Ren drank her coffee, looking outside. As PC glanced up, he noticed some more people had come into the restaurant. A man in a black suit sat in the corner by himself, occasionally looking toward PC and Ren. PC rubbed his face, wondering why a person would be wearing a dark suit on a day like this.

He put the paper down and pulled his wallet out of his pocket.

"Are we leaving?" Ren sulked.

"No," as he stood up. "Just going to use the bathroom." He put a hundred-dollar bill down on the table. "If the waitress comes back, pay her for me, I'll be right back."

She smiled. "Okay. Meanwhile, I'll look at your newspaper."

As PC headed across the room, he saw the black-suited man get up and head in the same direction. PC walked into the men's room, made a left, quickly hid behind the wall, pulled out his nine-millimeter, and held it high as the black-suited man came walking in. PC put the gun to the side of his head. The man stopped dead as PC pulled the trigger back.

"Surprise," PC said. He pulled the man's gun out of his gun harness. "My, that's a big cannon." PC shoved the gun behind his back, grabbed the man by the top of his jacket, and pushed him into the stall. "You want to tell me who you are?"

The man turned his head and leered from the corner of his eye with a smile. "Forget it."

"Okay," PC said. He checked the man's pockets and found nothing. "You don't carry much, do ya? Okay, time for you to go to sleep."

PC grabbed the man's shoulder close to his neck and squeezed with his fingers. The black-suited man's head went limp, hanging to the left. PC grabbed him from underneath his armpits. "Damn, you're heavy." PC put his gun away, spun the black-suited man around, sat him on the toilet, and leaned his head on the wall of the bathroom stall. PC locked the door and crawled out from underneath. He quickly went to the sink and washed his hands, dried them with paper towels, and threw them in the garbage.

He pulled the clip out of the man's gun, emptied the chamber, and threw the gun in the garbage. He put the clip in his pocket and walked out the door calmly.

He looked toward Ren, who was still reading the newspaper. He let out a big sigh, seeing that she was okay. "Oh, thank God." He walked over calmly, as if nothing had happened.

Ren looked over her shoulder and saw PC coming. She smiled. "There you are."

"Come on, let's go."

"Go? What's the rush?"

The server came, holding the bill in hand. PC handed her the hundred-dollar bill. "Here, keep the change."

The server was stunned. "Oh, thank you, sir!"

"You're welcome. Honey, lets go, our friends are waiting."

Ren read PC's subtle expression of warning. "Oh, yes, we must go find them." She waved to the server.

PC took Ren's hand. "Walk calmly out," he said in a low voice.

"What happened in the bathroom?"

"There was a black-suited guy sitting in the corner, watching us. He followed me in."

"I saw him. I thought it was weird he was wearing a suit in this weather. What happened?

"I neutralized him."

"Neutralized him? In what way?"

"It's difficult to explain."

"I'm listening."

"Have you ever watched Star Trek, the original one?"

"I have."

"Well, let's just say I gave him the equivalent of a Vulcan nerve pinch."

Ren raised an eyebrow.

"How long will he be out?"

"For a while. Meanwhile, we need to disappear."

"Do you think there are any more around?"

"I hope not, but we must be careful.

"Do you think he is a mercenary?"

"Could be. He's rough-looking enough to be one. Move over toward the receptacle."

PC motioned toward a garbage can, and he discarded the clip.

"What was that?" Ren said.

"Getting rid of evidence.

"What did you do with his gun?"

"Dropped it in the garbage."

Ren leaned toward the gift shop. PC pulled her back. "We need to get back to the vehicle and hang there for a while. It's best we stay away from the hideaway for now. It's early, and I want to wait till it's more crowded." He looked up at the sun. "It's a nice day, so people will come."

"So, we can get lost in the crowd."

"Yes. If anyone is watching us, I don't think they'll do anything stupid with a crowd of people."

They made their way back to the vehicle, which was well hidden in the trees and brush. Vehicles came in a few at time, then more as the morning progressed. PC sat with binoculars on top of the cart with Ren.

"Anything?" she asked.

PC scanned the parking lot. "No, nothing." He watched as a few people came walking out from the tunnel into the parking lot. "Oh, wait a minute."

"What, what do you see?"

"Our man in the black suit made it out of the bathroom."

"How does he look?"

"Hmm, a little dazed, like he's drunk."

"Guess that Vulcan nerve pinch does wonders."

PC laughed.

"Where is he headed?"

PC followed him with the binoculars deep into the parking lot. "He's walking way over to the other side." He saw a Humvee parked in the corner, painted military green. "Ah, yeah, he is a mercenary. PC handed the binoculars to Ren. "Look at what he is driving."

"Holy shit." She looked at PC. "Do you think that is a military vehicle?"

"Well, the military does use Humvees, but that must be his. Too painted up to be a military vehicle."

Ren scanned again. "He's leaving now. Seems to be in a hurry to get out."

PC grabbed the binoculars. "Yeah, yeah, that he is." He put the binoculars down. "He must have been the only one here."

"He will probably be coming back with reinforcements.

"Oh yes, he will be back with reinforcements."

"What do we do now?"

PC lifted his hat, scratched his head, and sighed. "Not sure. We do need to go to the gift shop to find what we need to get home, but I'm a little nervous someone might be hanging. We must lie low for a while. Let them think we're gone."

They sat in silence for a moment until Ren thought of something. "Hey, you said you have a house; why don't we go there for a bit and hide?"

"Well, I thought about that, but I want to use it as a last resort. Not sure if it's safe to go, since we have company watching us. Besides, I don't think Lambert wants us to wander far off course, like we have already."

Ren nodded her head. "Seems we're not alone anymore."

"No, seems eyes are on us." He looked at Ren. "We'll take it one step at a time." PC thought for a second and jumped off the top of the cart. "Be right back." He crawled into the cart, searching in his backpack.

"What are you doing?"

He pulled out a business card and pen and wrote on the back of the card. He put the pen back in the backpack and climbed back up on the cart. "Here." He handed Ren the card.

She examined it. "You gave me your business card, remember?"

PC turned the card over. "Yes, but on the back of the card is the address to my house."

Ren gave PC a curious look.

"If something happens to me, you go to this house. By the stoop is a rock with a false bottom. Inside is the key to the house."

Her brow furrowed. "How will I get there? I mean, I don't know this area."

"You need to come back to Field Four and go to the bus stop."

"Where is that?"

"Remember where we walked under the tunnel and turned?"

"Yeah."

"Well, instead of turning right to head for the beach, turn left. Walk toward the tower. There you will see the sign, and probably people waiting to take the bus, on the right side."

She looked at the card again and at PC. "Okay, but where do I go on the bus? Where do I get off?"

He pulled out another business card with writing on the back and handed it to Ren. "Follow these directions."

She read it and tucked the cards in her back pocket. "Nothing is going to happen to you."

"I hope not, but just in case..." He smiled at Ren, and she hugged him.

"You think we can walk on the boardwalk?"

PC broke the embrace and looked at Ren. "I think we're safe for the moment. But let's stay away from the gift shop for now. We know what we need is there, and we'll wait for things to cool off. They don't know where we are, anyhow."

Both jumped off the cart. Ren grabbed her nine-millimeter out of her backpack with the holder and hid it under her shirt. She smiled. "Just in case.

CHAPTER 40

P C and Ren made the right-hand turn from the path and up the steps to the board-walk.

"Just look casual and act like a happy couple," PC said.

Both had their sunglasses on with their floppy hats. Ren sighed, relaxed, enjoying the scenery, still holding PC's hand.

PC looked straight ahead, his eyes darting side to side.

"What are you looking for?" Ren asked without breaking her smile.

"Anyone standing around like they're waiting for something."

"Waiting for us."

"Exactly," PC said.

The boardwalk was filling, , with people in bathing suits or shorts with just a bikini top, enjoying the beautiful day.

"Hmm." PC leaned over and kissed Ren on the lips.

Ren smiled back. "Oh, that was nice."

He leaned back over and kissed her again. "I've spotted a couple of people of interest."

Ren continued her relaxed demeanor. "Where?"

"One is leaning on the wall near the restaurant."

"What does he look like?"

"Fat one with a red Hawaiian shirt."

"Oh, look at that over there." She pointed to a plane flying the banner for the local radio station WBAB-FM 102.3. As she pointed, she glanced surreptitiously at the red shirt. She noticed something sticking out from his waist. As she put her arm down, she whispered, "He's got a gun."

PC, not breaking face, said, "You saw a gun on him?"

"Yeah. That shirt doesn't fit him, being as fat as he is. Also, he is leaning up against the wall, which has exposed his weapon."

"Good eyes, girl."

"What about the other one?"

"He is to the right near the gift store, standing, reading a newspaper with a white short-sleeved shirt."

The man with the white shirt turned slowly as he looked at his newspaper. "He has a gun, also."

"How can you tell?" Ren asked.

"Well, when he turned, I could see the bulge near the waist."

Ren casually turned her head toward PC, but her eyes looked at the suspect. "Yes, I see the bulge. Do you think they noticed us?"

"Let's keep moving and see if they follow us. Let's hang a right here on the boardwalk and do some walking."

They made the right turn and walked down the boardwalk. They slowly weaved in and out of the crowd, still holding hands like a couple.

"Let's sit on the park bench." PC motioned to his right. They sat down. "Keep looking casual."

They watched as people passed them. No sign of the two men they had spotted. They sat for an hour; still no sign.

"We've been here awhile," Ren said. "Do you think they didn't see us?

"Seems that way. No sign of them."

"What do we do now?"

"I'm thinking of that right now."

Ren looked down at the boardwalk ahead of them. They didn't seem too far from the next field. She rubbed her neck as she looked down at the other end of the boardwalk. "Hey, I just thought of something."

"What's that?" PC asked.

"Do you think they are waiting for us at the next field?"

PC turned to Ren.

"I mean, we haven't seen them. How do we know they don't have someone waiting for us at the next field? They saw us turn. Instead of following us, they called ahead to the next field and are waiting for us."

PC rubbed his chin and looked at Ren. "It's a good thought. They may have done just that." PC looked around and stood up. "Come on."

Ren stood up. "Where are we going?"

"Back to where we will cut through the beach." PC started walking, but Ren grabbed his hand to stop him. "Wait, wait. I have another theory."

PC looked at her, confused. "Another theory?"

"Yeah, what if they have people at both ends of the beach just in case we double back or go toward the other field down the other end?"

PC rubbed the back of his neck and looked in both directions. "It's possible."

"Someone could be on the beach waiting for us."

PC looked toward the beach, still rubbing his neck. "Shit."

They both sat back down and looked around at the passing people. PC's face lit up, and he looked at Ren. "Come on!" He pulled Ren up.

"Where are we going?"

"Well, they may have us going forward, backwards and our left flank, but they don't have our right flank."

Ren looked to her right. "You mean through the dunes?"

"Right. We'll cut through the dunes and head back to the terrain. It's not that far."

Ren looked at the dunes with her hands on her hips. "Okay, let's go."

They moved through the dunes, walking around the high ones. In no time, they were near the parking lot and headed back to the terrain. They hid for the rest of the day. Dark clouds formed, and the beachgoers left in droves to beat the severe weather.

"Looks like the weather is scaring everyone away," Ren said.

PC eyed the sky as they sat in the cart. "Yeah, looks like it."

A big clap of thunder made them jump. PC looked at Ren. "That was nasty." He scanned the parking lot. "We need to find some shelter. This looks like a bad storm on its way."

"Let's get back to the hideaway."

"I'm still a little nervous about going back."

"We eventually must go back. I mean, it's pretty much our home in this world. And what do we do if we're still here and it starts getting cold?"

PC shrugged. "Hopefully, we won't be here when the cold weather comes."

"And what if we are?"

PC put his hand on her arm. "I promise you we won't be here when it gets cold. We have maybe another month of warm weather." Another loud clap of thunder shook the vehicle. "And we need to get the hell out of this. Not fond of being in a thunderstorm." PC turned on the vehicle and started rolling. "Looks like everyone is gone."

"Where are we headed?"

"For the tunnel. We can hide in there till the storm is over."

"And then what? We haven't eaten since this morning."

"Well, when the storm calms down, we'll head over the hideout and..." PC looked at Ren. "Take a chance that it is safe."

PC pulled the cart into the tunnel and drove halfway in. He turned the cart so they could see out of both directions if anyone came in.

"Okay," PC said as he folded his arms. "Now we wait.

CHAPTER 41

The rain came down hard for a steady hour, with the wind howling and thunder booming. PC and Ren sat quietly inside the vehicle, waiting for the storm to end.

"God, I'm starving," Ren said, rubbing her stomach.

PC felt his stomach rumbling, too. "Yeah, I feel your pain."

PC walked to the entrance of the tunnel to check the weather. They watched the rain from the sidewalk light.

PC turned to Ren. "Do you want to make a run for it?"

"You mean to the hideaway?" She looked up at the sky. "We're going to get soaked."

PC looked at his watch. "Yeah, but I doubt our friends are still waiting for us. They probably beat feet when it started raining."

Ren's stomach started growling again. "Let's get going before my stomach swallows me in."

They both jumped into the terrain and drove into the rain, ditching it in the same spot they'd hidden it before. They made a run back to the tunnel, backpack in hand, and walked to the end of the tunnel.

"Oh my God," Ren said. I'm soaked to the bone. Thank God it's not cold out." She pulled her hair back as PC wiped the water from his face.

PC stopped and put his arm out to stop Ren. He looked around to see if someone was lingering. "Looks like it's clear." They put on their backpacks. "Ready?"

"Ready."

They both jogged out in the pouring rain.

"Oh man, this sucks," Ren said in disgust.

It was dark now, with just a few dim lights shining from the boardwalk. They made their way off the path and stopped to look around. As they were beginning their turn onto the boardwalk, they were forcefully knocked off their feet by two other bodies.

PC lay on his back and felt the butt of a gun on his temple.

"Do not even move, dude, or you'll have a bullet in your head!"

PC did not move. He glanced up to see the guy with the red Hawaiian shirt. PC shifted his eyes left to see that the guy with the white shirt had a hold of Ren, twisting her arm behind her.

"Get up, asshole! I have had enough of being in the rain! Get up!" The red-shirted man pulled the gun away from PC's head. "You do anything, and the girl buys it!"

PC slowly sat up, put his hands on the ground to pull himself up, but swept his legs underneath the fat man, kicking him down like a ton of bricks and pulling out his nine-millimeter, mid-sweep, shooting the white-shirted man in the head. He fell back as Ren fell to the ground with him.

The fat man knocked the gun out of PC's hand and aimed his gun at him. PC heard a shot and jumped, thinking he'd been hit. He looked and saw the fat man fall forward and hit the ground, splashing a puddle of water on PC. Ren stood there with both hands still holding the nine-millimeter as the puddle turned red.

PC noticed Ren stood frozen with fear, looking down hard at the guy. "Ren. Ren!"

She pointed the gun at PC, still in a fog, and finally realized what she was doing. She lowered the gun slowly.

PC stood up, picked up his weapon, and holstered it. Ren dropped her arms and the gun to her side, staring down at the fat man.

PC, soaked from the rain, took the gun from Ren and holstered it for her.

She took a couple of steps away from PC and nodded to the white-shirted man. "Weren't you afraid you were going to shoot me? I mean, you could have killed me."

He shook his head. "No way. I knew you were not going to get shot. You didn't flinch one bit when I aimed the gun and shot the white shirt guy."

She stepped inches away from him. "I love a man with confidence, and I knew you would not miss." She touched his cheek. "I just had to ask."

They both hugged as the rain poured down on them.

Ren pulled away. "We can't leave these bodies here."

"No, they're not going to disappear like the others."

"What do we do with then? That fat one is going to be a bitch to move."

PC looked around as the rain continued.

"Not to worry, young ones," a voice said.

They looked behind them, and there stood the gatekeeper with rain streaming down his umbrella. "You go to your hideout and rest, get yourselves cleaned up."

"What are you going to do?" PC asked.

"Never you mind that. I will make sure no one discovers these now deceased men. You had to do what you had to do. Go now." He waved his hand at them. "Go and take care of yourselves. We'll talk again soon."

PC and Ren looked at each other.

"Come on, let's get to the hideout and get dry." PC took Ren's hand as they walked away.

Ren looked back at the Gatekeeper. "Thank you!"

They made it to the hideaway on the beach, lit a lantern, stripped off their wet clothes, found some towels in their storage area, and dried themselves off. Ren wrapped the towel around her body, and PC wrapped his around his waist. Both sat down and leaned on each other.

"Holy shit, that was horrible," Ren said.

"Ditto. Still hungry?"

Ren shook her head. "I do not know anymore. Just trying to process what happened to us out there. Do you think the gatekeeper will take care of those bodies?"

"Well, he said he is. Hell, I trust him more than I trust Lambert."

A voice from the back of the hideaway startled them. "After all we've been through?"

PC and Ren looked at each other and rolled their eyes.

"Come out of there, Lambert and show yourself," PC said.

Lambert came walking out of the dark, still with his mirrored sunglasses on and his grinning white teeth.

Ren wrinkled her nose. "Where the hell have you been?"

His smile disappeared. "I am sorry, my friends. We were shut out of this dimension, but have finally made it back in. Not sure how long it will last, but we should be okay for now." He looked over Ren and PC. "You both look like hell." He noticed the bandage on Ren's shoulder. "What happened to you?"

She rubbed her wet bandage, looking at Lambert. "Just a scratch."

"And what are you doing all the way back to your starting point? You should be up by the Montauk Lighthouse."

"We were," PC said. "But the soldiers drove us back. We came back here because the gatekeeper told us—"

"Gatekeeper?" Lambert looked at them both. "Who is this caretaker?"

"He is the gatekeeper for this dimension," Ren said. "He's been helping us to get back to our world."

"Well, he does not seem to be doing a good job, since he got you all the way to the beginning. Why did he send you back this way?"

"The only thing I can tell you is that he said there is a clue we need to find in the area we started from. That clue is going to help us get home."

"And you believe him."

PC raised his voice. "He has been nothing but honest with us. More than you've been. He even cleaned up a couple of guys we had to kill."

"Killed? Bodies? You mean they did not disappear?"

"No. These were not soldiers from another dimension. These were people living here, in this world. They are not going to magically disappear like the soldiers. Someone has managed to pay these mercenaries to kill us in this world."

"How do you know they are mercenaries?"

PC and Ren glanced at each other, then back at Lambert. "We had to kill a couple of them that were chasing us in our terrain gulf car."

"Car? What car? Where did you get a car?"

"The gatekeeper gave it to us."

Lambert looked at them blankly. He gave you a terrain car."

Ren shrugged her shoulders.

"Beats walking."

"And how did you know they were mercenaries?"

"It was in the paper. They identified the men as mercenaries."

"You just left dead bodies lying around."

PC raised his voice again. "We did not even know who they were when it happened. We figured they would disappear like everyone else. We did not know about it till we saw the paper the next day. It was a foggy night, and we were not going to check on casualties."

Ren got up in disgust. "You two battle this out." She looked at PC. "I think I'm hungry again; I'll go find us some food." She walked away from them and pulled her towel off her body to dry her hair. They watched her walk away, bare ass and all.

Lambert stared after her and finally turned to PC, who was trying to hide his smile, and shook his head. "Does she always walk around like that?"

PC nodded his head. "Oh yeah, she does. A lot."

"Amazing." Lambert made a circling gesture with his hands. "Do the two of you... you know."

PC stood up and abruptly said, "No!" He lowered his voice. "We don't."

"Why not? I mean..."

"We're too busy trying to not get killed and get home at the same time. Now that we have that settled, what news can you give me about us getting home?"

"Well, not much. They managed to close us down for a while from entering this dimension, but we fixed that, so it should not happen again—for now. Also, it's all over the news at home that the general is dead."

PC took interest. "Really? Did they say how he died?"

"They're trying to say some radical killed him from the other side. It isn't really flying with the public, since they know the general is a dirtbag, but there are some believers who are blowing it up online."

PC rubbed his chin. "Interesting." He glanced behind Lambert, searching for Ren. He was starting to feel hungry again.

"When do you think you will be starting back again toward the lighthouse?" Lambert asked.

"I do not know yet. We must regroup and make sure no more mercenaries are chasing us." He looked at Lambert. "Do you have any idea how people from this world knew who we were and came after us? The soldiers were easier to deal with than this group."

Lambert shook his head. "I do not know. This is news to me. Someone must have managed to get through and contacted these mercenaries. Could have been the general, I do not know."

"Can you shut it down so no one can slip through again to infiltrate this world?"

"Not sure. When I go back, I will have to report what happened and see what we can do. It's been a fight trying to keep the other side from destabilizing the two worlds. As you know, this was not supposed to happen. They miscalculated on their side, and we have been trying to correct it, but they've been fighting us." Lambert looked up, then back at PC. "I must go now. I will be back." He disappeared.

"I'll be here." PC stood alone.

Ren came walking back in with the towel wrapped around her again, with hamburgers and hot dogs and two bottles of water under her arm.

PC salivated. "Where did you get those?"

"In the back."

"And you cooked them already?"

She smiled and nodded her head.

"Yeah. On the little gas grill. Didn't take long. Come on, sit down, and let's eat. Lambert left us, I see."

They sat down on their sleeping bags. PC nodded. "Yeah, he's gone."

"Did you resolve anything?"

"Well, they were locked out for a while, but they kind of have things back to semi-normal." He picked up a hot dog, which already had mustard on it, and bit into it. He talked with his mouth full. "He wants to know when we will be moving again."

Ren had a mouthful of hot dog, too. "What did you tell him?"

PC cleared his mouth. "I told him we have to regroup, and he'll have to investigate the mercenary's situation."

Ren swallowed. "Does he think the general had something to do with it?"

"A possibility. He is going to investigate it." PC turned to look at the entrance as the rain continued. "Still raining pretty good out there in this weather."

"You think we'll be safe here?"

"I think so. Nobody else is out in this weather."

"Except the two idiots who tried to kill us."

"You know, they must have been offered a lot of money to sit out in the rain and wait for us."

"You think so?"

PC looked at Ren. "If someone offered a bundle of money to two cold killers, they would take the money. Anyhow, let's rest for now and figure out our next move."

Ren leaned her head on PC. "You're the boss."

CHAPTER 42

Morning had come. PC and Ren were sleeping quietly. The rain had stopped during the night. Ren rolled over and felt the urge to use the bathroom. She looked up and noticed the sun was up. She got out of her sleeping bag, crawled over to PC, and glanced at his watch as he continued to sleep.

"Eight a.m.," she said to herself. She put on a shirt and grabbed some flip-flops, and brushed her hair out so it didn't look like she'd just rolled out of bed.

She took the planks down, crawled out of the hideaway, and put the planks back in place. Walking up the steps, she stopped and sniffed the air. "Something's burning," she whispered. She noticed smoke coming from the gift shop. Her face went pale. "Oh, shit."

She turned around and headed back for the hideaway. She pulled the planks off and went inside. PC was still sleeping. She knelt next to him and shook him. "Hey, hey, hey, wake up."

"What, what, what." He lifted his head and looked at her, still half asleep. He sniffed the air. "Are you cooking? Smells bad, whatever it is." He put his head back down.

"No, you idiot, the gift shop is on fire."

"That's nice." Suddenly, her words registered, and he popped his head back up quickly. "It's on fire?"

"Yes, yes," she said, pulling on his arm. "Come on, hurry."

PC jumped out of his sleeping bag. "Let me get some clothes on." He grabbed what was there: shorts, a shirt, and some sneakers, and both crawled out of the hideaway, putting the planks back up quickly.

They ran up to the boardwalk. Smoke was billowing out of the gift shop. Sirens could be heard coming their way. They watched helplessly, with a few early beachgoers doing the same.

"Oh, no," PC said. He looked at Ren. "Were fucked."

They watched as the smoke continued to billow. The fire department came down the boardwalk in the fire truck, making their way to the steps, as far as they could go. They quickly ran with hoses and began to put the fire out.

Ren sat on the boardwalk with her knees up to her chin and her arms wrapped around her legs. PC joined her as they watched the fire department battle the blaze.

They sat in silence until the blaze was put out. Finally, PC spoke. "Come on, let's go."

"Where are we going?"

"Back to the hideout. Nothing we can do here." He stood up and held his hand out. She grabbed his hand, and he pulled her up. They walked back to the hideout quietly.

PC pulled the planks off, and both went inside. There, they found Lambert waiting for them.

PC growled, "What the hell are you doing here?"

Lambert smiled. "Just checking out my handiwork."

PC and Ren stared, shocked. "You. You set that fire? Why? What the fuck did you think burning that down would do?"

"We don't feel this gatekeeper has your best interest. We felt our plan is the best and needed to deter you from this gatekeeper to follow us. We don't know who this gatekeeper is."

"That's right; you don't, and we do. We trusted the old man from day one. He has been helping us get back to where you belong. He even bailed us out of trouble when we had to kill those two mercenaries. If he wanted us dead, we wouldn't be having this conversation. He directed us to the gift shop to get what we needed to help us get back, and you burnt the fuckin place down."

"And what was in the gift ship you needed?"

PC raised his voice. "We don't know! We were about to go in until you torched the place! Now we'll never know, thanks to your handiwork."

Ren grabbed PC's arms. "Take it easy; lower your voice. We don't want anyone to know we're here."

PC looked at Ren, then at Lambert. "If you weren't a hologram, you'd be down on the ground right now."

"Look, we're just trying to do what's right, and get you back home, and the universe back to normal."

"Yeah, well, it looks like you fucked things up. You know, we're tired of getting shot at and we just want to go home."

"And we're trying to get you home. The world is out of whack since you two ended up in a different universe."

"It certainly wasn't our idea." PC rolled his eyes at Ren. "Looks like we're back at square one."

She sighed and turned to Lambert. "We need some time to regroup. Come back in a few days."

"But..."

Ren snapped fiercely, "Come back in a few days." Her eyes were burning a hole through Lambert.

"Okay, I'll leave you two for now." Lambert disappeared.

PC shook his head and walked into the back of the hideout. He disappeared in the dark and started clattering around.

Ren struggled to see. "What are you doing?"

"Get your bathing suit on. We're going to relax on the beach and unwind from this debacle."

Ren put her two-piece suit on and threw on a T-shirt, then looked around for the sunscreen in her backpack. She picked up the beach blanket. PC came walking out with a small cooler and had his bathing suit on with two towels and an umbrella with a stand in hand. Ren put her sunglasses on and then slipped PC's on him.

"Thanks," he said. "Come on, let's go."

PC kicked the planks off with his foot and walked through with Ren behind him. Ren dropped the blanket and put the planks back up since PC's hands were full. She picked up the blanket up and looked at PC. "Ready."

"Okay. Let's go."

They proceeded to walk toward the water. They spied some early morning beachgoers. Some were looking at the smoldering gift shop from a distance. PC and Ren were no longer interested and kept walking.

"Here, stop here," PC said. "We'll park ourselves here."

Ren spread out the blanket as PC put the umbrella up. He pulled his shirt off, leaving just his bathing suit on, and Ren did the same. Both sat down on the blanket as they stared out into the ocean.

They stayed silent for a while to digest what had just happened and to get over the shock of the situation.

Ren slid herself closer to PC until she was touching him. Without looking, PC took her hand. Both were comfortable until they heard a voice.

"Hey there kids; how ya doing?"

PC and Ren cringed, and PC said, "Tell me it ain't so."

Ren peered over her shoulder slightly over PC's arm. "Yeah, it's Kevin."

PC sighed. "As if this day couldn't get any worse. Shouldn't he be in Indiana? Love to know what he is doing on Long Island."

Ren turned to Kevin, annoyed. "Kevin, what are you doing here? Why aren't you in Indiana?"

Kevin smiled at Ren. "On vacation."

Ren said under her breath as she looked at PC, "Yeah, seems he's been on vacation all summer."

"With us," PC said.

Ren pulled her shirt back down on her body, so Kevin wouldn't see the T-back bikini she was wearing.

PC noticed. "You pulled that on kind of quick."

"I don't want him to see me half-naked. I have to work with him."

"Yeah, but not in this dimension."

"True, but I still don't want him to see."

"Hey, you remember the Mrs.?" Kevin said.

The short, stubby lady with the one-piece bathing suit smiled and said hello as she spread the blanket down next to PC and Ren.

PC said in Ren's ear, "Well, at least they have their clothes on."

"Please, I haven't eaten yet today."

Kevin's wife said, "We're going to sit next to you and enjoy this nice weather. If you haven't eaten yet, we have some extra food."

Ren wanted to protest, but PC put his hand on her shoulder.

"Let's see what he has. I'm sure you're hungry."

Ren gave him an angry look. "I'm fucking starving."

PC held back a laugh at Ren. "Take it easy. I know it's been a bad day so far, but don't jump all over me."

Ren caught herself and sighed. "I'm sorry. Yes, been a long day, and it's just starting." She put on a practiced smile. "We're much obliged, Kevin."

Kevin put the cooler down next to PC and Ren. "Help yourselves. The Mrs. and I are going for a swim." He smiled as he walked toward the water with his wife, waving his hand. "Enjoy."

They stared after the couple. "Are there any sharks in these waters?" Ren asked wryly.

"Yeah, there are." PC shot her a surprised glance. "Oh, come on, Ren. I know he's a pain in the ass, but—"

"You're right, you're right. Besides," she smirked at PC, "I wouldn't want the sharks to get sick."

Their eyes gleamed at each other and they burst into laughter.

PC lifted the cooler lid up. "Let's see what they have." Inside, they found sticky buns wrapped in plastic like they were bought out of a 7-Eleven, granola bars, and a microwave meal with roast beef, mashed potatoes, and gravy.

They eyed each other and closed the cooler. "Holy shit," PC said. No wonder he's overweight."

"Holy junk food cooler." She started laughing. "Gross! He doesn't even have good junk food. It's all gross. And where the hell is he going to microwave that meal? It's the only good thing he has, and that's gross!"

"Wait a minute, what's this?" PC dug through the cooler with his hand and pulled out a can. "Ahh, a beer for me…" he put his hand back in and pulled out a plastic-covered glass. "And a glass of wine for you, my dear. It's too early in the morning for this, but, what the hell, I think we deserve it."

"Oh, let me have that. Haven't had any wine in—seems like forever." Ren looked to see what kind of wine. "Cabernet Sauvignon, my favorite." Ren quickly peeled the plastic off the top as PC opened his beer. They clinked their drinks.

"Salute, my dear."

"Right back at ya."

CHAPTER 43

PC and Ren passed out from their early morning drinks. With no breakfast, plus the first alcohol they'd had in quite some time, the alcohol went straight to their heads.

About two hours later, they woke up with Ren's arm across PC's chest. PC looked around him. He noticed Kevin and his wife were gone. "Oh, thank God," he whispered. He looked at Ren, who was still asleep. He scanned around some more and noticed the beach was wall-to-wall beachgoers. He gently rubbed Ren's arm to wake her up. "Hey, sleepyhead."

Ren opened her eyes slowly and looked at PC. "Are they gone?" she asked softly.

He smiled and nodded his head. "Yeah, they're gone. How are you feeling?"

She raised her head and searched the beach. "I'm okay. Just been a while since I had wine. Went right to my head." She looked at PC. "You?"

"Yeah, okay. Same as you. Seems like things have calmed down on the boardwalk."

Ren turned and nodded. "Oh, well, that's good. Hope no one was hurt. Just us, maybe."

PC looked at Ren and sighed. "We'll find another way. We've made it this far."

"Do you think we'll get stuck in this dimension? I mean, it isn't bad. It's our world, just a different dimension."

"Well, there is one thing I need to know. If we're in another dimension, there must be duplicates of us living pretty much the same life we live. My question is, are they here?"

"No, they're not," came a voice from behind PC and Ren. They both turned to see the gatekeeper. "They left this dimension like you left yours."

"Where are they?" Ren asked.

"They could be in your dimension, or they could be in another. I'm not sure."

"Going through the same thing we're going through, trying to get home," PC said.

The gatekeeper nodded his head. "I'm sure they're doing the same thing. But it's up to you two."

Ren gave him an inquisitive look. "How so?"

"You're the main body of this. When you were pulled out of your dimension, so were the other duplicates of yourselves. But you're the ones who needed to find the way home. When you do, the rest will fall back to their rightful dimensions. If you get stuck here, so will the others, where they are."

"Will it be difficult for them if they get stuck somewhere else?" PC asked.

"No more difficult than you. They will settle into society. Everything from their lives will be there. Their loved ones, jobs, money, and their homes."

"So, my home here on Long Island is here for me?"

"Yes, yes, it is. You can go to it if you wish."

PC looked at Ren. "Well, at least we know we can go there if we need to, especially if it starts getting cold."

PC pointed toward the boardwalk. "Well, I'm sure you know the gift shop was set ablaze by the same people who are trying to get us home."

The Gate keeper nodded his head. "Yes, I am aware of their miscalculated deeds, but the only thing they accomplished was slowing you down. For now, we have temporarily blocked your people from coming into our world. But if you need them for any reason, we will let them back in. We will not tolerate what they did. We'll let your people keep you supplied as usual, to keep you going. And they will be there if you decide to go to your home that you have here."

"Okay," PC said. "This is all good, but I must ask what happened to those men we had to kill last night."

"Please, don't worry about those men. We took care of their bodies and souls. They were evil men, and they won't be missed in this world."

"I'm fine with that," Ren said.

PC looked at Ren. "Okay, we'll leave that one alone."

He looked at the Gatekeeper. "Thank you for taking care of the mess we made. It's something we weren't looking to do."

"I'm aware that was not your intention. They wanted to kill you. You did what you did to survive."

"Can I ask you something?" Ren asked.

The Gatekeeper smiled. "Go ahead, my dear."

"Do you have your hot dog cart on the boardwalk? We haven't eaten since yesterday."

He laughed. "Unfortunately, I do not, but the restaurant is open, and they are expecting you." He winked at Ren.

"Oh." She smiled at PC. "What are we waiting for?"

"Thank you, Gatekeeper," PC said. "You've been a tremendous help."

"It's been my pleasure." The Gatekeeper bowed and disappeared.

PC looked at Ren. "Shocking that he disappeared like that." He stood up and pulled Ren to her feet. "Let's get our things, and you need to put some clothes on, so we'll go back to the hideaway."

"What's wrong with what I have on?"

"Well, you're half-naked, for one thing, with your ass hanging out."

"Oh, yeah." She smiled sheepishly. "Guess I can put a pair of shorts on."

They picked up their things, went to the hideaway, and came out dressed in summer wear, sunglasses on, with their floppy hats, and Ren just wearing her bikini top with shorts on.

PC put the boards back up on the hideaway and turned to Ren. "Let's go."

They walked up the steps to the boardwalk, and PC, feeling more comfortable with Ren, took her hand as they walked. Ren's eyes sparkled underneath her sunglasses. She looked at him and smiled as they walked toward the restaurant.

CHAPTER 44

As PC and Ren passed the gift shop, they saw the crime scene taped off, and the police and fire marshal standing, talking to each other.

"Do you think everything is ruined in there?" Ren asked.

"I would like to see if we could salvage any clues for us. But I'm sure it's a loss in there." He looked at Ren as they continued on. "Maybe we'll try to get in there tonight when everyone is gone."

Ren nodded her head. "Sounds like a plan."

They made their way to the restaurant door, and a young lady with menus in her hand, nicely dressed, greeted them with a smile. "Good morning, PC and Ren. We've been waiting for you both. It's good to see you."

PC and Ren looked at each other, a little surprised that the young lady knew who they were.

"We have your table ready. If you will just follow me."

They grinned and followed behind her to their table near the window. She sat them down and handed the menus to both. "A server will be over to take your order."

As she walked away, they looked at each other with amazement. "Wow!" Ren said. "They knew who we were, and we had reservations in our names. Do you think the Caretaker did all that?"

"He must have. We didn't make the reservations, and he did say they'd be waiting for us." PC relaxed. "Amazing. Nicest thing that has happened to us since we've been here."

"Yes, yes, it is! So, let's enjoy it," she beamed.

The server returned. "Hello, welcome to the Jones Beach Restaurant. What can I start you off with?"

PC nodded his head at Ren. "Coffee?" she nodded back. "Coffee for the both of us. Black for her, cream for me."

"Okay, I'll be right back." The server walked toward the kitchen.

Ren's smile disappeared as she looked around.

"What's the matter?"

Ren frowned. "Do you think we'll be safe in here? I mean, they tried to get us last time."

"True, but I don't think the gatekeeper would send us in here if something were going to happen. I think he wants us to get back as much as we do." He reached over and put his hand on Ren's. "We're safe here."

She smiled and took his hand. "Okay."

The waitress came back with their coffees, and they both ordered eggs with hash browns with toast.

As they waited for their breakfast, PC stared out the window, watching the fire marshal come in and out of the gift shop as the cops stood outside.

"What are you thinking?" Ren said.

PC rubbed the bottom of his goatee, eyeing the scene. "Wondering if the cops will be there when it gets dark." He turned to Ren. "We need to get in there and see if we can get some kind of idea what we're looking for."

"And if everything is ruined?"

"Then we'll have to go to plan B."

"And plan B is?"

PC looked away, then back at Ren. "I don't know. We'll have to make that up as we go along."

"Do you think we'll be S.O.L. if we don't find any clues?"

He looked at Ren. "There's always a way. We'll just have to keep trying until we find it."

Their breakfast came quickly. Being so hungry, they ate fast and ordered more coffee.

They chatted as they ate, mostly small talk. When PC asked for the check, the server said it had already been paid for.

"Who paid for this?" PC asked.

The server smiled. "The owner of the restaurant."

PC shot a look at Ren.

"Guess he owns everything," Ren said.

"Can we tip you, at least?"

"That won't be necessary." She smiled.

PC wiped his mouth with his napkin, and they headed to the gift shop.

They stood outside just on the boardwalk in the bright sun. Both put their sunglasses on. PC took her hand. "Come on, let's see how close we can get. Let's look like the happy couple, as always."

They strolled toward the shop with the two police officers standing near the entrance. The area was taped up between safety cones, about ten feet out.

They stopped by the tape, and PC caught the eye of one of the officers. "Hey, what happened here?" PC yelled out to him.

The officer came walking over. "Gift shop caught on fire this morning."

"Oh," Ren said. "What started it?"

"Fire Department is not sure yet, but the fire marshal is leaning toward arson."

"Wow, what a shame." Ren wrapped her arm around PC's. "I wanted to buy something special for my husband, but I guess not today."

PC stole a surprised glance at her, then looked back at the officer. "Well, we'll have to come back next year. I'm sure they will have it back up and running by then." He smiled. "Have a wonderful day, officer."

The officer smiled back, saying, "Enjoy the day, folks," and walked back to the front of the entrance.

As they walked away, PC said, "You want to get something special for your husband?"

"Well, you always say, 'look like the happy couple.'"

They laughed.

"Okay," PC said. "Let's enjoy the day, and we'll come back tonight and see if we can get in.

"Maybe we can do some fishing?"

PC nodded. "Good idea. Come on, let's head back to the hideaway and get the pole."

"Let's do it." They headed back to the hideaway.

CHAPTER 45

PC and Ren spent the day fishing on the beach, keeping away from the bathers so they wouldn't hook anyone. PC found a dead fish washed up on shore that he used for bait. They sat with their blanket spread out under the beach umbrella to keep the sun away, even though they had suntan lotion on.

After a long afternoon and no fish biting, they decided to stop for the day. The gathered their things and headed back to the Hideaway.

When darkness fell and everyone had left the beach, they came out and crawled along the edge of the boardwalk wall until they reached where they were closest to the gift shop.

PC popped his head up to see if the coast was clear. "Shit," he said with a faint voice.

"Is there someone there?" Ren asked.

He nodded his head. "One cop." He looked over again. "Sitting in his car."

Both sat down on the sand.

"Damn," PC whispered.

Ren looked over. "Do you think he will be here all night?"

"Probably."

"Maybe we can distract him, and one of us can get in."

PC rubbed his chin. "We can."

Suddenly, they heard a car door open and close. PC raised his index finger to his lip for them to be quiet. They both looked over the edge. The officer was stretching his legs and lighting up a cigarette.

Ren pulled PC down. "I have an idea. I'll be right back."

"Where are you going?"

Ren sped off, staying low as she headed back to the hideaway. PC looked over the edge of the boardwalk to see where the officer was. He felt a tap on the shoulder. He turned to see Ren with one of his pull-over shirts on. He looked her up and down. "What are you planning, Ren?"

Ren smiled and lifted her shirt with nothing on underneath, then dropped her shirt. "I'm going to give him a show like I used to, back in the day. Then I'll make him chase me; then you can get in."

"Not a bad idea. Okay, listen, stay close to the railing. If he gets too close to you, jump over the railing. The hideaway will follow you so you can disappear quick without him knowing where you went."

She nodded her head. "Okay. I left two of the bottom boards open so I can slide right in. But look quickly inside the shop. I'll keep his attention as long as I can."

"Okay."

PC looked up to see that the officer had walked behind his car and was leaning on the back trunk. PC turned and nodded his head. "Go, go and be careful."

Ren slithered up the steps and approached the officer quietly. PC watched, shaking his head. "Should be used to this. Crazy girl," he laughed to himself.

Ren approached the officer. She stopped a little more than halfway. She stood near a light pole and called out. "Excuse me? Can you help me please, officer?"

The officer turned around and took two steps away from the car to see Ren under the light. "Hey, what are you doing here?

"I seem to have lost my clothes and just have this to wear. Can you help me find my clothes, officer?"

She turned around and lifted her shirt up just a little bit so the officer could see her the cheeks of her butt.

"This beach is closed at dusk. You need to leave."

"Okay. But I need to find my clothes before I go." She pulled off her shirt and stood near the pole, bare as could be. "This shirt is too big for me." She dropped the shirt and wrapped one leg around the pole, bending her body backward and spinning erotically in a circle. She stopped and came straight up, hugging the pole between her breasts, facing the officer.

PC watched from the edge of the boardwalk, peeking his head over. "Holy shit," he chuckled. "What a crazy girl."

The officer sat stunned as Ren continued her dance with the pole. "Hey!" yelled out the officer, "You need to put your clothes on."

Ren turned with shirt in hand and said, "Well, why don't you put it on for me?" and she skipped away down the boardwalk.

Ren looked back and saw the officer coming towards her. "Oh shit!" Ren's skipping turned into full-fledged running.

PC nodded his head in surprise. "Pretty fast, limber girl." He watched them disappear into the dark and made his move. He jumped over the railing and headed for the gift shop. He stopped in front of it, noting that two pieces of plywood covered the doorway. He pulled off one of the pieces, pulled his flashlight out of his pocket, stepped in, and returned the makeshift plywood door.

Ren was still some distance from the officer. She saw a bench near the railing and figured it was time to jump over and ditch herself in the hideaway. She picked up speed and jumped in the air, landing her left leg on the bench. Lifting her right leg up for momentum, she went over the rail and disappeared.

The officer stopped at the rail, breathing heavily. He pulled out his flashlight and scanned the beach looking for her. "Where the hell did she go?" He placed his hands on his knees to rest, then stepped onto the beach, moving his flashlight from left to right. Nothing. "Damn it! Where the hell did she go?"

As the office looked for Ren, PC made his way out of the gift shop with a large plastic bag full of items that had survived the fire. He looked around to make sure the officer wasn't back yet. "Guess Ren had him running for his life," he chuckled. "Time to go."

He made sure the plywood door was shut just the way he'd found it. He looked both ways, ran toward the railing, and leaped over. He looked down at the beach and could see the officer looking for Ren. "Poor bastard."

He crept along the edge of the wall to the boardwalk until he came to the hideaway. He tapped on the wood. "Ren?"

"Yeah, I'm here," she said. She pulled the planks down, and PC crawled in, and they put the planks quickly back up.

"We'll have to sit in the dark for a while," PC said.

"Maybe we should wait till morning and let things settle out there."

"Yes, good idea." He looked at Ren as she put the shirt back on. He smiled at her. "Didn't know you were so limber."

She smiled back. "Yes, well, when you're a dancer, you have to be limber. And I exercise, too."

They looked through the cracks of the planks to see that the officer was still out there. They could see his light flashing and moving around the beach.

"He's not giving up," Ren giggled."

"Good job, girl. Let's get some rest and let the officer exhaust himself."

"Sounds good to me."

CHAPTER 46

PC and Ren watched as several police combed the beach looking for Ren. Two hours later they quit their search and left the beach, assigning extra officers to the gift shop.

PC and Ren woke up the next morning while it was still dark and moved down the shore to discreetly bathe themselves in the ocean; the showers were too close to the gift shop. They dried and dressed themselves on the beach and headed back to the hideaway.

When the sun appeared in the morning sky, they came out of the hideaway with the usual shorts, floppy hats, and sunglasses, and they made their way to the boardwalk.

"Make sure you keep your hat and sunglasses on, so the cop won't recognize you. And tuck in your hair under your hat."

Ren pulled her hair into a quick ponytail and tucked it under her floppy hat. She took PC's hand, and they continued walking. "When are we going to look at the goods you collected?" Ren asked.

"We will. Just want to make sure things have calmed down so we don't have to worry about the police."

"Do you think they will recognize us?"

"Me, no. You, maybe. It was dark, and the same cop might not be there anymore."

"So, what are we doing out here, then?"

"Breakfast, my dear. Always an important meal."

PC looked further down the boardwalk and noticed a big truck. "Hmm."

"What do you see?"

"Not sure. Looks like a food truck. Let's look."

They casually walked by the gift shop.

"Well, that's good, my friend is not there anymore. At least we don't have to worry about anyone recognizing me."

They proceeded toward the gift shop, stopped in front of the crime scene tape, and turned to the cops.

"Any luck on who did this, officer?" PC asked casually.

One officer shook his head. "No, but we did have some excitement here last night."

"Oh? What kind of excitement?" Ren asked.

The officer walked towards them. "Well, one of our officers was on duty here last night, and a young lady did a bare-naked pole dance for him, and then she ran for her life when the officer chased her."

Ren covered her mouth to hide her smile.

"Did he catch her?" PC said.

"No, she disappeared into the night. Vanished like the wind. The beach was searched, but no luck finding her."

PC nodded his head. "Too bad."

Ren pulled PC's hand. "Come on, honey, let's check out the food truck."

As Ren pulled him away, PC smiled. "Take care, officer."

The officer waved as they walked off. "Have a good day, folks."

Ren burst into laughter. "Guess I gave that guy the thrill of his life."

PC laughed. "Yeah, looks like you did. Something he will never forget. And that was quite a dance you gave him. I rather enjoyed it, myself."

She smiled back. "Did you! Well, next time I'll have to charge."

"Hope I get a family discount."

"We'll see." They laughed.

They reached the food truck. "Oh, looks like they are doing breakfast," Ren said.

"This is a good thing. Looks like we're the first customers."

"May I help you, young ones?" The gatekeeper stuck his head out of the window.

"Oh my," Ren said. "You're the jack of all trades."

"I like to keep myself busy, especially when I have to look out for my two friends." He held his hands toward PC and Ren. "You were highly creative last night. I commend you both."

"Thank you," PC said. "I just took one of everything that wasn't damaged from fire or water. Hopefully we'll piece something together."

The Gatekeeper turned his back to them and returned with a paper tray holding breakfast burritos and coffee. "Here you go, young ones; breakfast for two, and this is on the house."

Both smiled as Ren took the tray. "Oh, thank you. You've been so kind to us." She looked at the coffees—one black, one with cream. "Black coffee is for me!" She grabbed it.

"How can we ever thank you?" PC asked.

The Gatekeeper just smiled. "You already have. Just take care of yourselves and get home safe. You're getting closer, too, my young ones. Enjoy this wonderful day and get to work on the clues you have."

"We shall," Ren said.

PC noticed beachgoers headed for the food truck. "Looks like your day about to get busy."

"So, it seems." The Gatekeeper smiled at the oncoming crowd.

"Well, we'll leave you to it," PC said.

The Gatekeeper waved at PC and Ren as people crowded around him.

PC and Ren walked to the beach, sat down in the sand near the hideaway, and finished their breakfast.

"Okay, PC said. "Let's get the bag out of the hideaway and see what we have."

"You think that is a good idea, doing it out in the open?"

PC looked around. "Well, we're in the corner away from everyone, so I think we will be okay."

PC stood up and pulled the planks off, reached in, and grabbed the bag. He handed it to Ren as PC put the planks back up.

Ren reached in the bag. PC sat down next to her.

"Let's see," she said, "What we have here." She pulled out the first item. "A partially burnt book, on..." she read what she could of the burnt cover. "Witchcraft?" She looked at PC. "Seriously?"

He shrugged his shoulders. "Hey, it was dark, and I didn't have time to read anything or see what I was taking. Besides, we may have to put a spell on something or someone." PC smiled as Ren gave him a smirk.

"Yeah, well, maybe." She looked in the bag. "What else do we have?" She pulled out a long tube. "Hmm, what is this?"

"Must have posters inside."

Ren popped open the top and pulled out a poster. "You're right, we do have a poster here."

They spread it open on the blanket. "Hey," PC said, "this is the Montauk Lighthouse with a picture of the grounds and all."

"Yeah," Ren said, amazed. "And it wasn't even damaged in the fire." She looked in the bag and felt around. "Everything has some sort of damage from the fire." She looked up at PC. "Except this poster."

"But the book was damaged."

"True," Ren said. "But maybe we don't need the book."

"Maybe, maybe. But we'll keep it in mind."

Ren felt the poster with her fingers. "Awfully thick." Then she realized. "Hey, there are two posters here." She pulled out the second one. "It's the same one, but a little different."

PC looked at both posters. "Yes, you're right. Look, both seem to be hand-drawn, right? Now, look at this one, it's simulating that it's dark out with the moon in the background. The other is with the sun out, with people walking about."

They both examined the posters, deep in thought.

"One with the sun out, the other with the moon," Ren said to herself. She looked at PC. "Your thoughts?"

PC sat down next to Ren and stared down at the posters. He touched the poster with the sun, then the one with the moon. He turned and put his hand in the bag, searching for anything else and examining the contents. "I don't think there is anything of value except these three things."

"Do you really think this witchcraft book has anything to do with it?"

"I don't know, but we're going to have to go through the book to see what we have."

Ren sighed and said, "Yeah, guess we'll have to."

"Okay, let's get started."

Ren grabbed PC's arm. "I'm dying to solve this mystery, but first, I'd like to go for a swim."

PC nodded his head as he thumbed through the pages of the book. "Okay, you can go for a swim. I'll go through the book."

Ren grabbed his arm and turned his head to look at her. With a smile she said, "No, no, no darling, you see—I want to go for a *swim*." She pulled her sunglasses off, and her eyes twinkled at him.

"Oh, I get it, but you can't do that here. We'd have to walk down some to get to the clothing-optional part of the beach."

Ren smiled seductively. "Well, let's pack some things and start walking. It's a beautiful day and most of the heat is off us for the time being, so..." she raised her eyebrows up and down, "Let's have some fun and do a little skinny dipping."

CHAPTER 47

PC and Ren packed their backpacks, put on their bathing suits, sunglasses, and floppy hats, and headed for the clothing-optional part of the beach.

PC spread the blanket out and put the umbrella up as Ren headed for the water, bare body and all. He looked around to see if Kevin was around, but found no sign of him. "Thank God," he said to himself. He was beginning to feel the same way as Ren about Kevin.

He dropped his bathing suit and joined Ren in the ocean. They swam for a while, talking with some of the other bathers, then headed back to the blanket and dried themselves off, adding suntan lotion to protect their bare bodies.

As PC perused the book, Ren felt her legs with her hand. "You know," she said, "time for me to shave my legs." She looked at PC. "Beginning to look like a hairy beast again. Must do it tonight when it gets dark." She put her hand on his beard. "How about you?" Looks like you need a shave."

He rubbed his face, staring down at the book. "Yeah, I'll have to join you tonight."

Ren rubbed up against PC and looked at what he was reading. "Anything interesting?"

"Not yet, but I did find something for Kevin."

Ren started laughing. "And what would that be?"

"Well, we can turn him into a newt."

"A newt? It doesn't say that." She slapped PC on the arm. "And what movie is that from?"

PC smiled and looked at Ren. "You're getting to know me too well."

"Come on, fess up, what movie is that from?"

"Monty Python."

Ren threw her left hand in the air. "Monty Python. I should have known better."

PC closed the book and tapped it on his chin.

"What are you thinking? You're deep in thought."

PC nodded his head. "I am. This book and the posters are our clues. Just must connect them together."

Ren reached over to her backpack, pulled out the folded posters, and spread them out on the blanket. She studied them, looking at the differences. "One has the sun shining with people walking about, one is in the evening with no people, and the moon is out." She rubbed her chin.

PC stopped tapping the book and looked down at the posters. "The sun is out; the moon is out. People, then no people." He started thumbing through the book again. "Damn fire burnt away most of the chapter listings."

"Look to see if they have a glossary," Ren said.

PC turned the book over. "No, scorched on the back of the book also. Just everything else in the middle survived." PC closed the book and put it in his backpack. He stood up and held his hand out to Ren. "Come on."

"Where are we going?"

"For a walk. Can't think here."

"You mean, because we're naked?"

"Yes."

"Why? Nothing we haven't done before. Besides, everyone else is wearing the same attire as we are." Ren nodded her head and laughed.

"Ah, true."

As they walked along the shore holding hands, Ren held her arm up, examining it, and then her legs.

"What are you looking at? PC asked.

"I've never been this tan before. We must be the tannest people on the beach."

PC looked himself over. "You're right, I've never been this tan before." He turned and looked at his butt. "Wow, that isn't white anymore."

He looked back at Ren's butt. Yours too. From being on the beach all this time."

"What's going to happen to us when we get home?" Ren blurted out.

It caught him off balance, and he hesitated. He took a deep breath and looked at Ren. "I tell you, Ren, I've been more focused on getting us back home. I hear what you are saying, but I can't give you a clear answer because I don't have one. And I don't want you to take that in a bad way. My Army thinking has clicked in since the day we landed on the beach. I'm in survival mode, for the both of us."

Ren was silent for a moment, digesting what PC had said. "Agreed," she said. "I think when we get home and settle down in our lives again, it will tell us what to do." Ren stopped. "This has been quite an adventure. I don't know if I'd do it again, but it has been interesting. If I were to do it again, I'd do it with you."

They smiled at each other and hugged.

"Ditto, girl."

PC realized they had come to the end of the clothing-optional beach. "We better turn around. Looks like we've come to the end of our trail."

They turned around. "Oh shit," Ren said.

"Oh, shit is right. That's not usually a good sign for us when everyone disappears."

PC examined his ring finger. "And, we don't have our rings on."

They picked up their pace.

"Come on, let's get back to our stuff and the hideaway."

PC scanned the beach to look for soldiers. Ren was doing the same.

"I bet the soldiers didn't stay put at the lighthouse," Ren said.

"Yea, well, I guess they missed us," PC said sarcastically, scanning the beach.

They made it back to the beach blanket, threw all the backpacks in the middle, and PC wrapped up their belongings, including their clothes, in the beach towel, as Ren pulled the beach umbrella out of the sand and closed it.

PC looked up to scan the beach again. "We'll get dressed later. Let's get to the hideaway, fast."

They scurried away, searching for soldiers. They reached the hideaway and dove in, out of breath.

"Never ran that hard in the buff before," Ren said, heaving.

PC sucked air, his hands on his knees. "Yeah, well, first time for everything." He spun around, grabbed his rifle, and laid it down next to the entrance, ready for a possible attack.

Ren dressed. "Hey, put some clothes on at least." She tossed him some garments.

PC looked at Ren. "Wha? Oh, yeah. Here, just keep an eye on things while I slip into something more comfortable."

"Always the comedian," Ren said.

Ren took his position with her rifle and scanned the beach with the binoculars.

"See anything?" PC pulled on some shorts.

"Not yet."

PC finished dressing and lay down next to Ren. She scanned left, PC looked right.

"I'm not seeing anything," Ren said.

She shifted her binoculars to her right as PC got out of the way.

"Anything?"

Ren was silent for a moment. "I'm not seeing anything."

"What the hell?" PC scratched the back of his head.

Ren put the binoculars down. "What?"

"Strange. When there is danger, all the people on the beach disappear, yet no soldiers or any armor are coming after us."

"I know, it's strange. Well, for us it's strange."

PC glanced out as Ren continued to scan the beach, and his eyes focused on the ocean. Something was moving far out. He squinted to see but couldn't make out what was there. Something was coming out from underneath the water. "Hey," he said to Ren, "let me have those binoculars." He put them up to his eyes, and his mouth fell open. He took the binoculars from his face, looked out, and put them back up to his face.

"Okay, you want to enlighten me?"

PC shook his head. "Oh, Shit."

"What? Talk to me."

"Everything that has been thrown at us, and they came up with something new."

"What? What do you see?"

"A submarine."

Ren stared at him, stunned. "A what? A submarine?"

She pulled the binoculars from his face.

"Hey," PC said as she looked out toward the ocean with the binoculars.

She sat there for a moment, mortified.

PC looked at her open mouth. "Same way I felt."

"Holy, shit. What kind of sub is that?"

PC took the binoculars from Ren. "Looks like a U-boat."

"A U-boat?"

"Yeah, well, we have been running up against the past, so, what the hell, might as well throw a U-boat into the mix." PC studied it. "They got a big gun on deck."

Ren lay down on PC's back and looked out to the ocean. "How big?"

"Looks like a one hundred and four millimeter. Pretty accurate for its time. Used on IA and IX U-boat types."

"Same type of gun that almost got us earlier?"

"Yep. After 1943, most of the deck guns were removed. A few commanders were allowed to retain them. Of course, with our luck, we get one with a gun."

"What are they doing?"

"Just hovering out there. Wait a minute..."

"What's happening?"

"The captain is up in the tower, along with some other officers. Scanning the shore with binoculars."

"They're looking for us, no doubt," Ren said.

"No doubt, they are." PC kept a close look as the sub searched the shores. "I do see a marking. Looks like U-853. Hmm. I wish I had my U-boat book with me, to check what the fate of that sub was."

"The question is," Ren said, "what will be our fate?"

CHAPTER 48

PC continued to watch the sub as Ren fell asleep on top of his back. Ren was becoming a second skin, and he didn't mind it at all anymore. He kept the binoculars up to his eyes, never letting them down. The captain on the U-boat was doing the same thing. At one point, PC felt they were looking eye to eye. Neither wanted to move to let the other know they had an eye on each other. No one was blinking.

"What is it you are looking for?" PC whispered under his breath.

"Two souls lost in another dimension, would be my guess," Ren said sleepily.

"Oh, you are alive back there."

She stretched some and settled her chin on PC's head. "Are they still out there?"

"Yep. I have a bead on the captain. We're both waiting to see who blinks first."

"Are they aiming that big gun at us?"

"No, no one is manning it, which is a good thing."

"Good thing? They got us cornered like rats."

"Rats in a cage, my dear."

"What will we do if they decide to aim that gun at us?"

PC kept the binoculars up to his eyes. "While I'm playing chicken with this captain, pack our backpacks with what we need, get our guns together, whatever food and water we need, clothes, yada, yada. We may have to make a quick exit. They can man that big gun on deck quickly, and we need be gone like the wind when they start shooting. They can get fifteen to eighteen rounds off quickly."

Ren crawled off PC's back and loaded the backpacks, setting them near the entrance, along with their weapons. She strapped on her nine-millimeter and put PC's near his rifle. She then settled back on PC's back.

"Still playing opossum?" Ren asked.

"Yeah."

"How long are you going to keep this up?"

"Well, it's starting to get dark, and the ocean is getting rough. I'm guessing he will dive soon. They don't have any night vision binoculars like we do."

"Since they didn't have that technology back then."

"Exactly, dear girl. Hold on now."

"Did he blink?"

PC lowered the binoculars, beaming at Ren. "He blinked."

He put the binoculars back up to his eyes. "He's packing it up. All personnel are going inside the sub." He was silent for a moment, then said, "He's diving."

"Do you think he will come back?"

PC turned around to look at Ren. "I don't know. Maybe. He stayed there for a long time. He may have been scouting just to see our movements. He could have taken us out with the big gun, and he didn't. He may not have seen us, even though we were having a staring contest. He may not have been sure we were here and gave up. That's why I didn't move. If I had, he may have blasted us out."

"Hey," Ren said. "Look outside.

PC turned to look. "I'll be. The nightly people are walking the beach. So, the people are back, which means the sub is gone."

"For now," Ren said.

"For now."

PC put the boards back up for their privacy. He pulled out the two posters and the witchcraft book and spread them out on the ground. Ren sat next to him.

PC put one of the lanterns nearby since it was getting dark out.

They both stared at the posters, sometimes touching one with a finger, tracking the sky, sun, moon, people walking, trying to make sense of what they had.

"Maybe," Ren said, "maybe this is not what we're looking for. Maybe, it's something else."

"I don't know what else it could be. Most of the shop was charred up. I took what was still halfway good."

"Maybe we should do another midnight run."

PC face grimaced. "No, I don't think that is a good idea. They'll probably have extra help tonight after your little exotic dance you did and your streaking adventure." He rubbed his neck. "No, I think we have what we need. We just must figure out what we have."

"And if we can't?"

PC took a heavy sigh. "Well, we can just wing it and go straight after the soldiers."

"And if that doesn't work?"

"We'll have to adjust to life in this world as our world suffers from a would-be tyrant and our counterparts get stuck in different worlds."

"What about the sub? Do you think it will follow us as we move toward the lighthouse?"

"Most likely." PC nodded his head. "They will shadow us. But if they get out of hand and start shooting at us, we have a secret weapon in the back."

Ren gave PC an inquisitive look. "Secret weapon?"

"Yes, it's buried way deep in the back in one of the crates. I found it one night when you were out swimming in the ocean."

"What does it do?"

"It can do a lot of things. Can take out a plane, helicopter, boat," he smiled, "make a submarine disappear. That is our ace card. We only have one, and we must use it at the right time."

Ren was staring down at the poster as PC was talking, and she jerked her head up with her eyes wide and mouth open. "Disappear."

PC cocked his head. "Disappear?"

"Disappear," Ren said again. She looked down at the posters and ran her fingers on the sun, the moon, and the people.

"Sun, people, no sun, moon with no people. You see?" she said excitedly.

"Show me," PC said. Both were down on all fours looking down at the poster.

"See, the sun is out, and we have the people enjoying the nice day." She pointed to the second poster. "Here we have no people, and the moon is out. You see?"

He looked at Ren with interest. He turned around, pulled a plank off and looked at the dark skies. "The moon. The moon is coming up, and it's a full moon." He looked around on the beach. The people were gone. "Damn." He turned and looked at Ren. "The people on the beach have disappeared. Not a soul out there."

"That's why they disappeared," Ren said. It's going to be a full moon."

PC picked up the witchcraft book. "So, what is the meaning of this book for us?" He flipped through the pages. "I saw something earlier that may be of significance here." He fingered a page. "I think this is it."

Ren moved over toward PC and sat next to him. "What? Tell me."

"Well, it's this spell, but you can only do it when it's a full moon."

"What does it do?"

"Well, it makes evil people disappear. But it only works when there is a full moon." He kept reading. "Wow."

Ren grabbed his arm. "Talk to me."

"This could work, but there is one thing."

"And that is…"

"If there are any clouds and they block the moon, the spell will stop working." PC continued reading. "Hmm."

"What are you humming about?"

"Well, you have to light up this spell."

"Light up?"

"Yes, well, I mean you must light it up with a match." PC pointed with his finger on the page as Ren looked on. "Both must be together, meaning the moon must be showing in the sky, the spell must be lit. If the spell goes out or the moon goes behind a cloud, we're screwed."

Ren looked outside and saw the moon. "Okay, then. The moon is full now. How long before the next one?"

"Twenty-seven days. Will have to check a calendar to verify what day."

"Twenty-seven? That is almost a month. And it will be getting cold around that time."

"Yes, it will. We'll have to retreat to my house. Since we can't travel in a terrain vehicle on the main roads, we'll have to wait till morning."

Ren smiled. "Cool. It will be nice to go inside and get a decent shower."

PC laughed. "Yes, it will be nice. You're not used to living in the rough like I have."

"Actually, I never lived in the rough before, but it was an adventure to do."

PC grinned at her. "Ah yes, the adventurous one. You did adjust well, I must say. Most people couldn't adjust living off the grid like we have. At least we had supplies to keep us going."

"Okay, how are we going to get to your house if we can't take the terrain?"

"Well, we'll have to take a bus."

Ren stood up. "A bus?"

"Yes, they have a bus to the beach that stops at the town I used to live in, Wantagh. We just need to find a bus schedule in the morning."

"Wantagh?" Ren said. What kind of name is that?" she asked, curious.

"Wantagh was an Indian Chief."

"Really." Ren looked amazed.

"Yes, he was with the Merokee tribe, which was part of the Montauk tribe, and later he was the Grand Sachem of the Montauk tribe."

"Wow. How interesting. Must do some historical research of Long Island when we get back home. Okay, where do we get a bus schedule?"

"Well, should be one near the parkway where the bus stop is."

Ren stood up quickly and grabbed PC's hand. "Come on, let's go and find the schedule."

PC stood still. "What—now?"

"Well, yeah. Not like we have anything else better to do."

PC nodded his head. "Yeah, you have a point there. But we'll have to walk some to get to the bus stop near Field Four."

Ren pulled on his arm again. "Come on, let's go, then."

"Okay, okay. Let me grab my nine-millimeter and take yours too, just to be safe."

They hid their weapons underneath their shirts, holstered. Both came out of the hideaway, and PC put the planks back up. He looked around and saw some people walking on the evening beach as the moon had disappeared behind the clouds.

"Let's go." He grabbed her hand, and they walked together back toward Field Four to the bus stop, near the Jones Beach Water Tower. They enjoyed the pleasant evening weather.

"Should be up here," PC pointed. They saw the sign for the bus stop next to a park bench covered by a partition. Inside they found the posting of the bus schedule.

"Can you see that?" Ren said. "So dark."

PC squinted. "Barely," he said. "But I can make out some of it. Let's see." He squinted his eyes some more. "There's a nine-a.m. bus that leaves here tomorrow. How's that sound?"

"Perfect. We can pack up and be ready. Maybe have some breakfast at the restaurant."

"Sounds like a plan. Come on, lets head back to the hideaway, make some dinner, pack, and get some rest."

Ren smiled as they headed back. "I'm all for that."

CHAPTER 49

Both PC and Ren woke up early the next morning. They headed for the ocean to clean themselves up before they left, packed their backpacks with the items they would need, and headed out.

They noticed the police were no longer watching the now boarded-up gift shop. They had a quick breakfast, chatted for a bit, and headed toward the bus stop.

As they walked, PC looked up at the cloudy sky. "Hmmm," he said. "Pretty cloudy. Looks like we're going to get some rain."

Ren frowned at the ominous weather. "Well, that sucks. How far do we have to walk to your house?"

"Probably about a mile or two." PC looked at Ren. "Hopefully, it won't be raining when we get there."

"What if it is?"

PC looked up again. "Then," he shrugged, "we get wet. Besides, we've been wet most of the time, anyhow."

Ren nodded her head slowly. "This is true."

They made it to the bus stop and sat down on the park bench covered by the overhang. PC looked at his watch. "Should be here shortly."

With a squeal of brakes, the bus pulled up. Only a few people got off.

"I don't know why people would want to be here on such a crappy day," PC said.

They boarded the bus, and PC paid for the ride as Ren walked down the aisle and sat down.

They bus driver raised an eyebrow. "Leaving already?"

"Yeah, well, too crummy of a day," PC said.

"How did you folks get here? I didn't see you on my first trip here."

PC's suspicion kicked in. This was the first bus trip of the day. "Well, some friends dropped us off and we decided to go home since it's not a nice day."

The bus door closed. PC swallowed hard and sat down with Ren. The bus driver circled the Jones Beach water tower and headed north.

Ren said quietly, "How come you told him some friends dropped us off?"

He whispered to her. "He's not a bus driver."

Ren shot him a glance. "What?"

"Shh, keep it down."

"What makes you think so?"

"Did you hear what he said?"

"What?"

"He said I didn't see you on the first trip. This is the first trip of the day."

Ren's face blanched. "Oh, shit."

"Stand by." PC walked up to the driver, sat down behind him, and put his nine-millimeter to the back of the driver's head. "Time for you to pull over."

The driver froze.

"Keep your hands on the steering wheel and pull over on the grass."

As the driver was pulling over, PC noticed a bulge in the coat draped over the driver's seat. PC reached in and pulled out a gun. "Nice piece. Classic forty-five." PC tucked it behind his back.

Ren pulled out her nine-millimeter, both hands grasping the gun, and moved up a couple of seats.

The bus rolled to a stop on the grass. "Now what?" The bus driver said.

PC saw an insignia tattoo on the driver's forearm. "Military," PC said. "Interesting that ex-special forces would be driving a bus. Who hired you to take us out?" PC pressed the gun harder to his head. "I'm waiting," As he cocked the gun.

"Fuck you," the driver said.

"College educated, I see. Time to say goodnight." PC gave him the Vulcan pinch on his neck. The bus driver's head fell to his left shoulder as he slumped down.

Ren stood there with her index finger ready to fire, and slowly lowered her gun. "How do you do that?"

"I'll teach you one day." PC pulled the driver out of his seat.

"What are we going to do with him?"

"He will be out awhile. I'll drag him to the back and leave him there."

"Can you drive a bus?"

"No, but I can drive."

"Good; you're hired."

PC dragged the driver to the back of the bus and lay him flat on his back. "Rest in peace." PC gave him the sign of the cross.

He opened the doors, looked around, and threw the forty-five pistol into the nearby marsh. He closed the door and got in the driver's seat.

Ren sat behind PC. "You sure you know how to drive this thing?"

He looked back at Ren and smiled. "Piece of cake."

She smiled back. "I love a man with confidence."

PC put the bus in gear and rolled to the highway. PC glanced at Ren. "Just keep an eye on our guest."

Ren pulled out her gun and turned in her seat to see their passenger, out cold. "Are we just going to drive up to the bus stop like this?"

"No. Change of plans. We'll stop at a path in front of Cedar Creek Park. From there, we'll walk. We'll be a little farther from the house, but we'll manage."

"Yeah," Ren said. We have, so far."

They drove past the toll booth when a few drops spattered on the windshield.

"Oh, shit." Ren said. "Starting to rain." PC turned on the windshield wipers. Ren shot a glance outside. "Crap. Guess we're getting wet."

"Looks like it."

When they reached their destination, PC pulled over just before the path started. He turned the bus off, pulled the key out of the ignition, and got up. "Okay," he said, "grab your backpacks and let's go." He frowned as the rain started to pick up.

"What about our friend?" Ren said.

"He will be okay. Little bit of a headache, but okay. Come on let's go." PC opened the bus door, taking the keys with him so when the driver woke up, he couldn't go anywhere. "I'll dispose of these." He dangled the keys.

They made their way into the park as the rain started to pour. They came to a retention pond and PC threw the keys into the water. "No one's going to find that." They continued on.

Ren slicked her hair back as the rain came down harder. "How far, do you think?"

"Two, maybe three miles, since we're further away than where we were supposed to stop."

They made their way through the park and came out onto Merrick Road. They crossed the street and turned into a neighborhood.

"How come we're going through here?"

"Keep us off the main road for a bit so on one sees us."

"Do you think people are looking for us?"

"I am guessing yes, since we had that driver ready to take us."

They walked several blocks down the neighborhood until they came out onto the busy main thoroughfare, Sunrise Highway. They waited at the light for traffic to clear and walked across.

PC grinned. "Welcome to Wantagh."

Ren watched the Long Island Railroad train careen past. "Wow, where do those trains go?"

"Stops off to the different towns and ends up at Penn Station. The opposite direction to Montauk."

"Cool," Ren said. She tilted her head. "Penn Station?"

PC smiled. "New York City."

"Oh, wow! Never been to New York. Do you think we'll have time to go?"

"Another time. It's safer here."

Ren grabbed PC's hand. "Promise?"

PC looked at Ren. "What, promise to take to you to New York City?"

"Uh-huh."

PC smiled at Ren. "I promise, in the future, I'll take you to New York City."

"Okay, I'd like that."

They walked through the main town and made their way over a small bridge, with the parkway underneath them.

"What highway is that?"

"That, my dear is the highway we were just on, the Wantagh Parkway."

"They named the town after the Highway. How cool."

"I'm glad you find that cool." They both laughed.

"How much further?" Ren asked.

"We're getting there. Once we get over the bridge, we have about a quarter of mile before we turn on the street of my house."

"What's the name of your street?"

"Valentine Place."

"Valentine Place. What a nice name."

"It was great growing up as a kid on Long Island, especially in my town. Most of the neighborhood were kids. Everyone knew everyone. I think I knew everyone in a three-block radius."

The rain began to slow down, but PC and Ren were soaked to the bone. Ren held on to PC's arm and shook. "I'm starting to get a chill from being wet."

"Hang on, we're almost to our street." He pointed at the stop sign. "We'll be turning here."

They made a left-hand turn and continued to walk up the block.

"How much further?"

"Just a block and a half."

They made their way as Ren hung on to PC's arm, trembling.

PC looked down at Ren. "I thought you were a cold-weather girl."

"Yes, but it doesn't mean I have to like it."

PC looked up as the rain picked up again. "Hmmm, cooler weather starting to creep in already."

They finally made it to the house.

"This is it," PC said warmly, as they walked up the long driveway.

"This is nice. Nice neighborhood, too."

They stopped at the steps of the back door. "Wait here," PC said as he made his way to the garbage cans on other side of the steps.

"What are you doing?"

"Getting the key." He moved the garbage cans out of the way and reached down just to the right of the steps and pulled up a rock from the garden. He showed it to Ren. "If anything ever happens and you need to get back to the house, look for this rock just on the back edge of the garden."

"Okay." Her lips quivered from the cold.

PC turned the rock upside down, slid the small panel away, and pulled out the key. He opened the front door, and they slipped into the kitchen and out of the rain.

They took off their backpacks and popped their shoes off, then walked through the dining room into the living room with a fireplace.

Ren looked around with amazement. "Wow! This is nice. You grew up in this house?"

PC nodded his head. "Yep. It's changed a bit since I bought the house. I added the fireplace."

"So cool."

PC motioned toward the side hall. "Bathroom is right there, so you can shower and put some dry clothes on. Towels are in the hall closet." PC headed to the back door. "I'm going to do some things outside so no one bothers us for a bit. We must hang here for the next few weeks until we get a full moon."

Ren rubbed her arms. "What are you going to do?"

PC smiled. "I'll tell you all about it after you get freshened up."

"Okay." She raised her arms up and slapped them down on her sides and he stepped outside.

She walked into the kitchen and watched as PC opened the garage door. One of his neighbors from his backyard called out his name, and PC walked over to talk with him. She looked inside the open garage at his car. A black Challenger. "Nice," she said to herself. "He does alright." She walked out of the kitchen and headed down the short hallway to locate the closet. She pulled out a towel for herself and picked up her backpack with her belongings. She cracked open a door directly across from the closet and poked her head in. "Wow, this must be the main bedroom." She opened the door all the way and walked in. Queen size bed with a dresser and bureau. She opened the closet and pulled out PC's robe. "Oh, I need this." She headed for the bathroom.

PC waved to his neighbor, Mr. Lopez, as he always called him, and said they would talk again, then headed into the garage. PC rummaged around looking for some old glass jars. He came back into the house and grabbed the book from his backpack, so he could make the spell needed to protect them from any further danger. He heard the shower, and figured Ren was cleaning herself up, so he headed back to the garage.

About an hour later, PC came walking back in the house and found Ren lying on the couch in his robe and a towel wrapped around her head. "I see you found something comfortable to slip into."

"You don't mind, do you?" she asked, sitting up from the couch.

PC sat next to her. "No, not at all. I want you to be comfortable. Roughing it all this time on the beach with no shower except a sea bath, no bed, always out in the elements, getting shot at..."

"But I enjoyed it, really. I love adventures. You should know that by now."

"Yes, I do, and what an adventure it's been."

"What were you doing outside?"

"Oh, a spell I found in the spell book. I took four jars, and I knew I had the ingredients in the garage for this. I mixed them together and put one at each of the four corners of the house."

"What will it do?"

"Keeps evil away from us."

"You think it will work?"

"Well, I was never into witchcraft, but I'll give anything a try. Yes, I think it will. We'll be safe."

"I think so, too," Ren said. That book was left in the gift shop for us for that very reason."

"I believe you're right. Even though the Caretaker can't tell us what to do, he has pointed us to the doors we need to look inside."

Ren looked into his eyes and put her hand on his face. "You looked tired."

He shook his head. "Very much so." He looked around the house, then back at Ren. "Let me take a shower, put some dry clothes on, and maybe take a nap for a bit."

"I could use a nap, too." She looked into his eyes playfully. "I'll meet you in the bedroom." She kissed him on the lips and whispered, "You don't mind, do you?"

He looked at Ren, stood her up, disrobed her, and carried her into the bedroom.

CHAPTER 50

Ren woke up the next day to the sunlight peeking through the side of the shade. She put her arm out but did not feel PC's presence. "Hmm..." She sat up. "Wonder where he is?" She got out of bed and found the robe on the floor. She put the robe on and walked out into the hall. "PC?" She looked around and put her hands on her hips. "Where are you?"

She walked into the kitchen and found a note on the kitchen table. She picked it up and read it out loud. "Be back shortly."

She opened the refrigerator. "Nothing in here." She bent down and looked. "Just the condiments." She stood straight and closed the door. "Hopefully he's getting food."

She saw a coffee maker with coffee pods next to it. "Oh, thank god." As she was making the coffee, she heard a car pulling in the driveway. She looked out the kitchen window. "There you are."

PC exited the car with two grocery bags in hand and entered the house. "Good morning. How did you sleep last night?" He put down two plastic bags and she kissed him and nestled in his arms.

"I slept great. Best sleep I've had in many weeks. You?"

"After a little love making, like a baby. I feel so much better."

"What did you buy?" She released him and opened the bags.

"Well, we're going to need some provisions since we will be here for a bit before the next full moon. This will cover us for breakfast, and we'll go out later and stock up."

"Bacon, eggs, hash browns." She looked up to PC and smiled. "Sounds good."

He smiled back. I'll fix us breakfast and I'll let you make your coffee."

"Do you want a cup?"

"Please."

Soon the smell of bacon, eggs and hash browns permeated the kitchen as PC cooked.

"You're pretty good at this, I see."

He laughed. "Been on my own for some time, so you learn to fend for yourself. You've been out on your own too, for a while."

"I'm sure you do pretty good by yourself. You certainly have, in this strange adventure we have been on." She grinned and inhaled the coffee's aroma. "Yeah, I do alright. I've never had a man cook for me."

PC turned around. "Really? You must have met someone that cooked for you."

She shook her head. "No, no one. Some of the men and people in my life have been disposable friends."

"Disposable? Explain what you mean."

Ren took a sip of her coffee. "Oh, I don't mean that in a nasty way. Let me correct myself. I just meant that I like meeting people who aren't trying to turn a simple conversation into something more. Most people are searching for something. I prefer roaming around, being random." She took another sip of her coffee. "Have you ever sat at a bar and had an incredible conversation with someone? Then you just went your separate ways? I enjoy that kind of thing. Just meeting people and being with people without the whole 'Can I get your number?' or 'We should get together again.' It's just nice to meet other people without any demands or expectations." Ren noticed PC's intent look. "What?"

"Maybe I'm weird, but I love that."

"No, you're not weird. There's nothing weird about it."

He turned around and flipped the hash browns. "I didn't realize it until you said it, but it's something I've done myself." He reached over to his coffee and took a sip. "I walked into a bar by myself some time ago when I needed to get out. I sat at the bar and the girl next to me, who was by herself, started talking to me. We had a great conversation, bought each other drinks, talked the night away and we parted ways. Never saw her again." He paused for a second, then continued. "I think we were just enjoying the stimulating conversation without any strings attached." He turned around and smiled at Ren. "Who knows, maybe it was you I was talking to."

Ren smiled back. "Was this in Florida?"

"Yes, it was."

"It could have been, since I've been to Florida many times."

"I wouldn't know if I fell on her today, so yes, it could have been you." He turned his head, smiled, and winked at Ren, and turned around with two plates in his hand. "Breakfast is served."

He put both plates down and brought some silverware out of the drawer with napkins.

He sat down and looked at Ren. "Okay, we have a few weeks before the next full moon. It will give us plenty of time to plan our run to the lighthouse."

Ren talked with her mouth full. "What witchcraft do you have in mind to stop the soldiers?"

"Well, it's a potion where we have to actually set it on fire."

Ren looked up at PC. "Set it on fire. You said that before, about lighting it up."

"Yeah. It's like a Molotov cocktail."

PC stood up from his chair, walked into the living room, pulled out the map from the gift shop, and put it on the kitchen table facing Ren.

Ren studied the picture. "Long walk."

"Well, at that point I think we'll be okay."

"How are we getting there?"

"We'll use my car. I'll hide it in the brush. We'll have to stop at the hideaway and get the weapons we'll need."

Ren looked up at PC.

"Well?" PC said.

Ren nodded her head. "It's a plan, and we'll make it work. Meanwhile, what will we do for the next few weeks?"

PC sipped on his coffee and looked at Ren. "We will keep ourselves busy. Lots to do."

"Like getting a wardrobe for me."

"Yes, like getting you a wardrobe."

"Cool!" Ren said with a smile. "I noticed the lakes on our way here. Do you think we can do some fishing?"

PC looked at her. "So... interested in fishing?" He smiled. "Sure, we can do some fishing. But I want to give you something." He walked to the living room, came back with a little black bag tied closed with a knot, and handed it to Ren.

"What is this?"

"It has some herbs and sea salt in it."

She examined the bag in the palm of her hand. "What does it do?"

"It will keep evil away from you." He pulled another black bag out of his pocket. "I have one, too. Just keep it in your pocket and hopefully we'll be safe."

She nodded. "Hopefully."

"Well, I never tried this before. Can't hurt."

She put it in her robe pocket. "Okay, I'll give it a try."

PC sat back down. "Meanwhile, let's finish our meal, and we'll hit the lakes for some fishing."

Ren smiled. "Alright."

CHAPTER 51

PC and Ren kept themselves busy for the next few weeks. PC showed her Long Island. They went fishing at the nearby lakes many times, which Ren enjoyed, even catching a few largemouth bass, and fed the ducks. PC took her to the drainage ditch at night to catch eels. He walked her to his old high school and over the connecting footbridge, and even met his old track coach in the parking lot. They caught a Mets game at Citi Field, and PC took her to New York City, where she was awestruck. When they had dinner at home, PC did most of the cooking, and they also ate out at some of PC's old favorite restaurants. They even went to a few of his old bar haunts, where she met Louie the bartender at The Butt, where Ren had a good time.

All the while, they kept their eyes on the sky waiting for the next full moon.

Then the day came. They packed up what they needed, and PC locked up the house. It was almost dusk when PC pulled his car out of the garage. They drove back to the beach to go to the hideaway to pick up the weapons they needed. PC did not want to attract attention when bringing home high-power weapons of war.

It was dark, but the moonlight lit there way. No one noticed as they walked to the car with weapons in tow. Ren looked over at the big case PC was holding. "What is that? Our secret weapon?"

"Yep, it's our secret weapon."

"Does your secret weapon have a name?"

"Stinger missile."

"Stinger missile. I've heard of them. Nasty weapon?"

PC nodded his head. "It can be. I will show you how to use it just in case you must use it."

"What use would we need that for? Something big?"

PC looked at Ren and nodded his head. "Yep."

"Something big, like a submarine?"

PC smiled again at Ren. "You're a smart girl."

She laughed. "Well, I did see you reading your World War II sub book."

"Yes, I looked up that sub. In our dimension, it was sunk in 1942, not too far off Long Island. More toward Rhode Island."

"Oh? Well, do you plan to sink it here?"

"Well, I want to take out the gun on deck. I don't want it firing at us. It's a three-man operation and they can get us quickly, so I want to take that out. It will probably limp away and get sunk where it's supposed to be."

They made their trek back to the car with their haul. "Nervous?" PC asked.

"I don't know. I think I'm more stunned that we're finally coming to the end of this. It went fast—our time here." She took PC's hand. "Promise you will find me when we get home, or I'll find you."

"First thing I am going to do when I get home."

She studied his eyes and saw the glimmer of warmth beaming at her. Ren kissed PC. "Good luck to the both of us."

He smiled. "Yes, good luck to us both." PC revved the engine, and they made their way to Montauk Lighthouse.

It took them three hours to get to Montauk. PC hid the car in a shrubby area. When they got out of the car, PC motioned Ren over. "Watch me," he said as he bent down and pulled out a magnetic key hider. "The key to the car is in here. Something happens to me, and you need to get out of here in a hurry," he held the key box up, "This is where you will find the key." He knelt and put it under the bumper. He made Ren bend down and feel its location.

"Got it," she said.

"You have the directions to the house. If there's trouble, head back to the house."

"But what am I going to do if something happens to you?"

"Well, I don't plan on something happening to me, but you're smart. You'll figure out a way. But just in case, I left some money in the kitchen cabinet where the coffee cups are. There is enough to get you back home to Indiana where you can—well, start your life over, sort of, and continue your life. Plus, extra money for other things."

Her eyes glistened. "Promise me you'll be with me."

PC kissed her on the forehead. "I promise."

They strapped on their weapons. Ren checked her Remington and nine-millimeter, and carried the bag with the Molotov cocktail potion that would get them home. PC had his pistol along with his rifle and uncased the stinger missile, lugging it toward the lighthouse.

They crept through the brush, staying low. The moon was full and bright. They came to the parking lot, and PC noticed the parking lot was empty. He scanned the area for soldiers. "Hmm. Not as heavily manned as I thought it would be."

Ren tapped PC on the shoulder. "Hey, look over at the path going up to the lighthouse."

PC looked over. "A Machine gun nest." He pulled out night vision binoculars. "Looks like just two people." He turned to Ren. "We'll have to take that out. We'll need to throw our potion in that spot." He scanned again. "Come on. Let's go toward the water so we can see what is in the back."

They stayed low as they made their way near the cliff to catch a glimpse of the back part of the lighthouse. PC pulled out the night vision binoculars again.

"What do you see?" Ren asked.

"They have a machine gun back there, too." He put the goggles down. We won't have to worry about them too much; once we get the potion lit, everyone will disappear."

Ren looked out toward to ocean. The moon was bright, and she thought she noticed something. She frowned.

"What's the matter?" PC asked.

Ren strained her eyes. "I thought I saw something move out in the ocean." She grabbed the night vision binoculars and found what she was looking for. "The sub is out there." She noticed three men on the deck of the sub near the big gun. "Oh shit. Duck!"

A big gun blasted. PC and Ren hit the ground hard.

The round went over their heads and exploded about thirty feet from them. Dirt, sand, and other debris landed on top of them. "Don't move," PC said. "Let them think they got us." He slowly reached over for the stinger missile and pulled it close to him. Ren pulled some of the brush away. "Soldiers! headed for us!"

"How many do you see?"

"About seven."

He rolled to his side and held the stinger up to his chest. "When I say 'now,' I'm going to stand up and fire the stinger. You take out those soldiers."

Ren felt liquid draining down her thigh. She looked down, shocked. "Oh shit."

"What, what's the problem?"

"The potions bottle—a portion of it spilled out when we hit the deck."

PC pondered in silence.

"Oh, shit."

"Yeah. You already said that. Now what?"

"We're going to have to fight our way up."

"First thing's first." PC stood up and took aim at the sub which he could now see in the moonlight.

The soldiers saw PC stand up and aimed their rifles. Ren jumped to her feet and rapidly fired away with her Remington, mowing down all seven soldiers. PC fired the missile, and it whistled away toward the sub. It hit right where he wanted it to at the big gun, and the sky lit up with the explosion.

Ren turned to watch. "Wow. That did some serious damage."

"Yeah, like you always say, fucktard. At least they won't bother us now. But now we have our work cut out for us, with most of our potion gone."

"What do we do?"

PC looked around quickly. "We need some potato mashers."

Ren eyed the dead soldiers. "Quick, they haven't disappeared. Let's see if they have any."

They ran toward the dead soldiers, laying low and scanning the area. PC saw movement around the lighthouse.

"Oh shit," he said. "More soldiers."

They made it to the dead soldiers and found five potato mashers. "Quick," PC said, "put the potato mashers in my backpack and some in yours, too." Ren quickly tossed them in.

PC checked the front of the lighthouse and saw the machine gun nest. "Damn, we have to take that out," he said.

Ren threw the bag over her shoulder and noticed PC focused on something behind them. PC reached for his nine-millimeter, but Ren had anticipated what was happening.

Without taking her eyes off PC, she shot three oncoming soldiers from behind her. She stood frozen with the gun still pointing. "Got them?"

Astonished, PC slowly shook his head and said, "Got them."

He pulled his sniper rifle off his shoulder. "Quick, let's head for that high ground. I want to take out the machine gun nest in front of the lighthouse. Let's go."

Ren followed PC from behind. She quickly looked and noticed a lot of commotion and movement at the lighthouse. She turned toward the ocean and noticed the sub limping away in a cloud of smoke. "Guess that sub won't be bothering us," she said.

They made it up to the high ground. Both hit the ground as PC took out the night binoculars and checked the ground around the lighthouse. "Wow, they're like ants milling around."

Ren kept watch with her rifle out.

"Do you have a shot?"

"Yea, I got a damn good shot."

He turned to look at Ren. "Do you think we have enough of the potion?"

Ren looked at the bottle. "We'll have to get closer because we won't have a lot of time when this thing burns out."

PC nodded his head. "Okay." He lay down on the ground with his sniper rifle, peering through the fence. He put his eye to the scope to focus on the machine gun nest. "Get ready, Ren. I'm going to take out the machine gun nest in the front of the lighthouse. If soldiers come near us, throw those potato mashers at them. Use mine as well."

"What if I run out of mashers?"

PC raised an eyebrow. "Improvise. You have a gun."

"Oh, yeah," she smiled sheepishly.

PC went back to his scope. Two men were manning the machine gun. Other soldiers were moving around the area. PC took aim, stopped breathing, and exhaled as he pulled the trigger. A loud shot rang out. The soldier behind the machine gun went down along with a soldier standing nearby. PC smiled to himself. "Two for one." He aimed again and took out the second soldier behind the nest.

Ren was watching PC's back. She saw soldiers approaching and grabbed one of the potato mashers. "Get ready. Here they come."

PC concentrated on his scope. "You know what to do, girl. Make it so."

Ren waited till they were close enough. Five soldiers she saw. She had a good arm. she pulled the pin and threw it with confidence, and it flipped in the air end over end. The masher landed in front of the oncoming soldiers, exploded, and all five were taken out.

PC continued scanning. He wanted to take out as many as he could so it would be less of a problem getting to the back of the lighthouse door. So close, he thought to himself. He felt Ren pull another masher out of his back. "How are you doing, girl?"

As she threw the masher, she yelled out, "Just peachy!" and another explosion dropped troops dead to the ground.

Ren pulled out another masher and noticed soldiers coming from their left. She pulled the pin and rolled left as the masher went into the air. It landed between the soldiers, and the explosion took them out.

"How many mashers do we have left?" PC shouted out to Ren.

"Three."

PC fired his rifle and took out some more soldiers. "We're going to need at least two."

"Okay." She threw another masher and took out more soldiers. She pulled her rifle out as more solders came from the ocean side. She rapidly fired her Remington, mowing down soldier after soldier until they stopped coming. She turned to her right as more soldiers came. She rapidly fired every soldier down, with her adrenaline pumping.

She looked back and forth for anyone else coming. She heard PC's rifle go off again.

"How are we doing, Ren?"

She stayed focused and sternly said, "Outstanding."

PC rolled over and looked at all the casualties. "Holy shit. Must be thirty dead soldiers here." He looked up at her. "Okay?"

She nodded her head. "Okay."

They moved down the hill, laying low as they made it to the fence. The soldiers at the front had not spotted them yet. Ren pulled out the bottle with the little potion they had left. She popped the cork out and stuffed a rag into the top of the bottle.

PC took the bottle. "I'll throw this one. Light it up."

Ren pulled a lighter out of her pocket. Just as Ren was about to light the rag, the soldiers spotted them.

"Shit, they see us." She lit it quickly and yelled at PC. "THROW IT!"

PC tossed it high and far. They watched the potion as soldiers fired on their position. The bottle hit the ground, broke, and exploded into flames.

They stood up and looked around. It was quiet. Nothing moved.

"They're gone. It worked," Ren said with a smile.

"Come on." PC grabbed Ren's hand. "Let's go; we don't have a lot of time."

They both hopped over the fence and ran downhill toward the sidewalk. PC dropped his sniper rifle and pulled his other rifle off his shoulder.

Ren had her Remington ready. She looked up and noticed the moon. It was starting to disappear behind clouds. "Shit!"

PC looked at Ren as they continued their quick pace. "What?"

"Don't stop, the moon is going behind the clouds. Our potion will stop working. Let's hurry!"

The ran up the hill. They had to get to the back of the lighthouse and enter through the entrance. They both looked up as the moon began to disappear.

They ran by the Keeper's house. "Almost there!" PC yelled out. But as they were about to turn the corner to the doorway, the moon disappeared behind the clouds, and the soldiers reappeared.

As they turned the corner, PC ran straight for the machine gun nest and barreled right into the two soldiers who were manning it. Ren jumped over the sandbags with PC. She shot one of the solders dead as PC wrestled with the other one.

Ren looked up and noticed more soldiers coming at them. Too many to shoot down with her rifle. She dropped it immediately, manned the machine gun, and cut loose on the oncoming soldiers.

PC was still wrestling with the soldier and had had enough. He pulled out his nine-millimeter and shot him dead in the head. He looked up quickly to see that Ren was taking care of business. He pulled out the two remaining mashers, pulled the pin on one and tossed it, taking out more soldiers.

Ren was focused as she mowed down the soldiers. PC pulled the pin on the last masher, tossed it, and a loud explosion took out more soldiers. He picked up his rifle and looked toward the door. He watched as the door opened, and he saw a bright light from inside.

This is it, he quickly thought. He put his hand on Ren's shoulder. "Come on, Ren, it's time!"

She kept firing like she had never heard him. "They're still coming!"

He pulled on her. "We must go! The door is opened and they're calling us! Let's go!"

She stopped firing and stared at the light. "Home," she whispered.

PC pulled her up, but soldiers were still coming. PC and Ren bolted for the door. PC pushed Ren in front. "I'll follow you; go, go!" He raised his rifle and fired at the oncoming soldiers.

Ren reached for the door. PC wasn't far away, walking backward toward the door opening. They were almost there when a potato masher was thrown toward them. Ren was at the foot of the doorway facing out when the explosion occurred. The explosion threw her back, and she tried to grab PC. She screamed, "NO!" as she fell back, clutching at nothing but air. Everything went black.

CHAPTER 52

Ren fell back in a chair, gasping for air, her face still feeling the heat from the explosion in her face. Her eyes were wide as she held on to her chest, heaving. She looked around, disoriented. And then it hit her. "My office. I'm back in my office."

She struggled to breathe. She fell to the floor on all fours, her lungs seizing, and realized she was hyperventilating. She grabbed the liner from her trash can, dumped the contents, cupped her hands around the bag, and breathed in and out until could feel her control once more.

She put the bag down, still on all fours, and sobbed. Her head hit the floor, and she rolled on her side with one hand holding her stomach, and the other on her face.

She felt her pocket and sat bolt upright, wiping her face. "Yes, yes!" she yelled. She pulled out the business card PC had given her. "I still have it! Oh my god!"

She stood up immediately and fell back into her chair. "I must call; I must call. Oh God, please tell me he made it back home."

She picked up the phone, looked at the card quickly, and punched in the phone number frantically.

Suddenly there was a light knock on the door. Ren ignored it as she listened. "Pick up, pick up, oh please pick up." Tears ran down her face.

Another knock came at the office door but this time a little louder. Ren looked up. "WHAT!"

The door opened, and it was Kevin.

"What, Kevin? WHAT?"

Kevin stood in the doorway. "Hey, Ren. Are you okay?"

"Yes! I'm fine! Now get out!"

"Ren, you don't look—"

She yelled, "GET OUT!!"

Kevin closed the door quickly. He stood with his back to the door scratching his head, when he heard Ren yell out, "And stay away from the nude beaches!"

Kevin walked away quickly. "How did she know that?"

Ren listened as the phone rang on the other end. Finally, PC's voicemail came on. She sagged in her seat. She listened to the message and heard his voice. Tears came down her eyes. She heard the beep. "PC, PC, I made it back. Please call me and tell me you are okay. Please, please call me!" She hung up the phone, folded her arms, buried her head, and sobbed.

The office door opened quietly as Ren's friend Celeste walked in. She walked over to Ren's desk and put her hands on her shoulders softly. "Hey, it's me. Are you okay? What's wrong, Ren?"

Ren turned herself in her seat and hugged her friend.

Celeste held on to her. "Talk to me, girl."

"It's—it's my friend. Something has happened to him. I can't get a hold of him. I know something terrible has happened to him."

Celeste pulled Ren back and looked at her face, wet from crying, as tears continued to stream down her face. Celeste pulled a tissue from the box on Ren's desk. Ren took it and wiped her face. "Where is he? What do you think happened to him?"

Ren grabbed another tissue. "He's a soldier. He was in a battle. He was supposed to be home, and he's not. I'm afraid he didn't make it. I tried calling him and no one is answering."

"Well, that doesn't mean he didn't make it. He could be out somewhere, or he was delayed getting home."

"No, no, that's not it. It's a feeling. I feel something has happened to him."

"You two close? You've always been footloose and fancy free. I've never seen you hang on to anyone very long."

Ren stopped wiping her eyes and looked at Celeste. "It's hard to explain. All I can say is, it is a closeness. We enjoy talking to each other." Ren hesitated and continued. "We had an adventure. We did things together that most people couldn't imagine."

Celeste looked into Ren's eyes. She could see she was hurting. "Why don't you go home for the day? It's Friday, and it's slow here. Besides, I think you scared the crap out of Kevin."

They laughed, and Ren stood up and hugged Celeste. "I think I will go home." She found her handbag under the desk, said goodbye to Celeste, and left her office door with her head down, so no one could see her face.

She made it to her car and headed home.

She found the daily paper on her front door. She looked at the date, bewildered. It was the same date as the day she'd left. "God damn Lambert was right. Nothing has changed."

She opened the door to her home and dropped her handbag to the floor. She picked up the phone and tried to call PC again. It rang and went to voicemail. She lay down on the couch and began to cry again. She reached behind her to grab a tissue on the end table, and her hand hit something hard. "Ouch."

She sat up to see what it was. Her eyes widened. She pulled it out from near the end table. It was the Remington. She looked at it up and down. "This is the same gun I had on the beach." She looked around, mystified. "How did it get here?"

Ren put the Remington back where she found it and searched for any other reminders of her adventure. She found nothing. She lay back down on the couch. Her eyes closed slowly as exhaustion finally caught up with her, and she fell asleep.

CHAPTER 53

A month went by. Ren took a leave of absence. She flew down to Florida to find PC. She checked his condo, but no one had seen him for a while. Some thought he might be in New York. She even flew there and searched the beach for him. She checked where their hideaway had been, but it was nonexistent. She even checked his house, but PC's neighbor, Mr. Lopez, said PC had not been around in some time.

She flew back to Indiana and stayed home most of the time taking a leave of absence from work. She kept calling PC but always got his voicemail.

A Month had passed. Ren lay on the couch. The TV was on, but her mind was elsewhere. *He must be still there.* She didn't want to think PC was dead. Things hadn't changed much since she'd returned to her reality. The former President had just announced he was running for President again. The government was trying to press charges against him for inciting an insurrection. The country was split in two. She was beginning to feel that maybe she should have stayed in the other dimension. How could one person make that much of a difference, where not making it back in the world would set it off-kilter?

She let out a big sigh and stared off into space when there was a knock at the door. She sat up and looked out the window. She saw a man with a suit on and mirrored sunglasses.

"Who the hell is this?" She walked to the door and opened it.

"Hi Ren."

She recognized that smile. "Lambert!" Shocked, she poked his chest. "Are you still a hologram?"

"Nope, this is the real McCoy."

She felt a sudden rage. She grabbed him by his suit jacket, pulled him into her home, and threw him to the ground. Grabbing her Remington, she cocked the bolt and aimed it at him. She scowled, "Where is he? Where is PC? So help me God, if you don't tell me, I'll shoot you dead right here!" She aimed closer to him. "WHERE IS HE, GOD DAMN IT!"

Lambert lay on his side and held his arm up at Ren. "Easy! Easy! I'm here to tell you where he is."

"WHERE IS HE?"

"He's still stuck back in the wrong dimension. We've tried to get him back, but with no success. We've tried to send people in to get him. But something is stopping us."

"What's stopping you?!"

"We don't know. We think it's the Gatekeeper you met, but we're not sure. After the fire in the gift shop, we couldn't get back in. Something was blocking us. We couldn't figure out why."

Ren slowly backed up and lowered her Remington. "Gatekeeper. Yes, he blocked you out. He told us he blocked you out, and he would only let you back in if we said so. He wasn't happy with you setting fire to the gift shop."

Ren backed up some more until she was sitting on the couch with the gun lowered.

Lambert was still on the floor. "Can I get up?"

"What? Oh, yes, sit down over there on the chair."

Lambert got on his feet, straightened his suit, and sat down. He looked at Ren. "Even though you're back, the country is still not the same. I'm sure you been watching the news regarding the ex-president."

"Yes, unfortunately I have been watching the news. That tin pot wanna-be dictator who is slowly taking over the country. And to think I voted for that schmuck. What are you potheads doing about this?"

"We're doing something right now. We feel you're the only person who can retrieve PC. We need you to go back and get him back here. Once he is back, the timeline will fall back into place, the ex-president will disappear from the public eye, and things will be normal again."

"How am I to get PC back here?"

"We're not sure. We're hoping your Gatekeeper friend will help you out."

"He can't tell us too much. He can only open doors, and we have to figure out the rest. If he tells us too much, he may interrupt the timeline, like you said." Ren put the gun down behind the end table and sighed. "How will I get there?"

Lambert stood up and walked toward the front door, and Ren followed him. "Same way you got there last time." He stopped and looked at Ren. "It's unpredictable. It could happen any time, like last time. Be prepared."

He reached for the door and stopped. "One more thing I have something for you. The rift opened briefly the other day, not big enough to get PC through. PC managed to sneak this through before the rift closed. We think it's for you." Lambert walked outside as Ren stood at the door. He came walking back in with an animal crate.

Ren heard a soft meow. She recognized it right away. She touched the cage as tears filled her eyes. "Spotford! Oh, my God."

Lambert put the crate down as Ren opened the door. Spotford came out, looked up at Ren and meowed again. She picked him up and held him as he purred. She looked at Lambert with tears running down her face. "Thank you."

Lambert smiled as he walked away. "Be ready."